FROG IN A BUCKET

AN EDDIE COLLINS MYSTERY

Clive Rosengren

coffeetownpress

Kenmore, WA

coffeetownpress

A Coffeetown Press book published by Epicenter Press

Epicenter Press
6524 NE 181st St. Suite 2
Kenmore, WA 98028.

For more information go to:
www.Camelpress.com
www.Coffeetownpress.com
www.Epicenterpress.com
www.generontalbooks.com

Author website: cliverosengren.com

This is a work of fiction. Names, characters, places, brands, media, and incidents are the product of the author's imagination or are used fictitiously.

Design by Rudy Ramos

Frog in a Bucket
Copyright © 2021 by Clive Rosengren

ISBN: 9781603812627 (trade paper)
ISBN: 9781603812634 (ebook)

Printed in the United States of America

ACKNOWLEDGMENTS

Inherent in the life any writer is isolation. Now, with the terms "sheltering in place" and "social distancing" having become such integral parts of our zeitgeist, isolation has taken on new meaning for those of us facing the keyboard and the blank computer screen. Therefore, it is with great thanks I acknowledge and give a big shout out to the fans of Eddie Collins who have followed him through four books. Hopefully, you will soon again find him while browsing the shelves of your favorite bookstore.

My continued thank you to the folks at Coffeetown Press for hanging in there with my Hollywood actor, sometimes private eye Eddie Collins. Your ongoing support is greatly appreciated.

With the help of Zoom, sheltering in place and social distancing have not dampened the input of my intrepid writers' group, Monday Mayhem. Many thanks to Jenn Ashton, Carole Beers, Michael Niemann, and Sharon Dean for your continued support and input. Without your insights and help, this frog would have jumped out of the bucket numerous times.

1

Clay Dawson was a study in concentration. Even a crowded movie set didn't seem to faze the stocky, fifties-something actor, who wore John Lennon glasses and had a fringe of unruly salt and pepper hair surrounding his bald pate. And this was an especially crowded set.

The scene was a banquet, with tables scattered over the floor of the small soundstage on the Warner Bros. lot in Burbank. Clay and his onscreen wife, Janice Wilkes, an attractive brunette with piercing brown eyes were one-third of a table of guests. Sitting next to me was Bev Peterson, my movie wife. The other two diners were a black couple, Howard Fitzgerald and Ashley Brandt. The movie's title was *Terms of Power*. I had previously crossed paths with Clay and Bev, but the other three at the table were new to me. The six of us had established a rapport from the get-go, a fact that made the endless waiting on a movie set easier to withstand.

We three men were part of a city council and were dressed in suits and ties. My character's name was Greg Mason. The mayor of our fictional town, Byron Hessman, as played by Tony Gould, sat behind the dais, flanked by a row of corporate bigwigs. The purpose of the scene was for Mayor Hessman to lavish praise on them for funding a new civic center. Hushed up, however, was the fact that His Honor had funneled some of those funds into his own pocket. Ah, yes, the screenwriter's surprise, fodder for the final reel.

Clay leaned back in his chair and ran his hand over his bald dome. "Okay, Eddie, I've got Al Pacino, Paul Newman, and Cate Blanchett. I don't suppose you're going to give me a hint, are you?"

"Not on your life," I said. We were in the midst of a movie trivia game. The question in front of him was who are the six actors to have twice been nominated for an Oscar by playing the same character in two different movies. He'd gotten Al Pacino right off the bat with his portrayals of Michael Corleone in the first two installments of *The Godfather*. Paul Newman's Fast Eddie Felson in *The Hustler* and *The Color of Money* took him a bit longer, but he'd finally come up with the answer. He'd struggled with Cate Blanchett and her nominations for *Elizabeth* and *Elizabeth: The Golden Age*, until Janice leaned over and gave him help. He had three left to go, and I was pretty confident they would stump him. Faced with that possibility, he pulled out his cellphone and surreptitiously glanced down at the screen.

"Hey, hey, no help," I said, and he grinned before putting the device back in his pocket.

At that moment Steve Fischer bustled up to our little conclave of movie buffs. He was the Second Assistant Director on the shoot, and had pestered us the whole morning, a chore he relished. This was the first day on this banquet scene, and we were already sick of looking at fake rubber chicken, peas that were actually little plastic pellets, and small piles of fused Styrofoam that gave the illusion of mashed potatoes.

I've had my run-ins with fake movie food over the years, but this culinary deception defied believability. However, it came with the territory. My PI business, Collins Investigations, picks up the slack in my pursuit of the Hollywood brass ring, so I was glad for the booking. My contract stipulated three weeks, and by the looks at how this film was going, overtime could potentially be plentiful, thereby depositing more money in the pension fund. That thought was foremost in my head as our pesky second AD descended on us.

"Okay, guys, here's the deal," Steve said. "I'm gonna give you some additional dialogue to mutter when the camera rolls. Not loud, just kinda under your breath. Like sotted vocal, you know what I mean?"

Howard and I glanced at each other and did our best to stifle a grin at

Steve's rendition of "*sotto voce*." I don't know how long it had been since our second AD had encountered a bar of soap, but given the looks on the faces of Clay and his screen wife Janice, it damn sure wasn't this morning.

He stood behind them and leaned over. "Okay, you two are gonna say 'peas and carrots.' Got it? Lemme hear you."

Clay and Janice mumbled the words and Steve clapped his hands in approval. He then moved behind Howard and Ashley, who immediately put a napkin to her nose. "Okay, okay, good. Now you two say 'subberbroobub.' Got it?" When Steve heard the appropriate mutterings, he bounced on his toes and then scurried over to Bev and me.

"Terrific, guys, just terrific. Now you two—" He paused when he recognized me. "Hey, Eddie Collins. Good to see you again, man. Been a while." I said it had, recalling a week on a cop show I'd done a few months back where Steve, I think, had worn the same shirt he now had on his back. "Okay, Eddie, you and your gorgeous wife here are gonna say 'frog in a bucket.' Got it?" We nodded, and had to prove it by saying the phrase several times. Steve approved, and then had all six of us mutter simultaneously. He told us to take it down a notch, and when we passed muster, he gave us our cue, then bounced off, leaving us with looks on our faces like we'd just enrolled in a speech pathology clinic.

The sounds we were making most likely wouldn't end up in the finished film, but the sound engineers in post-production would be given more sources to create the illusion of a room filled with conversations. In reality, actual background dialogue would be turned over to a voice casting company that would go into a studio and create realistic dialogue. I have a friend who did that sort of work for a time and was constantly employed. He once told me they could carry on authentic conversations of anything from Eskimos to Australian Aborigines.

Our sextet did a little more practicing until the First AD barked over a megaphone that the camera was ready to roll and asked everybody to settle. As the movie spiel started, Clay leaned over the table and whispered, "Peter O'Toole in *Becket* and *Lion in Winter*."

"You got it," I whispered back. "But you're never going to get the other two."

"Five bucks says I do," he replied.

I agreed, and we listened to the First AD yell "Roll sound." The sound man responded with "Speed." A shout of "Background" prompted the waiters and bus boys, otherwise known as extras, to begin wandering among the tables. That prompt was also our table's cue and we began tossing gibberish back and forth in subdued tones that to any casual observer would provoke calls to men in white uniforms. A production assistant slated the scene with the familiar clapperboard and the director then took charge by shouting "And, action!"

Bev and I were facing the dais and watched the action while we frogged in a bucket. The camera was mounted on a dolly and moved along the length of the dais on a set of rails, stopping on Mayor Hessman and the fat cat to his left as they exchanged a few lines of dialogue.

The shot took three takes, each one, to my mind, exactly the same as the one prior. The director, a spindly young man by the name of Walt Langley, called "Cut. Check the gate." The cameraman made sure there was no lint or any other offending matter in the lens, then informed the director it was clean. As Howard and Clay continued tossing our ad-lib gibberish to each other with various accents, the First AD and the director conferred. My two fellow councilmen had been goofing off like this all morning, and I had to confess that their antics had lightened the boredom. We finally heard the AD utter the welcome words of "All right, everybody, that's lunch. One hour."

The six of us pushed our chairs back and headed for the stage door and the chow line. Before I could take even two steps someone bumped into me from behind, shoving me into Bev. I turned around, but all I could see were bodies in motion, their backs to me.

"Sorry, Bev," I said. "Mention food to an extra and you've got a stampede on your hands."

"Boy, don't you know it," she said. "I worked on a set with five hundred of them once. It made the parting of the Red Sea look like a tea party." I laughed, and as we filed out of the soundstage, she hooked up with Janice and Ashley, her fellow movie wives, and disappeared into the throng.

I've seldom found movie lunch tables lacking in both quality and quantity, and *Terms of Power* was no exception. I stood in line and finally arrived at the ordering window of the roach coach. Tray piled high with a sizable piece of snapper, salad, and rice, I joined my fellow councilmen at a table under a blue canopy. There was no sign of our wives. Birds of a feather, I suppose. They'd probably had enough of the three of us.

Howard unscrewed the top of a bottle of Snapple. "Man, I thought I'd never say this, but I am damn glad to see some broccoli."

"I know," Clay said. "I think those peas in there could double as ball bearings." He sliced into a chunk of chicken breast, then leaned into me. "Okay, Collins, four down and two to go. Is number five a man or a woman?"

"A hint, Clay? Where does it say you get a hint?"

He turned to Howard. "Look at this guy, breakin' my balls."

"Okay," I said. "It's a man, but you're still not going to get it."

"Modern? Or before Technicolor?"

"Not that far back," I said.

He shook his head and returned to his chicken. We discussed the morning's shooting, Steve Fischer's lack of hygiene, and various aspects of the business, both pro and con. I'm in my late forties, and have been in Hollywood for twenty-seven years. Clay and Howard have similar backgrounds, although they haven't been here as long, both of them coming out from New York a few years ago. After we finished our lunch, a production assistant eventually started to circulate among the tables telling us that we "were back," movie jargon hinting that we should return to our banquet of plastic peas and Styrofoam potatoes.

Fortunately, we learned that the scene had moved into an after-dinner mode, so the plates had been removed and replaced with coffee cups filled with colored water. While we waited for Mayor Hessman to address his constituents, my five table-mates and I made small talk about all things Hollywood. Clay and Howard also had three-week contracts, but this was the last day we were going to be favored by the presence of our wives.

Clay's participation in our conversation was spotty. He had a faraway look on his face as he tried to come up with the last two answers to the trivia question. At one point, he leaned back in his chair and a huge grin broke out on his face as he said, "Okay, Collins, here it is. John Wayne."

"For what?"

"Rooster Cogburn in *True Grit*, and then the sequel *Rooster Cogburn*."

"Good try, Clay, but no dice. He won for *True Grit*, but wasn't nominated for the sequel."

"You sure?"

"As I'm sitting here."

"Dammit," he said.

The five of us laughed and Ashley leaned over to me. "How did you get to be such a movie junkie, Eddie?"

"Many hours in darkened theaters."

"I heard that you're also a private eye," Howard added.

"You heard right," I replied.

"Dangerous work, isn't it?" Janice said from across the table.

"Well, sometimes," I said, and immediately flashed back to an incident some months ago up at Lake Arrowhead that for a time had made me think my ticket was on the verge of being punched.

Clay set his water glass down and chimed in. "If he comes up with any more of these cockamamie trivia questions, it's going to get real dangerous."

The table erupted in laughter and I put up my hands in surrender. "All right, Clay, look. Here's a little hint. This guy is probably better known for being something other than an actor."

"Thanks a lot. How the hell's that supposed to help me?"

He didn't get much sympathy from us, because at that point our pesky second AD came up to the table and said we men should remove our jackets and drape them over the backs of our chairs. The three of us stood and complied. As I did so, I felt something in one of the side pockets. I reached inside and pulled out a brass key about two inches in length. It had several gouges on it and was attached to a round metal ring, along with a circular metal disc the size of a silver dollar. Etched into the disc was the image of a box, its lid open, and the word 'Pandora' stamped below it. I hung my jacket over the back of my chair, sat down and looked more closely at the key.

Bev saw the puzzled look on my face and asked, "What's the matter, Eddie?

"I just found this key in my coat pocket. It wasn't there when I suited up this morning."

"Are you sure?"

"Yeah, I think so. Could be that I missed it, though."

"These men's costumes are probably rented. Maybe it belongs to whoever wore it before."

"Good thought," I said, and stood up and removed the coat from the back of the chair. I looked at the inside pockets and saw a tag sewn into the fabric of the left side. On it was the name 'Ken Thompson.' Underneath that were the words 'Crash and Burn.' I showed the tag to Bev. "What do you think? A title and the name of an actor?"

"I'd bet on it," she said. "They told me in wardrobe that they rented a lot of stuff from SunCoast Costume."

"Not from Warner Bros. stock?"

"According to my agent this film is an independent. They're renting studio space from Warner's. That probably goes for wardrobe as well."

"Yeah, I'll have to check with them when we're done here." For my own reference, I pulled a notebook out of my shirt pocket and jotted down the name 'Ken Thompson' and the title *Crash and Burn*, then stuffed the key into a trousers pocket. Suddenly another thought occurred to me. "Hey, Bev, when I bumped into you earlier, someone had jostled me from behind. You didn't happen to see who it was, did you?

"No, I didn't." After a moment she continued. "Are you thinking someone slipped that key into your pocket?"

"It's possible," I said. "It was a madhouse there for a couple of minutes and somebody pushed me pretty hard."

"Maybe, but I'd check with wardrobe."

"Yeah, you're right," I said, and replaced the jacket over the back of my chair. SunCoast Costume has been part of the Hollywood support system for more years than I can remember. They rent clothing for not only the movie and television industry, but also to private individuals for Halloween and other such occasions. I wasn't sure if someone had bumped into me and put the key in my pocket, but I was also uncertain as to whether or not it was in the pocket when I got dressed this morning. SunCoast Costume was going to have to sort it out. As I sat down again the first AD shouted out for everyone to settle. The mayor was about to address the multitude.

Hair and makeup crew members flitted around Tony Gould, patting, pampering, and combing. After a consultation with the director, Tony cleared his throat, sipped from a water glass and stood behind the lectern. The same pre-shooting sequence was repeated, the room fell quiet, and we all turned our attention to the His Honor.

Tony Gould had been around Hollywood forever, playing everything under the sun. Whenever I watch a movie that has a scene filled with sober, middle-aged gentlemen sitting around a conference table, Tony Gould is bound to be there. He had a mane of silver hair. A bit of a paunch added to his gravitas. He ran his hand over his tie, buttoned his coat and adjusted the microphone.

"Ladies and gentlemen, welcome to a celebration of the marriage of civic pride and dynamic business leadership. On behalf of the city council and the citizens of Pine Bluff, I'd like to express my deepest appreciation for the generosity extended by Ridgeway Enterprises." Tony paused and sipped more water. "Without their infusion of both financial and engineering aid, this beautiful new facility we're sitting in would not have been possible."

Again Tony paused to sip more water. He stepped back from the mic, cleared his throat and adjusted his tie. Then he stepped back to the lectern, his face turned ash white, and he collapsed to the floor.

2

Stunned silence filled the room. After a moment or two the director shouted for the camera to be shut down and the on-set doctor summoned. Behind the dais, the other actors in the scene backed off as the first AD scurried around the end of the table and bent over Tony. A doctor carrying a black medical duffle bag rushed through the door of the soundstage and disappeared behind the table. A man who'd earlier been identified as the line producer had a cellphone to his ear and called for an ambulance.

The six of us at our table looked at each other, at a loss for words. After a moment or two, Howard voiced the possibility of something being wrong with what Tony had eaten for lunch. We all vouched that the meal had set well with each of us, but we also agreed that that could be a possibility. About ten minutes elapsed until finally Steve Fischer got on a bullhorn and told everyone in the scene to exit the soundstage. Extras were told to return to the background holding area and principals—meaning the six of us—were instructed to return to our trailers and await further word on what would transpire from this point on.

People started filtering out through the huge main door, whispered conversations trying to assess what had just happened. Howard, Ashley and I made our way to dressing room trailers that were lined up along a Warner Bros. backlot street. Howard and I shared one trailer. He occupied one half of it and I had the other. We heard the sound of a siren entering the lot as Ashley said she'd see us later and continued on to her trailer. I stepped inside my makeshift cell, removed my jacket and looked again at the label

I'd discovered earlier. There wasn't any indication of a date ascribed to the title *Crash and Burn*. As I pulled out my cellphone, someone knocked on the trailer's door. It was Howard. I stepped back and invited him in.

He climbed up the stairs and said, "What do you think, Eddie? We wrapped for the day?"

"Beats me."

"Do you know the guy?"

"Not well. I've auditioned with him a few times over the years. Matter of fact, he's taken his share of roles away from me. Always seemed like a decent guy, though." I opened the mini-fridge and pulled out a couple bottles of water and handed one to him. "What about you? Ever work with him before?"

"Nope." He unscrewed the top of the bottle and took a long gulp. "What do you think happens next? They re-cast?"

"Always a possibility, I guess. Depends on what's wrong with him. We've got other stuff that doesn't include Tony. I imagine they'll shoot around him if they can." I gestured for Howard to have a seat and he sank down onto an end of a padded bench underneath one of the windows.

"Well, I hope it's nothing serious," he said. "I'd hate like hell to have a job pulled out from under me."

"I hear you, man."

"You know, I've been intrigued by your movie trivia question this morning. Mind if I take a crack at the answer?"

"Be my guest," I said, and grinned with a bit of smugness as I tipped up my bottle of water and took a healthy swallow.

"Bing Crosby," he said, his eyebrows arched in anticipation.

I almost choked on the water. "How the hell did you know that?" I said, unable to disguise the surprise in my voice.

"Oh, man, I've been a huge fan of Der Bingle my whole life."

"So I suppose you know the movies?"

"He won it playing Father O'Malley in *Going My Way* in 1945. And the next year he was nominated again for *The Bells of St. Mary's*."

"Damn, Howard, I'm impressed. You're going to keep it to yourself, though, right? I mean, there is a five spot riding on it."

"Absolutely. In fact, I think I've got a question that'll stump both you and Clay."

"Try me," I said.

Before he could, there was a loud knock on the door. "Yeah," I said. It swung open a foot or so and Steve Fischer stuck his head through the opening.

"All right, here's the skinny, guys. The doc thinks Tony had a heart attack. He's in an ambulance on the way to the hospital. So that's a wrap for today. We'll let your agents know what's happening by end of day, okay?"

We agreed and Steve disappeared. Howard said he'd hold onto his trivia question until hopefully seeing me tomorrow and then left my little home away home. At least that's what I hoped it would be for the next three weeks. The collapse of our fictional Hizzoner, however, could put a damper on that.

I finished off my bottle of water and tossed it in a small wastebasket. The bottle landed on a cardboard tag with my name on it, and a safety pin through a hole punched in the tag. I remembered that when I'd started to get dressed earlier the safety pin had been slipped over the hanger. I'd taken it off and discarded it. For a moment I debated whether or not I should replace the tag on the hanger, but decided to leave it for the wardrobe people to deal with. I got out of costume, dressed, made sure I had all my valuables, including the key I'd discovered, and left the trailer.

The *Terms of Power* wardrobe department was a long trailer that sat next to a smaller one housing the hair and makeup crews. I knocked on the door, heard someone call out for me to enter, and stepped inside. On one side of the trailer long racks of clothing were suspended from the ceiling. Several wheeled racks full of various costume pieces were shoved up against the opposite wall. At the end of the trailer to my left was a desk, behind which sat Melissa Ailes, the wardrobe mistress on the production. She was a heavyset woman, with streaks of lavender running through her dark hair and enough bling on her fingers, wrists, and earlobes to set off the best metal detector on the market.

"Can I help you?" she said.

"Yeah. Did the production rent wardrobe from SunCoast Costume?"

"Depends on the costume. You're...Collins, right? Eddie?"

"Correct."

"Lemme check." She picked up a clipboard and flipped through a couple of pages. "Yeah, yours is from SunCoast. What's the problem? Something doesn't fit?"

"No, it's fine," I said, and pulled out the key I'd found earlier. "This was in one of the pockets."

She looked at it for a long moment. "Wow. SunCoast is usually pretty thorough about the stuff they rent. They must have missed it."

"The jacket has a name tag and what appears to be the title of a production sewn onto one of the pockets. Do you know if they keep records of everything they rent?"

"Gosh, Eddie, I don't. I'd call out there for you, but I'm so swamped here I don't know my ass from a bucket. Pardon my French. And now with what just happened, it's even worse."

"Understood," I said. "I can call them. I was just wondering if the costume came from them. Thought maybe you got it from Warner's."

"No way. Their rental policies suck."

"Thanks. I'll give SunCoast a call." I started for the door and had my handle on the knob but stopped and said, "Any word on what's happening with the shoot?"

"*Nada*," she said, and sipped on a cardboard to-go cup of coffee. "The guy's in most of the damn movie. A big monkey wrench on the horizon, if you ask me."

"No biz like show biz, right?" She nodded and put one finger to the tip of her nose. I grinned and opened the door.

"By the way," Melissa said, "I like your porkpie. More guys should wear them."

I voiced my agreement and stepped out of the trailer.

It was a sunny crisp November day in Burbank, the only cloud being the figurative one hanging over *Terms of Power*, putting in question three weeks of employment. Collins Investigations keeps me and my secretary, Mavis Werner, afloat, but not enough to the point where I have to forego the lure of movie fame and fortune. Neither has knocked on my door of late, but a pension fund continues to accumulate and I manage to stay eligible for health insurance, so the pursuit persists.

As I strolled to the parking garage on the Warner lot, I checked my cellphone for messages. There were none, but there was a text from Carla. That would be Carla Rizzoli, an actress I've been involved with for a little over a year. We'd worked together years ago, and she'd come back into my life by hiring me to locate her brother. I was married to an actress years ago, and getting involved with another one caused friends to warn me about making the same mistake twice. But our relationship hasn't set off that alarm, and as the months have gone by, we seem to be on pretty solid ground.

Her text read, "*hey, Shamus, your working actress sweetie checking in. hope your shoot is going well.*" Carla had been fortunate enough to land a television series, playing—of all things—a private detective. It would be natural for me to be green with envy, but I've resisted the urge and am totally happy with her success. I stopped walking and replied to her text, not with thumbs flying, but rather one finger poking out something coherent. I told her I'd call her later.

An elevator that qualifies as an antique lumbered to my floor and I stepped off to encounter Dr. Leonid Travnikov, one of my neighbors. The good doctor was Russian and a man of few words. I don't know how many patients he has, since it seems like communicating with him presents challenges. He wore a dark suit and a black fedora.

"Afternoon, doctor," I said.

"Yes, it is," he replied, his Russian accent inescapable. "You are well, Mr. Collins?"

"I am, thanks."

"Is good. Stay that way. Eat more vegetables."

With that, he stepped into the elevator. As the door closed, the hint of a smile broke out on his stolid face.

I pushed open the door to Collins Investigations to see Mavis behind her desk and on her computer. She's my trustworthy gal Friday, always willing to pull my covers and keep me from making a fool of myself.

"Guess what?" I said.

"What?"

"Travnikov just smiled at me."

She looked up at me. "You're sure he wasn't about to sneeze?"

I cracked up, doffed my hat and hung it on a peg in my office behind hers.

"I thought you were shooting at Warner's?" she said.

"I was. We ran into a snag." I filled her in on the snafu as I looked through the mail on my desk. Even though the Internet is capable of finding any needle in any haystack, it sometimes doesn't replace the good old Yellow Pages. I pulled our copy of the tome off a shelf and turned to the "P" listings. My finger moved over the pages, finding only a florist and a day spa with "Pandora" in the name. I attached a Post-It note to the edge of the page and laid the directory on the corner of my desk.

On my last birthday a few months ago Carla and Mavis had conspired to bring me onto the Internet highway by buying me a laptop computer. It was an Apple, their device of choice, and I was getting pretty used to it. I wasn't in danger of being adept enough to do any hacking, by any means, but have mastered the rudiments. I flipped it open, made sure I had an Internet connection, and opened up the IMDb website, an invaluable aid in finding everyone and everything having to do with the movie industry.

I typed "Ken Thompson" in the search window. Four names appeared, one a screenwriter, another an electrical technician, and the other two actors, one listed as "Ken T. Thompson." Clicking on Ken T. and scrolling through his list of credits didn't result in one called *Crash and Burn*. The Ken without the "T" yielded a photo of a man with a long face who appeared to be in his fifties. His eyes were dark, deep-set, above a prominent nose. He had a look of intensity on his face. *Crash and Burn*, a film from eight years ago, was among the list of Ken Thompson's credits. I clicked on the title and started scrolling through the cast list. Ken Thompson was pretty far down the list, which didn't surprise me.

But what did surprise me was an actor playing the part of "Judge Faraday." The actor's name was Tony Gould.

3

When I first opened Collins Investigations a few years back it was out of necessity. The idea of keeping a cinematic career afloat by tending bar, substitute teaching, driving cab, selling real estate, or any of the other subsistence jobs we non A-list actors are faced with did not appeal to me in the slightest. Thus, with the benefit of having been an MP, came the private eye business and the tendency to stick my nose into places it probably shouldn't belong.

The sensible thing for me to do would have been to take the key I discovered in the pocket of my jacket and run it up to SunCoast Costume and be done with it. Better yet, give it to Melissa Ailes and let her worry about it. But then along comes a link between Ken Thompson, Tony Gould, and a film called *Crash and Burn*. Serendipity. A wonderful word. One that, for a private eye, raises an itch that begs to be scratched. I picked up the key and looked at it for a long moment.

The metaphorical implications of what was stamped on the disc didn't escape me. In fact, they were almost too obvious. In Greek mythology, Pandora opened up a box that unleashed a torrent of ills and misfortunes. I turned the key over in my hand and wondered if that was what I was doing. Stirring up a mess for myself?

Key clasped in one hand, I closed my laptop and walked into Mavis's office. She supplements her Collins Investigations salary by buying and selling antiques and collectibles, mostly on eBay. I'm constantly amazed by the stuff she traffics in. However, what I saw on the screen when I leaned over her shoulder caught me by surprise. It was a photo of Fred Astaire and Ginger Rogers, no doubt a still from one of their legendary dance numbers. But what made the photo more interesting were what appeared to be signatures.

"Is that signed?" I asked.

"You got it. By both of them."

"Wow, that's gotta be worth some shekels, right?"

"Depends on where the bidding goes. Right now it's stalled. But I'm hanging in for the long haul."

I went around to the front of her desk and sank into one of the chairs. She looked up and said, "What's up, boss man?"

I held up the key. "First impression. What do you think this is for?"

She held out her hand. I gave it to her and she looked at it closely. "I don't know, but it's obviously got to be related to someone or something involving Pandora."

"How about a room key? Say, hotel or motel?"

"I doubt it," she said, as she handed it back to me. "I think they've all gone to those key cards."

"Unless it's one that's not expensive."

She gave me a look that could only be described as skeptical. "Like some seedy flophouse with hourly rates and no mint on the pillow?"

I shrugged. "Yeah, maybe. Who knows?"

"Where did you get it?"

"It was in the pocket of my costume this morning."

"Whose is it?"

"That's the sixty-four thousand dollar question. The suit was once worn by a guy by the name of Ken Thompson on a production by the name of *Crash and Burn*."

"So give it back to the people in wardrobe. What's the big deal?

"Tony Gould, the guy who keeled over on the shoot? He was in the same production."

She looked at me for a long moment and the trace of a grin broke out at the corners of her mouth. "And you can't resist."

"What do you mean?"

"I know you too well, Eddie. You don't believe in the word coincidence. You're bound and determined to make a mountain out of a molehill."

"I'm just curious."

"And your curiosity is going to get you in trouble."

I tossed the key into the air and caught it. "Well, you're a lot of help." I stood up and walked back into my office.

"Give the key back to the wardrobe people. Save yourself the trouble."

She was right, of course, but it did nothing to dispel my curiosity. I've worn a lot of rented costumes over the years, but have never found something in one of the pockets. Either that key was left there by the previous actor, or someone slipped it into my pocket when I was jostled while heading for lunch.

I flipped open the Yellow Pages, found the phone number for SunCoast Costume and dialed. The usual menu listings left me uncertain which key to hit, but I lucked out with my first choice.

A woman's voice with the trace of a New York accent answered. "Can I help you?"

"Hi. I'm calling on behalf of an actor friend of mine. He worked on a movie a few days ago. His costume was rented from you folks and he left something in a pocket. How would he go about getting it back?"

"Well, first of all, we'd need the name of the production he worked on."

"Okay, I'll pass that along to him."

"Just out of curiosity, sir, what is the item?"

"I'm not sure. But he said it was valuable. Something his girl gave him. He doesn't seem to want to bother about it, but I told him she's gonna be real pissed when she finds out it's missing."

"I see," she said, and paused, making me wonder if she'd seen through my ruse. "Tell him to give us the name of the show, his name, and a description of the item. We'll go from there and see what we can find."

"So if you found something like that, you'd hold on to it?"

"For a period of time."

"How long?"

"Usually six months. Unless it's something we could use in our stock, we'll generally put it up for sale or donate it to Goodwill. Some place like that."

"Is there a possibility someone from SunCoast could have overlooked it after it was returned?"

"I suppose, although we're generally pretty thorough. But with the volume of rentals we do, I would think it might be possible."

"My friend also told me there was an actor's name and the title of a film or TV show sewn into one of the pockets. Do you guys do that?"

"No. If the production wants the piece identified, they'd have to do that themselves. And remove it before returning the costume to us."

"So, this name and title my friend saw should have been removed before SunCoast got it back, right?"

"That's correct."

"But it wasn't. So it could be that you guys might have overlooked that as well?"

There was a pause on the end of the line. I think I may have caught SunCoast with its pants down, as it were.

"Look, sir, I'm not going to pretend that we might not make a mistake here and there. As I mentioned, we handle a tremendous amount of rentals. That tag should have been removed. And as far as the item your friend lost, we'll do our best to see that he gets it back."

"Well, that's good to know," I said. "I'll tell him to give you a call. Thanks for your time."

"You're welcome," she replied, and ended the call.

I replaced the phone in its cradle and looked up to see Mavis leaning against the doorjamb of my office.

"Why didn't you just tell them the item belonged to you?"

"Because it doesn't. And I'm not sure if it was left in my jacket or if someone slipped it into my pocket."

"Why would someone do that?"

"That's another sixty-four thousand dollar question, kiddo."

"Which is reason enough not to get your nose out of joint over a stupid key."

"It opens something. Wouldn't you want to know what?"

"You're the private eye, not me."

"Spoken like a worthy sidekick, Mrs. Werner." She shook her head and went to answer her phone that had just rung. I brought up the contacts on my cellphone, but before I could punch in a number Mavis interrupted me.

"Eddie, it's Morrie."

I picked up my handset and said, "Morrie Howard, my favorite agent."

"Your only agent, bubbeleh," he said, using a Yiddish nickname he bestows on almost everyone. "How's my favorite gumshoe?"

"Not bad. We had a little episode this morning on *Terms of Power.*"

"So I heard. That's why I'm on the phone. They've got a call time for you tomorrow at eight o'clock."

"Did they say anything about what they're going to do?"

"Not to me."

"Okay, I'll be there," I said, and hung up.

I went back to my cellphone contacts and dialed the number for Reggie Benson, an Army pal of mine I'd rescued from homelessness and a life on the streets a couple of years ago. He was a Military Policeman with me, and I've kind of given him the profile of my operative, as it were.

"Hey, Eddie, how ya doin'?"

"Good, Reggie. How's yourself?"

"I'm all right. What's up?"

"It's four-thirty," I said, looking at my watch. "Feel like some pizza?"

"Pizza? Yup, yup, always up for pizza."

"Great. I've got something I want to run by you. Pick you up in, say, what? Fifteen?"

"You bet. I'll be outside."

After stowing the cell in my pocket, I plucked my hat off its peg and walked into Mavis's office. "What's the status of Fred and Ginger?"

"Some butthole from Denver outbid me."

"Damn."

"You off to see Reggie?"

"I am. Going to bat some ideas around about this key. And with me tied up on this film, maybe he can do some leg work for me."

"Well, say howdy, but I still think you're whistlin' Dixie. What time's your call tomorrow?"

"Eight."

"Check in with me later?"

"Will do," I said, and with that I went in search of pizza. In the elevator on the way down to my car I thought over what my conversation with the woman at SunCoast costume had revealed. Two reasons remained as to how this mysterious key had found its way into my costume. An oversight by someone at the rental company was entirely possible, and their admission that the tag with Thompson's name on it should have been removed made it more evident that there was a link between Thompson and the key. But that raised the question as to why someone would stick it in my pocket. The jacket had Thompson's name in it, not mine. I'd removed the cardboard tag with my name on it from the hanger when I put the costume on. True, that left the identity of the costume as belonging to Ken Thompson. But surely the wardrobe department knew there was no one by that name in the cast. Odd, and puzzling enough to keep me wanting to scratch the itch.

Home for Reggie Benson is an apartment above a funeral parlor. Bernie Feldman, a friend of mine and the owner of the place had a college student living there as a sort of night watchman until the kid took a powder. When I decided to get Reggie off the street, Bernie came through with a job that included a place to live.

I pulled into the driveway and saw him sitting on the bottom step of a flight of stairs leading up to the second floor. He had a baseball cap pulled low on his forehead and wore a red polo shirt over jeans and sneakers. He jumped to his feet and opened the car door.

"Hey, Eddie. Good to see you."

"Same here, buddy." I pointed to a red Subaru parked in front of one of the doors to a two-car garage. I'd recently come into some money and had bought it for him, another step in getting his life back in order. "How's the car running?"

"Great, man. Darn good wheels."

I backed down the driveway and drove to a little hole-in-the-wall place we'd frequented a few times. There were only six tables. I tossed my hat on one of them and we ordered a meat lover's pie, along with a glass of beer for me and a diet soda for him. When I found Reggie, I'd marveled at the fact that he hadn't resorted to drugs and alcohol, a choice he still adhered to.

We picked up our drinks and sat down at the table. Soft rock music filtered through the room, along with the aroma of fresh pizza. Reggie took off his cap and fluffed his full head of hair. "Whatcha been up to, Eddie?"

"A movie," I replied, and told him about the *Terms of Power* shoot, Tony Gould's collapse and finding the key. I pulled it out of my pocket and showed it to him. "What do think this might be for?"

"Oh, man, it could be anything." He turned it over in his hand. "It's a Schlage. That's pretty common." He ran his finger over the metal disc. "Pandora. That's something to do with mythology or something, ain't it?"

"Greek mythology. Pandora opened this box and released all sorts of crap."

"Wow. And there's a box on this thing." He handed the key back to me. "Looks to me like it's kinda ominous, don't you think?"

"I don't know. Could be."

We leaned back as a waiter laid the pizza in front of us. We dug in and ate for several minutes. "So, Eddie, say someone did slip that key into your pocket. Why you? When the room was full of people?"

"Good question. He might have gotten my name from the wardrobe people, but that still leaves the question of why."

We pulled a second slice from the pie and chewed and sipped from our drinks, momentarily lost in our own thoughts. Reggie got up and refilled his drink from the dispenser, then came back to the table.

"So what do you think I should do with this key?" I said.

He shrugged his shoulders and stirred his glass of soda with the plastic straw. "Well, common sense would probably tell me to take it to those costume people and let them deal with it."

"That's exactly what Mavis said."

"I figured she might." He grinned and pulled a piece of pepperoni off his slice and put it in his mouth. "But then..." He left the sentence hanging and looked at me over the top of his glass.

"Yeah? But then...?"

"Well, it's gonna be pretty hard to find out what kind of lock that key fits," he said. "That leaves you trying to find out who it belongs to."

"I looked in the Yellow Pages. Pandora only came up with a florist and a day spa."

"Well, you got that fancy computer for your birthday, Eddie. You could get on the Internet."

"Is that what you'd do?"

"Might be kind of interesting," he said. "If somebody put it in your pocket, it had to be for a reason."

"Exactly."

"Did you feel someone's hand going into that pocket of yours?"

"Hard to say. There was a crush of people."

We gnawed on pizza for a couple of minutes and Reggie said, "What about this Ken Thompson guy? Do you know him?"

"Nope." I pulled out my cellphone, got on the IMDb app and showed him the picture. "I've never seen the guy."

"He looks like he's got something to hide."

"Why do you say that?"

"Aw, I don't know. Just a gut reaction." He handed the phone back to me. "Maybe somebody thought you were him."

"Yeah, could be," I said, and munched on some pizza. "Well, hell, I'll probably take yours and Mavis's advice and turn the key in tomorrow."

"But still wonder why you found it, right?"

I nodded. "You took the words right out of my mouth."

He laughed, we bumped knuckles, finished our pizza and headed for the car.

As I turned off Sunset, I glanced at him as he kept time with Merle Haggard's Okie drawl coming from the disc player. "How's things working out with Bernie?"

"Oh, great, man. He's a real standup guy. Even had me out to his place a couple times for a cookout. They've got a swimming pool and everything. Yup, sure glad you got me hooked up with him."

He reached over and squeezed my shoulder and I looked at him. It felt good to see him happy like this. Who knows what would have become of him if I hadn't run into him out at the Santa Monica Pier? Reggie had flirted with becoming a cop after he got out of the service. It never took, but it left him with instincts that I've come to appreciate and rely upon.

I pulled into the funeral parlor's driveway. Before closing the car door, he leaned down and stuck his head inside. "If you change your mind, Eddie, and can't resist the urge, you know where I am if you need some help."

"Thanks, man. Talk to you later."

Two thirds of my Collins Investigations support group had given me advice I wasn't exactly ready to embrace. That left the third member. I pulled over to a curb and dialed her number.

With the success of Carla's television series, and I suppose throwing financial caution to the wind, she'd bought a condo in the heart of Hollywood just off the Boulevard. We'd flirted with the idea of buying the two-bedroom unit jointly, but our lingering tendencies to be lone wolves had so far resulted in each of us maintaining our own living space. Nevertheless, I had a key to her place. I drove into the underground garage and parked in one of her allotted spaces next to her Honda Fit.

The aroma of Chinese food tickled my nostrils as I opened the door. She sat cross-legged on the sofa, dressed in cut-off sweats and a tank top. Her flat screen television was on, and a script lay next to her. Little cardboard to-go containers were spread out on the coffee table.

She'd moved her furniture from the little house she'd rented a stone's-throw from the Sony lot in Culver City, and given the difference in square footage, she was still in the process of adding pieces. Besides the beige sofa, two new puffy armchairs flanked the coffee table. The room had windows facing an interior courtyard, and in the mornings sunlight poured into the living room.

In the months we've been together, the sight of her always brings on a surge of emotion, making this lone wolfishness of mine tenuous. I leaned over and gave her a lingering kiss as she wound her arms around my neck.

"Mmmmm," she murmured. "I've been thinking about that all day. I'd ask if you're hungry, but you taste like pepperoni."

"I just had some pizza with Reggie."

"Awww, tired Reggie. Is he doing okay?"

"He's fine. How was your day?"

"Good. I had a light load. Sounds like you had a little excitement, though."

"Yeah. But I've got an eight o'clock call for tomorrow, so I don't know what the hell they're going to do."

The character Carla plays on her television show, *Three on a Beat*, is a private detective by the name of Billie Guardino. When I called her earlier, I'd briefly told her about finding the key, so I pulled it out of my pocket and handed it to her. She looked at it closely and turned the disc over in her hand.

"Okay, Detective Guardino, I need some advice."

"Lay it on me, Shamus."

"What the hell should I do with that key?"

"Turn it into wardrobe," she said, as she handed it back to me, then shoveled some moo shu pork into her mouth.

"That's it? No curiosity? No sense that the game's afoot?"

"A little. But listen, Sherlock, despite the disc with the box and Pandora, that's a very common key. How the heck do you think you're going to find what it's for?"

"But there's a reason it wound up in my costume."

"Could just be an accident, Eddie."

"And you're not at all curious about the link between this Ken Thompson and Tony Gould?"

"You don't even know them, do you?"

"I know Gould a little." I pulled out my cellphone and called up the IMDb site. "This is Ken Thompson," I said, and showed her the photo.

She looked at it for a long moment, and laid her chopsticks down. "Wow, this is weird."

"What?"

"This guy looks a little familiar."

"How so?

"I'm not sure. Maybe from the Follies."

She referred to Feline Follies, a gentlemen's club Carla once danced at under the name Velvet La Rose, a subsistence job that hopefully could be forgotten, given her television success.

"There, you see! Reggie said the guy looked like he had something to hide. And now you think he looks familiar. I think there's an itch there that needs scratching."

"I've got just the thing for your itch," she said, as she batted her eyelashes at me. She picked up the remnants of the Chinese food and carried them into the kitchen.

"Well, I don't know," I said. "Maybe I'm nuts, but instinct tells me there's something more there than meets the eye."

Carla came back from the kitchen with a glass of white wine and a bottle of beer that she handed to me. "You've got three weeks on this movie, provided they continue shooting. Don't let your instinct interfere with your wallet."

"Says the co-star of her own television show," I said.

She sipped from her wineglass, set it on the coffee table, snuggled up to me and put her arms around my neck. "Besides being a good actor, you're also a good detective, Eddie. But just as the actor needs a script, a detective needs evidence. I don't know that you have it. But I could be wrong. Maybe you can convince me."

She kissed me on the cheek and I set the bottle of beer down on a coaster on the coffee table. "What time's your call in the morning?"

"Seven," she said.

"Well, then, I'd better get busy," I said, as I took her in my arms and kissed her.

4

Carla and I parted company in her garage the following morning. She, along with both Mavis and Reggie had basically told me to forget about this infernal key. I mulled over their advice during my shower and shave at my apartment. The innate Collins stubbornness refused to be washed away.

Despite a traffic snarl in the Cahuenga, Pass I made it to the Warner's lot a half hour before my call. The coffee was hot and the scrambled eggs with sausage and hash browns were sublime. I spotted Clay and Howard at a table under the blue awning and straddled a chair across from them.

"Morning, guys. Anybody know what we're doing?"

"Haven't heard," Howard said. "Steve Fischer has been flitting around here, but hasn't offered anything."

"And no word on Tony's condition?"

"Not that I'm aware of," Clay said. "There wasn't anything on the news." He cut off a chunk of a breakfast burrito, chewed, and reached into his pocket. He separated a five-dollar bill from a money clip and handed it to me. "Okay, look, Collins, I give up. Who the hell is the actor who's more famous as something else? I didn't look it up, and it's driving me fuckin' nuts."

I laughed, accepted the Abe Lincoln and gestured to Howard. "Allow Mr. Fitzgerald to enlighten you."

Howard grinned and said, "Think *White Christmas*."

Clay's mouth stopped working and hung at half-mast. "You gotta be kidding me. Bing Crosby?"

"Won for *Going My Way*, nominated for *The Bells of St. Mary's*," Howard replied.

"I'll be damned," Clay said, and shook his head as he finished his mouthful of burrito.

"But that still leaves you with number six," I said. "This one might surprise you."

"What surprises me," Clay said, "is how much useless information you've got stored in that head of yours, Collins."

"Useless? I just picked up five bucks from you," I said. "But I'll tell you what. I'm willing to go double or nothing."

"Against my better judgment, you're on," Clay said.

His brow furrowed in concentration as Howard and I filled our coffee cups and chatted about people in the business we both knew. I glanced over at Clay and decided to quit prolonging the torture.

"Yo, Clay, how you doin' with that name?" I said. Howard looked at me and nodded slightly, telling me that he knew the answer.

Clay paused in mid chew and looked at both of us. After a moment, he slammed his fork down on the table. "Oh, for crissakes, you gotta be kiddin' me. Stallone?"

"First time for *Rocky*," I said, "and then supporting actor for *Creed*." I reached in my pocket and handed him a sawbuck. "I couldn't stand to see you in any more agony, Clay. Don't spend it all in one place."

"Yeah, yeah," he grumbled, and went back to his burrito.

"However, Howard here says he's got one that's going to stump both of us," I said. "So lay it on us, man."

Howard took a sip of coffee, and with little conspiratorial glances to his left and right said, "On what movie was the Steadicam first used?"

Clay and I looked at each other. A good question, I thought. The Steadicam is a cantilevered camera mounted on the body of the operator, allowing much more movement and flexibility. I was pretty sure the budget on this picture wouldn't allow one, but I'd seen it in operation before and was amazed at its use.

After a moment Clay said, "Hell, that's easy. *Touch of Evil*. Orson Welles."

"Good try, Clay, but no cigar," Howard said.

"No? Come on, that first shot? It's gotta be over three minutes long."

"It is, but the movie came out in nineteen fifty-eight. Far too early for the Steadicam."

Clay and I stared at each other like a couple of idiots. Finally, he asked, "You gonna give us the director?"

"Hell, no," Howard said. "I've told you it's after fifty-eight. That's enough of a clue."

I sipped on my coffee and racked my brain, but couldn't come up with anything. This was a stumper, one that would require much more thought. However, it was going to have to go on the back burner, because at that point Steve Fischer bounced up to us, trying to look important. He slapped his thigh with a clipboard and had on a different shirt, perhaps an omen pointing to more pleasant interactions with his co-workers.

"Mornin', guys. Can I ask you to finish up and come into the soundstage? Bring your coffees with you. The producer's got more info on where we're at."

"How's Tony?" Clay said.

"More shall be revealed," Steve replied, and walked over to the next table.

We pushed our chairs back, gathered up our trays and bussed them. It looked like the production had only called about twenty-five extras. They remained in their holding area and listened to Steve as we made our way into the soundstage. I counted only fourteen principals in the room, among them Bev, Janice, and Ashley. They spotted us and walked up.

"Hi guys," Bev said. "Bet you thought you'd seen the last of us, right?"

"And the day is ever so much brighter for your appearance," Clay said, as he put an arm around Janice's shoulders. "Did they tell you what's going to happen?"

"Not a word," Ashley replied.

We sipped our coffees and made small talk for a few minutes until Warren Davidson, the line producer, called for our attention. We took seats at one of the banquet tables and watched as Davidson huddled with the director for a moment, then addressed us.

"Good morning, folks. First of all, I have some sad news. Tony Gould passed away at five o'clock yesterday." The announcement caught everyone by surprise and after a moment of silence, whispered conversations floated among those of us seated at tables. "However," Davidson continued, "the production is going to continue. I'm sure that's what Tony would have wished."

How in the world Davidson would know that was beyond me, but I suppose the statement was made as some sort of attempt at camaraderie. Hollywoodspeak for "everybody's sorry as hell, but the show must go on, so let's get on with it."

After a sip of coffee Davidson continued. "We're in the process of recasting the role, and as soon as we've made our decision, we'll let you know. Needless to say, our shooting schedule is going to be altered somewhat. The assistant directors will huddle with you in a few minutes."

He turned to a gentleman in a dark suit and tie who sat at a table next to him. "But first, I'd like to introduce Detective Harold Meyerson from the Burbank Police Department." I turned to glance at my tablemates, all of whom copied my look of puzzlement.

Meyerson stood. He was a solidly built man, well over six feet tall. His hair was jet black and closely cropped. A lanyard displaying a badge hung around his neck. He had cop written all over him. He looked vaguely familiar, but I wasn't sure why. Over the years I've had occasion to come into contact with the Burbank PD when I've been on a case, but I didn't remember specific names. I tried to recall where I might have met Meyerson before, but my efforts collided with Howard's infernal Steadicam trivia question.

The detective set his coffee cup on the table in front of him and addressed us. "Thank you, Mr. Davidson, and good morning, folks. Just to give you a heads up. Preliminary toxicology tests performed on Mr. Gould yesterday at Saint Joseph's suggest the possibility that his death may have been due to something more than just a heart attack."

Once again, murmurs and the buzz of conversation floated around the room. Meyerson went on. "Our aim is not to interfere with you folks, but please be advised that there will be a team of detectives here today trying to piece together Mr. Gould's whereabouts on the set yesterday. We would appreciate your cooperation."

With that he yielded to Davidson, who explained what was going to transpire for the rest of the day. We were told to standby while an assistant director would come around with more detailed information.

"Toxicology tests?" Janice said. "That suggests poison, doesn't it?"

"Could be," I said.

Howard chimed in. "Looks like our suspicions about Tony's lunch might be true."

"His chow came from the same roach coach as ours, right?" Clay said. "Anybody get sick last night?"

We all replied that we hadn't and began to offer opinions as to what may have happened. Our conversation stopped when Steve Fischer came up to the table and handed us a revised shooting schedule for the day, along with pages of dialogue. A new scene had been scripted with the three couples discussing the city council's decision to build the new civic center. We were told to get into costume and report back as soon as possible.

As we filtered out of the soundstage and made our way to the trailers, Howard and I compared notes on previous examples we'd encountered where a production had been disrupted like this. I shared one experience where a death had occurred, but Howard said he'd never run across one.

Before entering our respective halves of the trailer Howard said, "Now no cellphone consulting on that Steadicam question, Eddie."

"Not even a casual conversation with our camera operator?" I said.

He laughed and grabbed the doorknob of his cubicle. "Only under my supervision."

"I'd ask Steve Fischer, but I'm afraid he'd be no help." He chuckled and I opened the door and stepped into my dressing room.

I wasn't prepared for what greeted me.

A gangly young white man with grungy brown dreadlocks and a scruffy beard was pawing through the pockets of my costume. He wore jeans and a short-sleeved denim shirt. His back was to me and when he heard the door open, he whirled around and froze like he'd been caught looking through his sister's lingerie drawer.

"Can I help you?" I said.

"Uh...yeah, I...uh, was looking for something."

"And what would that be?"

He ran one hand over his beard and his eyes darted around the room like he was looking for a means of escape. "Ah...a key. You happen to find a key?"

So my mysterious key now concerned someone else. "No, I haven't seen a key. Who's looking for it?"

"I don't know, man. I was helping to clean out Mr. Gould's dressing room and someone on the crew told me there was a key missing."

"What made you think you'd find it in here?"

He looked very uncomfortable and shifted his weight from one foot to the other. "I was supposed to get it from Ken Thompson." He pulled back the lapel of the costume jacket and pointed to the tag inside. "That's you, right?"

There was no tag on the hanger indicating Collins. The name of the character an actor plays is usually displayed next to the door of his trailer. "Did you see 'Ken Thompson' next to the door?" I said.

"Ah, I don't know, man, I never looked."

"It says 'Greg Mason,' not 'Ken Thompson.'"

"Oh, okay. So you're not him then?"

"No, I'm not. Who told you to go looking for this key?"

"Look, what's with all the fuckin' questions? You find a key or not?"

"No, I didn't find a key."

"Fine," he said, and threw up his hands, shoved me aside and stormed through the door, slamming it behind him.

I immediately pushed it open and shouted after him. "Hey, wait a minute! What's your name?" I didn't get an answer and the guy disappeared around a corner. I shut the door and picked up the wastebasket. Empty. Transportation had cleaned out the dressing room overnight, taking with it the cardboard tag with my name on it that I'd removed from the hanger yesterday.

I slowly started to get dressed, my head full of questions about who the hell this kid was. When entering one's dressing room on the morning of a movie shoot, an actor usually finds a call sheet with a list of the scenes being shot that day and cast members who will be used. Unless I'd misread this morning's sheet, there was no Ken Thompson working on *Terms of Power* on this particular day. But that's not to say that he couldn't be in other scenes of the film. And yet that still didn't explain why his name would be on a label sewn on my costume. Surely this guy with the dreadlocks would have known that, if indeed he was employed by the production. Also, if he was on the costume crew, he would have known 'Greg Mason' translated to 'Eddie Collins,' not 'Ken Thompson.' Despite what Mavis, Reggie, and Carla had told me, I couldn't help but wonder what the connection was between the dearly departed Tony Gould and Ken Thompson.

The itch persisted.

5

The young man with the dreadlocks had tried his best, but didn't convince me that he worked on *Terms of Power*. This damn key I'd found was an obvious link between Tony Gould, now deceased, and a Ken Thompson, but what the hell was it? As I continued to get into my costume, questions rolled around in my head until I heard a knock on the door.

"Yeah?" I said.

A young woman pulled it open a foot and poked her head through. "Hair and makeup are ready for you, Mr. Collins."

"Okay," I said, and made sure all my valuables—including the key— were transferred from my street clothes to my costume, then stepped out of the trailer, new script pages in hand.

"Hi, my name is Debbie," she said, as she stuck out her hand.

"I'm Eddie," I said. We shook hands and started walking toward the makeup trailer. Debbie carried a flat legal-sized metal box that served as sort of a clipboard with what I assumed were call sheets and other production papers inside. She wore jeans and a USC sweatshirt and had a radio clipped to a fanny-pack belt circling her waist. A mic hovered near her right ear. She pushed a send button on the radio and relayed that she had Mr. Collins and was taking him to makeup.

"Guess you guys had quite a surprise yesterday, huh?" I said. "With Tony Gould's passing, I mean?"

"Yeah, no kidding."

"Any idea who's going to replace him?"

"I don't know," she said. "But I imagine there's plenty of actors in town that need the work, right?"

"Can't argue with you there." We dodged a hellbent messenger on a bicycle who barreled around a corner. "Let me ask you something, Debbie. Have you got a cast list in that clipboard of yours? For the whole film?"

She flipped open the top of it. "Yeah, somewhere I think."

"Is there a Ken Thompson on it?"

She rifled through some papers and stopped to look at one of them. "Nope. No such name. Friend of yours?"

"Yeah, from a while back. I ran into him at the audition for this. Just thought he might have landed the job."

"It could be that the list will be added to," she said. "I'll let you know if I get an update."

"Thanks," I said.

She closed the lid on the metal clipboard as we came to the makeup trailer. She pulled open the door and stuck her head inside. "I've got Mr. Collins for you, guys," she said, then opened the door wider and continued, "Nice to meet you, Eddie. I'll be back to get you."

I stepped up into the trailer and took an empty ersatz barber's chair. Crystal, a rotund black woman with a huge smile was ready for me. She looked at me, one hand on a cocked hip and said, "Good morning, sunshine. What did we do to you yesterday?"

"Made me irresistible," I said.

She broke into a huge laugh. "Oh, honey, you don't need us for that." She pulled some tissues from a box and stuck them over the rim of my collar, then opened a round container of pancake makeup and started dabbing it on my face with a small sponge. "Some excitement around here yesterday, huh? I mean, what happened to Mr. Gould?"

"Boy, you're not wrong there," I said. "When you guys worked on him, did it seem like there was anything wrong?"

"He wasn't in my chair," she said, and then turned to the other makeup person in the room, a slim young man dressed completely in black who had a tattoo of a snake running up his left arm. "Randy, did Mr. Gould act like anything was wrong with him when you worked on him yesterday?"

"Sure didn't. He cracked me up telling me stories about his arthritic cat. He was one funny dude."

Crystal and I continued to chat as she powdered me down and then told me I was good to go. Just in time, Debbie opened the door and said they were ready for me on set. With tissues still protruding from my collar, I got out of the chair, said my thanks to Crystal, and Debbie and I started for the soundstage.

"Got another question for you," I said.

"Shoot."

"Do you know all the people in the wardrobe department?"

"Not everyone," she said. "We're fairly early in the schedule."

"Earlier today I saw a young man hanging around the trailers. Dreadlocks? Beard? Real thin? He looked like a guy my sister dated at one time. Ring a bell with you?"

Debbie thought for a moment. "No, but that doesn't mean anything. Have you checked with Melissa, the wardrobe mistress? She'd be the one to ask."

"Yeah, good idea. I'll pop my head in there later."

We reached the door to the soundstage that had a revolving red light above it, which, when lit, indicated the camera was rolling. Debbie pulled it open and we stepped inside and waited for our eyes to adjust. She directed me to a group of six director's chairs, where my fellow cast members were gathered, cardboard coffee cups and script pages in hand. I claimed the empty seat and pulled my pages from my pocket. Clay and Howard also had tissues stuck in their collars. The three of us looked like wannabe courtiers unable to afford the lace for our doublets.

"How you doin', guys?" I said. "Ready for another morning of magic?"

Clay let out a guffaw and said, "Yeah, right. I need some magic to come up with an answer to that damn question. You figure it out, Collins?"

"Not yet," I replied. "I would have gone with *Touch of Evil* too."

He looked at Howard. "And no clues, I suppose?"

"No clues."

Clay then turned to the three women. "Any ideas, ladies? The first film where the Steadicam was used?" They looked at each other and shook their heads. He shrugged and said, "Looks like it's you and me, Collins."

"It'll come to me, Clay, but in the meantime we'd better work on this new dialogue, right?"

They all agreed and we started running the lines until we felt fairly comfortable with them. We took a break and Janice and Ashley walked over to the craft services table, then returned with pieces of pastry. I turned to look at one corner of the soundstage where Detective Meyerson was huddled with the director and line producer. I stared at the cop for a long moment, but still couldn't place where and when I'd seen him before.

"Has that Burbank cop talked to any of you?" I said, turning to my cast mates.

"Not to me," Howard said. The other four all indicated the same.

Bev sipped on her coffee and leaned over to me. "You find anything else in your costume this morning?"

"Nope. It remains a mystery," I said. "I'll have to run it up to the people at SunCoast. Let them deal with it."

She agreed that that would be the right plan of action, even though I had no intention of doing so. At least, not yet. The six of us continued running lines for a few more minutes until Steve Fischer appeared and told us to follow him to the set. We took our seats at the banquet table and waited while hair and makeup people did touch-ups. Sound and camera chimed in that they were ready, and we plunged into the scene on the "action" cue.

The first take went off without a hitch. Walt Langley, the director, gave us a couple of minor notes, and we did it again. Then once more for good measure. Finally he ordered the take to be printed, and we were told to relax, but to stay on the set. We filled more cups with coffee and reclaimed our director's chairs. Phones emerged, as did mine, but there were no texts or emails for me.

Clay was lost in thought, looking intently at the floor. "What's the matter, Clay?" I said. "You look like you've lost your last friend."

"Truth be told, Howard's Steadicam question is driving me bat-shit crazy."

The rest of us burst into laughter, and Howard patted him on the back. "Come on, Clay, it's not that big a deal."

"That's what you think," he said. "I'm the undefeated Trivial Pursuit champion on my cul-de-sac. My reputation is on the line."

"In your own mind," Janice said. "None of us are going to spill the beans if you give up."

"Never!" he replied, thrusting a finger into the air with as much fake bravado as he could summon.

"Okay, look," Howard said. "A bit of a hint. The director of the film where the Steadicam was first used started out as an editor."

"Well, hell, Howard, that's not much help," Clay said. "Most directors start out as film editors." He shook his head, slid off his chair and went in search of more coffee.

Howard shrugged and said, "Jesus, I didn't think I was going to ruin his day."

We laughed and assured him he was just being a tad melodramatic and not to take him seriously. As Clay came back with his coffee, Detective Meyerson approached and pulled up another chair. He had an air about him that gave one the impression he was damn proud of his badge and wasn't going to let anyone think differently.

"Good morning, folks. Detective Meyerson, Burbank PD. I'd like to ask you all a few questions."

Each of us introduced ourselves. When it came to my turn, I offered my hand and as he shook it, Meyerson looked at me with the trace of a scowl.

"Collins," he said, "You wouldn't by any chance have a PI ticket, would you?"

"I do," I replied.

"Yeah, I thought so. I remember you from that Hendrickson case a few years ago."

There it was. The answer. I flashed back and recalled a case I'd picked up where I'd been hired to tail a wandering husband who got caught up in a Burbank PD sting that involved human trafficking, of all things. It was a pretty sordid scene and I wound up making zero friends with the cops when I inadvertently stepped into their stakeout.

"That's right," I said. "Glad you got your man."

"No thanks to you," he said.

"I was just doing my job, detective. We were all on the same side."

"Well, that's a matter of opinion." He pulled a notebook from his pocket and flipped it open, his attitude telling me I most likely wouldn't wind up on his Christmas card list.

My fellow actors were silent, like they'd eavesdropped on a family argument. "As I mentioned yesterday," Meyerson continued, "preliminary tests are being done on the deceased. While there aren't any definitive results, I want to get a sense of his routine while he was on the set. Did any of you happen to have either breakfast or lunch with mister Gould?"

We all said we hadn't and Clay offered the opinion that Tony seemed to take his meals in his trailer, as opposed to joining the rest of the company. Meyerson asked several more questions, then closed his notebook and was about to get off his chair when Janice piped up.

"Detective, I just remembered something," she said. "After I was through with lunch I bussed my tray and started to walk back to my trailer. I had to pass Tony's. As I passed by the door, it opened and a guy stepped out with a lunch tray full of plates and silverware. It looked like he was returning mister Gould's dishes."

"Did you see him deliver the lunch tray?" Meyerson said.

"No. I'd never seen him before," Janice replied.

"Can you describe the guy?"

"He was tall, thin, with a beard, and had those braids all over his head. You know? Those things that look like strands of rope?"

"You mean dreadlocks?"

"Yeah, I guess that's what they're called."

Meyerson entered the information in his notebook and I turned to Janice. "Was he wearing a denim shirt and jeans?"

"Hmm, I'm not real sure, Eddie. He might have been."

Meyerson threw another scowl at me and once again turned his attention to the group. "Did any of the rest of you see this guy?"

"Yeah, he was in my trailer this morning," I said.

"You sure it was the same man?"

"Those dreadlocks are hard to forget."

"What was he doing there?"

"He was going through the pockets of my costume and said he was looking for something."

"What?"

"He didn't say," I replied, deliberately holding back the fact that dreadlocks had been looking for a key. Meyerson had pissed me off with his attitude over what had transpired between us in the past. Being a burr under the saddle of someone in law enforcement comes with the territory for a private investigator, and there's no doubt I've caused my share of irritation. On that case in particular, I was apologetic and subsequently cooperative with the Burbank PD. However, today I was going to be stubborn. And uncooperative. My interest lay in finding out what that key signified, not the death of Tony Gould.

"So, this guy with the dreadlocks," Meyerson said, "he's on the wardrobe crew?"

"That I don't know," I said. "You'd have to ask them."

"Which I'll do, Collins, okay?"

"You've got the badge," I said, returning the glare he leveled at me.

Meyerson thanked us for our time, closed his notebook and walked off. I sipped on my coffee and let the silence sink in. It felt like the six of us were at a funeral. After a moment Howard and Ashley got off their chairs and threw their coffee cups into a trash bin.

"If I was you, Eddie," Clay said, "I'd avoid being picked up by the cops in Burbank."

"I don't plan on it," I said.

Bev again leaned over to me and said, "How come you didn't tell him about the key?"

"Frankly, the guy rubbed me the wrong way. Besides, I don't think finding that key has anything to do with Tony's death."

"I hope you're right," she said.

I hoped I was too. And if I wasn't, I'd find some other Burbank cop to tell them I was wrong.

6

The rest of the morning consisted of various camera angles involving the six of us. They were tedious, and I began to wonder if ultimately they were even necessary. I had the distinct impression that the director and his crew were improvising until a decision had been made about Tony Gould's replacement.

At eleven-thirty, we finished another scene, after which the director announced to everyone on the set that that was a wrap for Janice Wilkes, Bev Peterson, and Ashley Brandt. Our screen marriages had come to an abrupt halt. The three ladies accepted hugs and thanks from the director and his first assistant. I put my arms around Bev and told her it was good working with her again.

"Same here, Eddie. I hope you find out where that key of yours belongs."

"I'll shoot you a text when I do."

She said she'd look forward to it, and then said goodbye to Clay and Howard. I did the same to Janice and Ashley and the three women left the soundstage, leaving their three cinematic mates to soldier on.

Our director told us he wanted to get one more shot before lunch, a scene that took place in a men's restroom. Of course it had to be a men's room. The obligatory shot of guys standing at urinals, pretending to do what men have to do, all the while uttering innocuous dialogue. Then a hunch of your shoulders, a fake zip-up and the washing of your hands. It's become an overworked cliché in movies, and I always wonder why men have to be so congenial when engaged in such a private moment. The only element missing in our scene was the bad guy bursting out of one of the stalls, catching the unsuspecting men with water on their hands and egg on their faces.

The scene was going to use an actual men's room in one of the adjacent office buildings. But it had to be lit, so while the crew moved equipment, Clay, Howard and I were released and told to hang out in our trailers and we would be summoned. Before leaving the soundstage, we ran the lines a couple of times, and agreed we were on top of them.

Clay and Howard walked off, Clay pestering Howard about clues to the Steadicam question. Taking advantage of the break, I made my way to the wardrobe trailer and pulled the door open. Melissa Ailes was nowhere to be seen. Instead, a young blond woman stood on a three-step ladder pawing through costumes hanging on one of the racks suspended from the ceiling. She wore a black tee shirt with the logo of the Hard Rock Cafe on the back of it. She had cargo shorts on and sandals covered her feet. A floral tattoo was splayed across one of her calves. She looked over her shoulder as I stepped into the room.

"Can I help you?" she said.

"Is Melissa around?"

"Not at the moment. I'm Ginger. Something I can help you with?"

"Yeah, I'm in the cast, playing Greg Mason. The name's—"

She interrupted me with, "Right, you're Eddie Collins. What do you need?"

I was impressed that she knew my name by the mere mention of my character. But then, wardrobe departments generally have photos and names right alongside a character's name, so I suppose actor and role become almost synonymous. In any case, I had a sense I was probably asking the right person.

"Do you know all the people on the wardrobe crew?"

"I'm pretty sure I do. You looking for someone in particular?"

"Well, there was a guy in my trailer this morning looking through my costume. Tall? Skinny? He had a scraggly beard and his head was full of brown dreadlocks. I didn't get his name, but he looked like a guy that dated my sister at one time. You happen to know what his name is?"

She backed down off the ladder with a dress on a hanger. "Boy, I don't know of anybody with that description. You sure he was in wardrobe?"

"Not really. He left abruptly. Didn't seem to be very talkative."

"Maybe he's in another department? Props, maybe?"

"Yeah, could be," I said. "I'll ask around. Thanks, Ginger."

"You bet," she said, and laid the dress on a table as I opened the door and stepped out of the trailer. Given the fact that Ginger had known my name without ever having met me, I had a hunch that her not knowing my dreadlocked visitor was proof that he was not on the wardrobe crew. I began to wonder if he was even involved with the film shoot at all. If so, what the hell was he doing coming out of Tony Gould's trailer? And why was he looking for a key with "Pandora" inscribed on it?

Howard, Clay, and I were stupendous in front of our respective urinals. Walt Langley only needed two takes and the three of us were then released for lunch. The production's roach coach offered Mexican food or a pasta dish. Clay and I settled on the former, while Howard opted for the latter. We straddled chairs under the blue tarp and I caught sight of Detective Meyerson lurking around the perimeter of the lunch area. At one point when he was on his cellphone our eyes met and the look on his face still gave me impression he thought my photo should be hanging on the wall of the nearest post office.

Clay still agonized over Howard's trivia question, and his agony was exacerbated by Howard's smugness. I was also clueless, but then, I hadn't thought too much about the answer. We bussed our trays, poured ourselves cups of coffee and again took seats as we waited for our next shot.

"Okay, guys," Howard said. "Out of the generosity of my heart, I'll give you another little hint."

"Well, whoop-dee-doo," Clay said. "Don't bust your balls, Howard."

He chuckled and said, "This director died in 1988 at his home up in Malibu."

"Of what?" I said.

"Pancreatic cancer."

"Eww, tough one," Clay said.

Clay and I sipped our coffees and racked our brains, trying to avoid Howard's smugness. We batted some names around for a few minutes until Steve Fischer came up to the table.

"Hey, guys, good news," he said. "You're released for the day. We're still trying to figure out what the heck we're doing. Be sure and stay in touch with your agents, okay?"

We said we would, disposed of our coffee cups and headed to our trailers.

"I'll have the damn answer by tomorrow, Howard," Clay said, as he pulled open the door to his dressing room.

"I'll look forward to it," Howard replied.

I said I'd see both of them tomorrow, pulled the door shut and changed clothes. My watch said two o'clock. I had plenty of time to return to Collins Investigations and do some sleuthing on my computer, something that a few months ago would have been as foreign to me as doing needlepoint.

7

Mavis doesn't do needlepoint. Not to my knowledge, anyway. But what I saw on her desk in front of her as I opened the door to Collins Investigations could lead one to believe otherwise. Two pillows, both of them approximately a square foot in size, lay on the desk, waiting to be placed in a cardboard box, whose bottom seams were being covered with duct tape.

"Hey, boss man, done for the day?"

"Yup." I picked up one of the pillows that had two faces on them, one male, one female. "Who are these guys?"

"Come on, Eddie, that's Roy Rogers and Dale Evans."

"Oh, yeah, right." I picked up the other pillow with the images of two horses' heads on it. "And I suppose these are Trigger and Buttercup?"

"Buttermilk, Buttermilk! For cryin' out loud, weren't you a fan of Roy and Dale?"

"Not really. Gene Autry was more my guy. Besides, Champion could kick Trigger's ass any day of the week." She let loose a noise somewhere between a snort and a sigh, then yanked the pillow out of my hand and placed it in the box on top of Roy and Dale. "Who's the lucky buyer?"

"A gal down in Torrance. Would you believe they still have a fan club?"

"If you say so," I said, as I walked into my office, once again marveling at the necessity in some people's lives for all things trivial. "Any calls?"

"Telemarketers. I assume you're not interested in laser spine surgery?"

"Not this week." I hung up my hat and plopped down behind my desk. Today's *Hollywood Reporter* and *Los Angeles Times* lay on one corner. I sent

Carla a text that said I was done for the day, and asked if she wanted to get some dinner later. I pulled the Pandora key out of my pocket and laid it in front of me. Focus, I reasoned.

"I go on Google if I want to look up something, right?" I said, as I pulled the laptop in front of me and flipped it open.

Mavis appeared in the doorway. "Oh, my God, stop the presses! The private eye is finally on the Internet. A red-letter day."

"Yeah, well, don't push your luck. I may need help."

"What are you looking for?"

I held up the key. "Despite what you, Reggie, and Carla may say, I think this key wound up in my costume for a reason. I aim to prove it."

"Well, good luck," she said, and then grinned and went back to her taping. I pulled up the Google site and typed in "Pandora." The hits I got were intimidating enough to cause me to paw through the beaded curtain into my apartment for liquid fortification. Foaming glass of beer at my elbow, I dialed the number for the floral shop that had popped up earlier when I'd looked at the Yellow Pages. I was told they didn't have any key like the one I described.

When I asked the young woman who answered the phone for Pandora Day Spa if they had individual lockers that might be missing a key, I was told that patrons of the place brought their own locks and keys while on the premises. No help there, so I started scrolling through the Google results. They were dominated by entries pertaining to the music service. Several listings for jewelry outlets also popped up. I began to think this search wasn't going to yield anything useful, so I pushed the laptop to the edge of my desk and picked up the newspapers.

Both the *Times* and the *Reporter* ran obituaries of Tony Gould. They reported that his death was apparently due to natural causes. I found it curious that the obits would appear so soon after his death, but then remembered that a reporter friend of mine had once told me that early in his career he was assigned to writing obituaries for people who were still alive, so when they passed, bang, the obit was all ready to go. The

Times didn't have a long piece about the actor, but the *Hollywood Reporter* delved more specifically into the various projects he had been involved in over the years. I took a sip of beer, propped my feet up on the desk and leaned back in the chair.

It was obvious that Tony Gould had had quite an exemplary career as an actor, and had also occasionally directed a project. But what I didn't know about him brought my feet off the desk and made me bolt upright. A few years ago Tony Gould also wore the hat of a producer and had his own production company.

It was called Pandora Productions.

"Aha!" I shouted, which, after a moment, brought Mavis from around the corner.

"What?"

"Tony Gould, recently deceased? Tony Gould, who keeled over on the set of *Terms of Power*? You remember?"

"Yeah, yeah, so what?"

"He also had a production company." I paused and looked at her with the best smug face I could muster. "Would you like to know the name of it?"

She glared at me, and when it became apparent I wasn't going to offer the answer she said, "Okay, I'll bite. What?"

I picked up the key, and swung it back and forth from its metal disc.

"You're kidding? Pandora?"

"You got it, kiddo."

"I'm impressed. Where does that leave you?"

"I'm not sure. But this morning there was a guy with a head full of dreadlocks pawing through my costume looking for this key. The wardrobe department knows no such guy. Then he's seen carrying dishes out of Tony Gould's trailer not long before Gould keels over on the set. Now you tell me. Enough to pique your curiosity?"

She pursed her lips and looked at me for a long moment. "Maybe. But how are you going to follow up on it when you're still working on this movie?"

"I've got Reggie. And you, when you're not selling cowboy pillows."

She laughed and shook her head. "Whatever you say, Eddie." She turned around and went back to her desk with the parting shot of, "But I still think you're whistling Dixie."

I took another swallow of beer and figured it wouldn't do me any good to rebut her comment, so I went back to the laptop. The IMDb site also has another subscriber version called IMDb Pro, providing more in-depth information on all things Hollywood. I went to the site and entered "Pandora Productions and Tony Gould." It brought up a link with several film projects attributed to the company, some of which were familiar to me. I noodled around the site for several minutes, following links that led me to the personnel involved in the production company.

All at once my eyes froze on the screen.

Listed as a co-producer on a film from eleven years ago by the name of *Circle of Deception* was one Ken Thompson. I clicked on his name and scrolled through his credits. It was the same Ken Thompson who was in *Crash and Burn*. Along with Tony Gould. Two films together, one of them produced by Pandora, a name found on a key that I happened to discover in a pocket of my costume. A key that was subsequently sought by a guy in dreadlocks, who may have been one of the last people to see Tony Gould alive. Questions swirled around in my head, kicking and wrestling with the term coincidence. They stopped when my cellphone chirped. The screen said Carla Rizzoli.

"Hey, you," I said. "How's the day going?"

"Okay, I guess."

Her usually upbeat voice was missing. "What's the matter?"

"Oh, nothing. Just a little blue, is all."

"How come?"

"Today's Frankie's birthday."

The Frankie she referred to was her brother, an undercover cop who Carla had hired me to find some months back. I'd been successful, but the end results hadn't come out to her satisfaction. Nor mine, for that matter.

"Still missing him?" I said.

After a long pause she sighed and whispered, "Yeah."

"How about I take you out for a nice dinner? I've got a big shoulder for you to cry on."

She managed a small chuckle, then said, "I don't feel like going out, Eddie. Why don't you pick up something and come over here? I'll call you when I'm done."

"You got it. I'll pop into Ralph's and raid their deli."

"Ralph's? Really?"

"Why not?"

"I was thinking more along the lines of Whole Foods."

"Okay, Whole Foods it is," I said, wondering what the hell was wrong with Ralph's, but quickly ceding the fact that I wasn't going to win the argument. "Any special requests?"

"Surprise me," she said, and hung up.

I sipped on my beer. Despite what had happened to her brother back then, Carla's always been an upbeat person, not prone to moping. She currently had a role on what looked to be a successful television series, which was giving her a lot of optimism, not only about her career, but her personally as well. Hopefully some TLC and good, solid comfort food would help with the blues.

After taking my empty beer glass back into my apartment, I turned on the small boom box that sits behind my desk. There's a sort of retro-oldies-folk station I tune into periodically. The familiar strains of *Tom Dooley* by the Kingston Trio filled my office as Mavis appeared in the doorway, her box of pillows under one arm and her purse over the other shoulder.

"Was that Carla on the phone?"

"It was. She's a bit down. Today's her brother's birthday."

"Oh, dear. You better cheer her up."

"That's my plan."

"What time's your call tomorrow?"

"I don't know yet. Waiting to hear from Morrie."

"Okay. I'm off to put Roy and Dale in the mail. My love to Carla."

"You got it," I said, and she turned and left the office.

I pulled my Rolodex in front of me and found the number for Dennis Engels, a producer friend of mine who's shuffled around the Hollywood maze for a number of years. We'd gotten to know each other on a television pilot for Universal a while back that unfortunately went nowhere. He, however, had parlayed the project into some lucrative positions down the road. A woman answered the phone, and after giving her my name and my reason for calling I was put on hold. A couple of moments passed and Dennis came on the line.

"Eddie Collins. Long time no hear from. How ya doin'?"

"Good, Denny. Still waiting to become a household name."

"You and me both, pal. But you're still hanging out that PI shingle, right?"

"I am indeed. That's the reason for the call."

"What can I do you for?"

"In your checkered past, you ever hear of a production company by the name of Pandora?"

"Oooh," he said, then paused. I could hear voices in the background. "Despite all the brain cells I've destroyed, I seem to recall a company by that name."

"It was run by one Tony Gould," I said.

"Yeah, right." After a moment he continued, "Wait a minute. Didn't I just read that he kicked the bucket? On a set, or something?"

"*Terms of Power*. I'm working on the thing."

"Christ, there's easier ways of getting a good role, Eddie," he said, and followed it up with a hearty laugh.

"Not that desperate yet," I said. "What else do you remember?"

"Oh, man. Let me think." He paused. "Seems to me there was something hinky about the outfit."

"Hinky? How do you mean?"

"Somebody sued them, I think."

"For what?"

"That I don't recall, Eddie. But tell you what, let me ask around. See if I can shake anything loose."

"I'd appreciate it, buddy," I said. "What have you got on your plate lately?"

"Couple things. In the wind, you know?"

"My SAG dues are current, Denny."

"I hear you. You're always on my list, pal."

We gabbed for a couple of minutes and I finally hung up, after exchanging cellphone numbers with him. Dennis was a good guy to know. He had indeed called me in on a project or two in the past. Whether or not that continued was anybody's guess, but it doesn't hurt to grease the wheel, as some purveyor of clichés once said.

With Pete Seeger and his banjo in the background, I returned to the laptop. My Internet surfing abilities still remain somewhat inept, but I had a passing knowledge of Wikipedia. I brought up the site and entered Pandora Productions. Bingo! There wasn't much, but enough for me to discover that the company had had some legal problems before disbanding nine years ago. Two years after *Circle of Deception*. The site listed links to a couple of references, but after looking at them, I didn't find any more information as to what the legal proceedings were. I surfed a little more, but finally gave up and called my Gal Friday.

"What's up?" Mavis said. I could hear the sound of traffic in the background.

"Are you driving? I'll wait for you to pull over."

"Bluetooth, Eddie. Hands-free telephone. That's your next project. Every self-respecting private investigator should have one."

"I'll take it under advisement. Hey, listen, this Pandora outfit apparently got into some legal trouble a few years back. I can't for the life of me figure out how to find out what it was. Can you, in your vast and unchallenged knowledge of all things computer, help me out?"

She chuckled and said, "You do have a handle on the powers of persuasion. I'll give you that. Leave the specifics on my desk and I'll get to it in the morning."

"Thanks, kiddo," I replied, and I hung up, wondering what that did to her Bluetooth.

I'd no sooner finished the call with Mavis than Morrie phoned with my call time of seven o'clock in the morning. Pretty early. Maybe they were finally getting their act together on *Terms of Power*. It could also mean they'd found a replacement for Tony Gould. While I finished scanning the papers, Carla sent a text saying she was done at four. They were shooting an exterior and in danger of losing their light. My watch said it was three-thirty. That gave me an hour to get cleaned up and pick up some good old-fashioned comfort food. I texted her back and told her I'd meet her at her place.

I shut down the laptop and threw the newspapers on Mavis's recycling pile. Then I filled a notebook page with what I wanted her to look for and left it on her desk. As I reached to turn off the boom box that was belting forth Woody Guthrie's version of *Old Dan Tucker*, I stopped and my face broke into a huge grin.

I had the answer to Howard's Steadicam trivia question.

8

If I ever have a burning desire to hobnob with the hip, slick, and cool of greater Los Angeles, Whole Foods Market fits the bill. I stood in line at the deli counter behind two young women whose wardrobes probably consumed several pictures of Ben Franklin. They couldn't decide what kind of sushi they wanted. One leaned towards Sashimi, the other fancied Temaki. After several eye-rolls and a gentle reminder from the counterman that someone was behind them, they finally compromised and ordered both. While they waited for their bait to be wrapped, they apologized profusely and then launched into a conversation about their most recent tummy-tucks. A fender bender between a Porsche and a Prius made the parking lot a zoo, which, as a result, caused me to be late getting to Carla's with our dinner.

My tardiness didn't bother her, but I could tell her melancholia hadn't left. Despite oven-baked chicken with parmigiano reggiano crust, smoky collard greens, and tomato-basil freekeh salad sitting in front of her, she picked at her food. At one point I filled our wine glasses with a nice red whose name I couldn't pronounce and reached out and squeezed her hand.

"Thanks for the food, Eddie. There's enough here for three days."

"You can always take it with you to your trailer. A break from the roach coach."

"Not a bad idea," she said, then sipped some wine and looked down at the table. "I'm sorry I'm such a party pooper."

"Hey, no problem. I haven't forgotten about Frankie either." And I hadn't. The memories of what had happened to her brother that day at the

Farmers Market, along with what a bullet from my gun had done were still firmly entrenched in my consciousness.

"My mom called this morning. She really misses him, too."

"Yeah, I can imagine," I said. I didn't know what else to say, so I suggested she go and relax in the living room and I'd take care of the remains of dinner. She said okay, we both stood, and I took her in my arms. "Cherish his memory, honey. You'll always have that, and sooner or later losing him will be easier to deal with."

"Yeah, I guess," she said, as she laid her head on my chest and put her arms around me. The tone of her voice indicated that she didn't fully agree.

I kissed her, and she picked up her wineglass and went into the living room. After taking care of the food and dishes, and with wine bottle and glass in hand, I joined her on the couch. I slid an arm around her shoulder and pulled her into me. She'd turned on the television and for a moment or two we looked at some innocuous reality show until she switched it off and picked up her glass.

"I'm glad you found out something about that key of yours," she said.

Over dinner I'd told her what I'd learned that afternoon, but even so, she'd said she couldn't see where that information would lead me. I confessed that I didn't either, but that I thought it was enough to propel me to keep looking. She put her glass back on the coffee table and sank into the sofa. She was quiet for a long moment, a faraway look on her face. After a moment, she reached for a tissue and dabbed at the corner of one eye.

"Something else is bothering you, Carla. Come on, out with it."

After a long sigh, she said, "Aw, crap, I wasn't going to tell you this, but something else happened today that's also bummed me out."

"What?"

"I got hit on. To put it bluntly, someone grabbed my ass."

I set my glass down and turned to her. "Really? Who?"

"One of the line producers."

"You're kidding."

"I wish I was. His name is Artie Young. It happened on the lot." Carla's show, *Three on a Beat*, was being shot at Raleigh Studios, not far from Paramount. "We'd finished a table read," she continued, "and were on a break. He came up behind me at the coffee pots when I felt it. I turned around and got in his face. He said it was accidental, but I know damn well it wasn't."

What she told me immediately stirred up feelings of disgust, not only because it involved someone I deeply cared for, but also the fact that, in the wake of Harvey Weinstein and the whole #MeToo and Time's Up movements, one would think the days of the casting couch and sexual misconduct would be left in the past.

"For crissakes," I said. "Hasn't the guy read the news? That kind of behavior should be suicide in this day and age."

"You would think so," Carla said. "He knows that I used to dance. In fact, he mentioned one time that he'd seen me at the Follies."

"So because of that he thinks you're used to it, or something?"

She shrugged and picked up her glass. "I guess. But that was performing, Eddie. Yeah, from time to time some guy would get a little frisky, but we learned to expect it, and did our best to discourage it. If anyone got out of hand, they were thrown out of the club on their asses. This isn't like that. It's a whole different workplace."

"And one where that stuff is totally inappropriate," I said. "Did you tell Marsha or Alison about it?" Marsha Bailey and Alison Jackson were her two co-stars on the show.

"Yeah, both of them," Carla replied.

"What did they say? Anything like that happen to them?"

"Alison said he'd been awfully 'friendly' with her on a couple of occasions, but nothing like what he did to me."

"Did you tell anybody else about it? An executive producer, for instance?"

She put her wineglass back on the coffee table and tucked her legs underneath her. "Not yet. The thing is, I'm kind of afraid to. I don't know

for sure what kind of power Artie has. I don't want to jeopardize this job."
She pounded a fist into a knee. "Dammit, I've got a good thing going with
the show."

I reached out and grabbed one of the fists she had made. "Listen,
honey, that's exactly how creeps like this want you to feel. They think
they're invincible because they can hire and fire. But thanks to ol' Harvey,
there's little tolerance for this kind of crap anymore. What do you think
you should do about it?"

"I don't know. Any ideas?"

I picked up my wineglass, sipped, and took one of her hands in mine.
"First of all, you should probably keep your distance from this asshole."

"I will, as much as I can, anyway."

"I don't know what kind of relationship you have with the executive
producers. They might cover for him. But then again, maybe they'll fire
his ass."

"Yeah, I don't know either," she said.

"But don't let it get in the way of what you're doing. You've got Marsha
and Alison in your corner. Strength in numbers, if the three of you stand
up to him."

"Yeah, they were both pissed when I told them."

"What you should maybe do, besides keeping your distance from this
schmuck, is talk to someone in the union. It seems to me the Guild is
pretty on top of this stuff."

"That's a good idea. Somebody from SAG was on the set one day a
while back, but I didn't get his name."

"Let me see if I can find a number and I'll text it to you."

"Thanks. Is that going to put me in any kind of jeopardy?"

"No, not in the least. The show is signatory to the Guild's contract,
and if there's any sexual misconduct, the employer is going to hear about,
believe me."

Carla put her wineglass on the coffee table, then leaned into me and gave
me a kiss. "Thanks for listening, Eddie. I'm glad you're in my corner too."

"So am I," I replied. We hugged each other for a long moment, and finally she leaned back.

"Are you called tomorrow morning?"

"Yeah. Seven o'clock."

"Me too," she said, as she grabbed another tissue and made a swipe at her nose. She picked up her wineglass, sipped, then looked at me and broke into a welcome smile. "Kinda neat, isn't it? Both of us in front of the camera at the same time?"

"Let's hope it happens more often. In the meantime, keep that asshole at arm's length. From personal experience, I know you can do that."

"What? What personal experience?"

"Let's just say I've gotten to know the Rizzoli wrath." She scowled and tossed a pillow at me. I was kidding, of course, and I only said it to playfully provoke her into getting back her Italian feistiness. It worked.

We refilled our wineglasses and gabbed about our respective film jobs. Since we both had early calls, we agreed that I should trundle off to my own lair. I picked up my hat from a table by the door and we wrapped our arms around each other, holding the pose for a wonderful long moment. She raised her face to me and I kissed her.

"I'm sorry you had a bad day, kiddo."

"Yeah, well, it comes with the territory, I guess," she said, as she tugged on the brim of my hat. "But you've got a terrific knack for cheering a girl up, Shamus."

"My pleasure, ma'am," I said, and gave her another kiss. "I'll touch base with you tomorrow. Sleep well."

"I will. You, too." When I turned to grab the doorknob, she patted me on the rump. "Ooops," she said. I looked over my shoulder and she giggled, her hands over her mouth like she'd said a naughty word in front of her Sunday school teacher. I gave her a smirk and closed the door behind me.

One of the rituals of living in Los Angeles—and I suppose anywhere nowadays—is that you lock your car door. I don't have one of those fobs that you push and your car chirps and beeps when you lock it and unlock it. Great for finding a misplaced auto, but the underground parking garage at Carla's place wasn't big enough to lose a bicycle, let alone a car. As I approached my road-weary vehicle, I peered through the window and saw something was amiss. The glove compartment was hanging open and CDs and papers were strewn all over the front seat. I pulled a handkerchief from my pocket and gripped the door handle. It was unlocked. I'm generally very diligent about locking the car when exiting, but I'm only human. I'd had Whole Foods dinner on my mind and it occurred to me that I could have had a moment of forgetfulness.

I pulled the door open and leaned down to look inside. Nothing was destroyed; the disc player and radio were still there. Upholstery was undamaged. But somebody had definitely been looking for something. I popped the trunk and moved to the rear of the car. The cardboard box that contains various costume pieces I use for auditions had been turned upside down and the contents strewn over the interior of the trunk. The metal box with a digital lock that I keep my sidearm in had been moved from its usual position, but hadn't been jimmied open.

I stuffed the costume pieces back in the box, repositioned the metal safe and shut the trunk. The passenger side of the car showed no damage, no sign that some punk had keyed the paint job. The passenger door was locked.

Carla's Honda Fit was parked next to me. I looked inside and didn't see a sign of anything disturbed. I knew she had an alarm on the car, so I didn't try to see if the door was locked.

As I leaned against my car with the door open, a debate rolled around in my head. Chances were that there might be latent fingerprints on the door and the glove compartment, but since nothing seemed to be missing—disc player and CDs, I thought it a good bet that whoever ransacked my car had worn gloves. Getting the police involved seemed like a waste of time. Chalk it up to life in the urban jungle. I called Carla and told her what happened, and suggested that she keep her eyes peeled when going to and from her car.

Before climbing into the front seat, I looked back at the entrance to the garage. Wooden barriers with black and yellow stripes spanned both the entry and exit. One had to punch in a four-digit code to raise the barriers. So someone hadn't driven in; they'd scooted under the barrier. That meant either someone had been following me and had seen me drive in, or else a thief was on a random spree. As I looked around the garage, I couldn't detect any evidence of anybody else's car being ransacked.

After the CDs and papers were reassembled into some sort of order, I drove out of the garage with the thought in my head that someone had been looking for something specific in my car, thus no theft or damage. Maybe I was being paranoid, but I had a hunch what it might be.

A key and a metal disc with "Pandora" etched on it.

9

Tony Gould had been replaced. I found that out when I stepped into my dressing room and glanced at the call sheet for the day. The actor the producers had hired to play Mayor Hessman was a fellow by the name of Tom Sanderson, a name unfamiliar to me.

I had a new costume hanging from the rack. A different colored suit and shirt and tie. Paranoia notwithstanding, I went through the pockets, hoping like hell there wasn't another key or some other misplaced trinket in one of the pockets. They were empty, and there was no label with a previous actor and production sewed into the lining. A clean slate.

On my drive into Warners I found myself mulling over the events of the previous evening. I had no proof that Dreadlocks had made an encore appearance by ransacking my car. Since access to Carla's parking garage was open, I reasoned that the intruder could merely have been somebody on a spree of mischief. Still, the fact that it was my car, and not anyone else's, bugged the hell out of me.

Clay and Howard had already secured their breakfasts and were sitting at a table, shoveling away. With a plate full of scrambled eggs, bacon and a dollop of hash browns, I straddled a chair and joined them.

"Mornin," I said. "I see we've got a new mayor."

"Yeah," Howard replied. "I worked with the guy before. He's got the chops."

I cracked open the little packets of salt and pepper and sprinkled my eggs. "Well, I have some monumental news, guys."

"Oh, yeah?" Clay said. "You finally learned your lines?"

"Not only that, but I know the answer to Howard's trivia question about the Steadicam."

The two men looked at each other, forkfuls of breakfast burrito halfway to their mouths. I nibbled on a slice of bacon and waited for a response.

After a moment Clay said, "Well? What the hell is it?"

"*Bound for Glory*. The Woody Guthrie story, with David Carradine."

Howard pointed his fingers at me as if he were aiming a pistol and said, "Bingo. Directed by Hal Ashby."

"Crap," Clay said. "I've seen that movie. Where the hell was it?"

"Garret Brown, the guy who invented the Steadicam, was the operator," Howard said. "Haskell Wexler was DP. The camera is on a crane that swoops down. Brown steps off and follows Carradine through a crowd of Okies. And then, after he talks to Randy Quaid, they turn around and walk toward the camera, and the operator walks backward. Amazing!"

"Damn, that's right," Clay said. "I remember that shot now."

"It took almost two minutes," Howard added. "And won Wexler the Oscar."

"Good going, Collins," Clay said, as we exchanged high-fives. "But I seriously think both you guys need a hobby. And maybe you should get laid while you're at it."

The three of us laughed as Howard looked over my shoulder and gestured to someone approaching.

"Hey, Tom, grab a chair," he said.

I turned around and saw who I assumed was Tom Sanderson walk up. He was a short man. Closely-cropped gray hair covered his partially-bald head. A mustache filled his upper lip, and blue eyes peered through a pair of rimless glasses. The face was familiar to me, no doubt from one of the countless auditions I've been on over the years in pursuit of the Hollywood brass ring. He had a cup of coffee and a bowl of fruit in his hands. He set the coffee down and grabbed Howard's outstretched hand with a burst of enthusiasm that belied his lack of height.

"Howard, how the hell ya doin'?" he said, with the trace of a southern accent. "A nice surprise to see your name on the call sheet. It's been a while, boss."

"Indeed it has," Howard said, and then gestured to Clay and me. "Meet Eddie Collins and Clay Dawson."

Sanderson shook hands with both of us, pulled out the fourth chair and sat down. "Pleasure to meet y'all."

"Welcome aboard," Clay said.

"Thanks," Tom replied, as he looked at me. "Eddie, I think we've crossed paths before. Some audition, somewhere."

"Yeah, I thought so," I said. "I couldn't tell you what it was, though."

"You got me. They all blend into one after a while, don't they?"

We continued to chat as we ate our respective breakfasts. When questioned about his slight accent, Tom informed us he'd grown up in New Orleans and come to Hollywood after a stint at LSU. He said he was glad when *Terms of Power* came along, but wished that it had come under different circumstances. He went on to say that he'd known Tony Gould and had worked with him on a couple of occasions. We'd refreshed our coffees and were filling Tom in on the shoot thus far when Steve Fischer walked up, clipboard slapping one of his legs. I was glad to see he wore different clothes from yesterday. Evidence of hygienic progress, no doubt.

"Mr. Sanderson, I'm Steve, one of the ADs," he said. "Hair and makeup are ready for you. If you'll follow me." He turned to the three of us. "You three can chill for a while. First up is the scene with the mayor addressing the banquet. What we'd already shot with Mr. Gould."

"Oh, boy, I'm the first one in the barrel, huh?" Tom laughed, picked up his coffee cup and fruit bowl and followed Steve.

I excused myself from the table, and after getting more reluctant kudos from Clay about the *Bound for Glory* answer, went back to my dressing room and left the door open to get some fresh air into the place. After looking over the dialogue that I had for the day, I pulled out my phone and found the website for SAG-AFTRA. After poking around the site for a minute or two, a number popped up to call if one wanted to report sexual harassment issues. I texted it to Carla and was halfway through a digital crossword when there was a knock on the screen door. I turned to see Detective Meyerson peering through the screen.

"Yeah, come on in."

Meyerson pulled the door open and stepped into the trailer. "Morning, Collins. You got a couple of minutes?"

"Sure. Have a seat."

He pulled a chair out from the small table in the room and took out a notebook, then looked at me for a long moment, his demeanor appearing less confrontational than yesterday.

"What's up?"

"Hey, listen, I was out of line yesterday. About what happened on that Hendrickson deal."

"No problem. Not the first time it's happened to me."

"What? Getting in the way of an investigation?"

Maybe he wasn't going to be as non-confrontational as I had thought. "No, having a run-in with cops."

"You make a habit of it?"

"Look, Detective, it's no big secret that those of us who hold a private ticket aren't exactly drinking buddies with you guys. In that Hendrickson episode, I didn't have clue one that Burbank PD was anywhere near the scene. That's a testament to your proficiency, I suppose, but it sure as hell doesn't make me public enemy number one."

"Point taken," he said. "Water under the bridge. So, we good?"

"We're good. Now, what can I do for you?"

"We've got a new wrinkle in the Gould case. I need to ask you some more questions."

"What's the new wrinkle?"

He brought up one hand and scratched the back of his head, giving me the impression he really wanted to clam up. He gestured to my hat and said, "Keep this under your porkpie there for the time being, but it looks like we've got a homicide with Gould's death."

"How so?"

"The coroner says he died from an overdose of insulin."

"So he was a diabetic?"

"Apparently. His medical records confirm it."

"Could be accidental," I said.

"True. But his wife says he's been on it for several years. Seems to me he would have known what the hell he was doing with respect to a needle." He flipped a couple of pages in his notebook. "Tell me again about this guy with the dreadlocks."

"Like I said, I found him in my trailer going through my costume. He said he was looking for a key."

Meyerson consulted his notebook. "You didn't say anything about a key yesterday."

"No, I didn't."

"Why not?"

"Truth be told, Detective, you'd pissed me off and I was being uncooperative."

"Thought we were beyond that?" he said.

"We are now. We weren't then."

Just the smallest trace of a grin broke out, and he nodded. "*Touché.* What kind of a key?"

"He didn't say what it was," I replied, still determined to keep to myself the existence of the Pandora key. "He said he was cleaning out Gould's trailer and somebody on the crew told him there was a key missing. That he should get it from a Ken Thompson."

"Who's that?

"I don't know," I said, and went on to tell him about finding the label inside my costume with Thompson's name on it and the title *Crash and Burn*.

"How did he know to look in your trailer?"

"Good question. I can only assume he went through every trailer until he found the costume he was looking for."

Meyerson made some notes and kept clicking the top of his ballpoint. "The wardrobe people don't know anybody on their crew who answers to that description."

"I know. And a PA I talked to said she wasn't aware of anybody by the name of Ken Thompson working on the movie."

"So who the hell is this dreadlocks guy?"

"Your guess is as good as mine, Detective. But if he was seen coming out of Gould's trailer with lunch dishes, chances are he might have been one of the last people to see the victim."

"Exactly. But if he's not on the costume crew and isn't in the cast, how the hell would he even get on the lot?"

"He could have come in with someone else. Gould, for instance. Maybe he told the gate guards he had an audition, or was delivering something. I think those gates tend to be somewhat porous."

Meyerson made a couple of final notes, then closed his pad and stuck it in a pocket. He pulled out a business card and handed it to me. "Thanks for your help, Collins. Give me a jingle if you come up with anything else."

"Will do," I said.

He stood up and stuck out his hand. "And again, I'm sorry for getting in your face yesterday. I've run into private guys before who seem to think they can damn well do whatever they please. Doesn't sound like you're one of them."

"I try not to be," I said, as I handed him one of my cards.

He glanced at it and stuck it in his shirt pocket. "So what's your 'day job,' so to speak? This, or being a private eye?"

"For three weeks it's this," I said. "After that, who the hell knows?"

He laughed and stepped to the door. "Fair enough. Let me know if you see Dreadlocks again."

"You got it."

He opened the door and stepped down out of the trailer and moved off. I was glad the bridge hadn't been burned. Despite my obstinance in not revealing my possession of the key, I figured it wouldn't hurt to have john law on my side.

Before I could get back into my crossword puzzle, another PA appeared at the door and said hair and makeup were caught up and that I might as well take advantage of the lull, sit in the chair and be ministered to.

Back in my trailer, I suited up and again pulled out my phone to see that I'd gotten a text from Denny Engels. *Asked around about Pandora. Back in 2010 an actress who'd worked for them sued the company. She later disappeared. That's all I know. I'll keep my nose to the ground.*

I returned his text, thanking him, then sat and stared at Denny's text for a long moment. This damn key with Pandora etched on it was pulling me into a pool full of questions, for which I had few answers. My quandary was whether or not I wanted to get out of the pool or continue to flounder.

A knock on the door and a summons from Debbie, the production assistant, delayed further thought. More movie magic awaited me.

Howard was right when he said that Tom Sanderson had the necessary acting chops. For the rest of the afternoon we filmed three scenes where hizzoner vehemently defended his support of the new civic center using taxpayer money. Tom was letter-perfect with the dialogue and projected a sense of feistiness totally in keeping with the character. Since we didn't have the benefit of comparison to Tony Gould, Sanderson's addition seemed to be spot-on casting.

We wrapped at a quarter after five. Tom received kudos from the director and his crew, along with those from the three councilmen with whom he'd been sparring all afternoon. As the four of us walked back to our trailers, I booted up my phone and discovered I had texts from both Mavis and Carla. Before I had a chance to read them, Clay insisted on a movie trivia rematch.

"Come on, guys," he said, "you've gotta give me a chance to regain my crown."

"Clay is a sore loser, Tom," Howard said. "He claims to be the movie trivia king of all Burbank."

"No, just Studio City," Clay replied.

"Okay," I said. "What have you got?"

"Give me your cellphone numbers. I'll text you one tonight. Obscure and unsolvable."

The three of us laughed and gave him the numbers, then peeled off and went to our respective trailers. Carla's text said they were going to go late that evening, but she'd try and connect with me later. Mavis's text read, *Found some interesting stuff for you about Pandora. Left it all on your desk. Catch you later.*

As I changed clothes, Steve Fischer knocked on the door and gave me a seven o'clock call for tomorrow morning. Traffic was backed up at the main gate into Warner Bros. I sat in my car, watching the guards and wondering if one of them had seen a tall lanky guy with dreadlocks coming through their domain. I was tempted to ask them that question, but decided that was Detective Meyerson's bailiwick, not mine. I pulled out onto Barham Boulevard and headed for Hollywood, listening to Tom T. Hall's rendition of *I Like Beer.*

That was a bailiwick I was familiar with.

10

Surviving yet another perilous ascent by my building's elevator, I stepped onto my floor to see Lenny Daye, one of my neighbors, locking the door to *Pecs 'n Abs*, the magazine he runs. As the title indicates, the periodical is geared toward readers who have a healthy appreciation of models with well-defined examples of those particular areas of the male physique.

"Hey, Lenny, what's going on?"

He turned and stuffed the key into the back pocket of his red, white, and blue, skin-tight trousers, whose colors practically demanded that one wear sunglasses. His shirt was solid red and unbuttoned down to his navel. The usual array of piercings ran up the outer edges of both ears.

"Eddie Collins, my favorite actor. Tell me you're coming home from some steamy emoting on some torrid Hollywood soundstage."

"Steamy and torrid, no, but emoting yes. Where you off to?"

"Party time, honey. Wish me luck."

I did, but wasn't sure what I was wishing for. Lenny strutted to the elevator, turned back to me, winked, and set off on his adventure. Where it might carry him I did not want to know.

Mavis had left her desk lamp on, and a note was lying underneath it detailing what she had found on her Internet search. I walked into my office, hung my hat on its peg and briefly looked through the mail. A sheaf of papers lay on my desk, waiting for me. First things first. I pawed my way through the beaded curtain into my apartment and grabbed a sample of what Tom T. Hall had been singing about. With two fingers of bourbon and the beer on the desk in front of me, I started looking through the papers.

In June of 2010, a Meredith Paulson had filed suit against Pandora Productions, an LLC located in North Hollywood, California. I looked at the names of the defendants cited. Tony Gould was one of them, and, no surprise, so was Ken Thompson. The suit alleged mental cruelty and emotional duress due to sexual harassment during Paulson's employment as an actress while working on a film called *Just in Time*. The plaintiff, Paulson, charged Pandora with essentially blackballing her within the industry because of her lawsuit. The case went to trial and a jury found in favor of the defendant, Pandora Productions. As per usual, Mavis had done some additional digging, revealing more about the case and its aftermath.

I continued to read.

Three months after her lawsuit, Meredith Paulson disappeared. Barbara McAndrews, the girl's mother, filed a missing persons case with LAPD. Mavis had found a Sunland address for McAndrews. No arrest was ever made, and the case was left unsolved.

I sipped from my libations and leaned back in my chair.

Nine years ago, based on Meredith Paulson's allegations, the entertainment industry's salacious secrets had apparently still been in play. Ever since the dawn of Hollywood, rumors surrounding the casting couch have swirled and been whispered about, but never confirmed, never admitted. I've done enough reading about old Hollywood to know it was pretty common knowledge that Jack Warner, Daryl F. Zanuck, Harry Cohn, and other power brokers frolicked with young, aspiring actresses whenever they felt like it. Consequences be damned. Meredith Paulson had tried to blow the whistle, expose the lechery, but hadn't succeeded. And even now, from what Carla had told me last night about this line producer on her show, consequences apparently still don't matter. In today's climate, sexual misconduct has been pounced upon and brought into the glare of exposure. However, it seems old habits don't die easily. It takes time to turn the ship around, and this Artie Young character proves the point that there's still work to be done.

My cellphone interrupted my reverie. It was Carla.

"Hey, kiddo, you still working?"

"Yeah, we're up in Glendale. Looks like we're going to be a while."

"What's happening?"

"We're shooting across the street from a nightclub. They refuse to tone down the music and keep ruining shots."

She cited an all too familiar problem film companies encounter in greater Los Angeles. Despite permits being granted, and concessions extended to homeowners and businesses, disruption is a constant problem. Reasons remain puzzling. Envy for not being in front of the camera? Just general orneriness? Who the hell knows?

"Glendale PD can't do anything about it?" I said.

"They keep trying. The noise stops for a while, and then starts up again."

"Sounds like you might get some overtime as a result."

"For sure. We're on golden time pretty quick. And we've only got the location for today."

"So I guess dinner's out of the question?"

"Yeah, I'm sorry, Eddie, but I don't know how long I'm going to be."

"Hey, no worries. Did you get my text with the SAG number?"

There was a bit of a pause before she said, "I did, but I haven't had a chance to call it yet."

"Well, keep track of it," I said, detecting a tone of hesitation in her voice. "Use it when and if you want."

"I will."

"Has that butthole been around today?"

"I haven't seen him."

"Well, you tell him if he doesn't keep his hands to himself, you know a tough guy who's going to find him and break both his thumbs."

"Oooh, my knight in shining armor."

"You got it, babe."

"You wouldn't be full of bluster, now, would you, Shamus?"

"Well, maybe a little," I said, which provoked laughter on her end of the line.

We chatted for a couple of minutes until I heard a voice in the background and she said she had to go. I laid the phone on the desk and wondered if she was going to call that SAG number I'd given her. It wasn't my place to tell her how to handle the situation. I just had to be supportive of her. My bravado was for show only. She had recourses she could follow without me getting involved.

As I scanned more of Mavis's computer printouts, I mulled over whether or not I wanted to get further involved in this Pandora key business and the questions surrounding it. There wasn't much I could do about the disappearance of Meredith Paulson, but the fact that she had worked for Tony Gould, who was now dead, perhaps as a result of a homicide, was puzzling. Furthermore, a dreadlocked guy, who might have been the last person to see him, and was trespassing in my dressing room looking for a key with the name Pandora on it was just too damn coincidental. And just too easily prodding my curiosity.

The cellphone chirped and revealed a text from Clay Dawson. He had a trivia question for his three amigos: *There's an actor who made only five films. All of them were nominated for a Best Picture Oscar. Who is the actor, and as a bonus, what are the five films?*

Good question, Clay. I had an inkling of an answer, but decided I needed nourishment to flesh it out. Computer printouts under one arm and porkpie on my head, I locked the office door behind me, wondering about the connection between a brass key and the disappearance of an aspiring actress. Pandora's box, for damn sure.

11

Tom Sanderson and I were the only two actors called for the first shot of the day. The scene consisted of my character, Greg Mason, in the mayor's office, discussing with His Honor a financial plan that had just been presented to the city council of this fictional town that provided the setting for *Terms of Power*.

I'd overslept a little and only had time to grab a cup of coffee and a bagel from craft services. I changed into yet another new costume and had just finished the bagel when Debbie, the production assistant, knocked on the door.

"Good morning, Eddie. They're still lighting the set, and now they tell me they've got a problem with the camera, so we're running a few minutes behind. If you need to get breakfast, go ahead."

"I'm good, Debbie."

"Then why don't we get you into hair and makeup while we've got the time."

"You got it," I said, and with jacket over one arm, I grabbed my coffee and told her I was on the way.

When I opened the door of the trailer and stepped inside, I heard some light jazz coming from a small boombox sitting below the mirrors. Crystal, the makeup lady, sat in the chair sipping on a cup of coffee. Her colleague, Randy, with the snake tattoo running up one arm, sprawled in the other chair, poking his cellphone.

Crystal saw me in the mirror, got up and said, "Well, good morning there, sunshine." She set her coffee down as I sank into the chair. "You're lookin' pretty chipper, honey. I could almost get away with combin' your hair and sendin' you on your way."

"And deprive me of your sweet smile and infectious laugh?"

She cocked her head to one side and pursed her lips. "Oh, lordy, listen to him, would you, Randy? If he ain't the charmer. Like to make me blush."

Randy paused in the assault on his phone and looked over at us. "You should see her before she gets her coffee. You'd maybe change your tone, Mr. Collins."

Crystal laughed and tossed a makeup sponge at him. "You hush!" She stuck some tissues around my collar, then grabbed another piece of sponge and began dabbing pancake on my face. "Randy don't know what he's talkin' about. I'm sweetness and light from the minute I get outta bed. My mama taught me that a long time ago."

"I don't doubt it for a minute," I said. And I meant it. There's a curious thing that happens when an actor crawls into a makeup chair, desperately wishing for another hour of sleep. Sometimes you'll encounter a person like Crystal, who displays a joy in what she's doing and does everything possible to lessen the agony of getting up at the crack of dawn. Other times an actor will get a makeup artist who has all the personality of a mud fence, exacerbated, in many cases, by strange odors, like the lack of a few minutes with a toothbrush and a dose of mouthwash. Over the years I've come to the conclusion that the friendlier the makeup person, the easier it is to face the camera with enthusiasm and confidence.

The door to the makeup trailer opened and Tom Sanderson appeared, already in costume. Randy got out of his chair and swiveled it around in his direction. Tom clapped me on the shoulder as he walked past me.

"Mornin', boss. How ya doin?"

"I'm good, Tom. Did you get Clay's trivia question?"

"I did, but I can't come up with an answer. You?"

"I think so. Not entirely sure, though."

"What's the question?" Randy said, as he stuck tissue behind Tom's collar.

"There's an actor who only did five movies," Tom said, "and each one of them was nominated for a Best Picture Oscar. Who's the actor and what are the films?"

Randy paused, sponge and makeup in his hands. "Five movies? That's not much of a career."

"You're right," I said, "but he died after the fifth one."

Crystal stopped working on my face. "Now, Randy, don't that make you look like you got egg on your face? Yeah, only five movies, but I bet five good ones."

"Whatever," he said, and went back to working on Tom's face. It was obvious that he had long ago given up on trying to debate his colleague.

"Damn good career, you ask me," she said. "Speaking of dyin'. When I came in this morning, everybody and their mother was talkin' about Tony Gould. Rumor has it that he died of an overdose of insulin. You guys know 'bout that?"

"News to me," Tom said. "You hear anything, Eddie?"

"First I heard of it," I said, keeping in mind Meyerson's request yesterday to keep the cause of Gould's death to myself.

"I don't know, but that kinda sounds like some of that foul play stuff to me," Crystal said. "I bet that Burbank cop's goin' to be hangin' around a lot longer now. Don't know 'bout you, but that guy gives me the creeps."

As she turned back to the mirror, I couldn't hold back a grin. I've learned over the years that makeup trailers are prime sources of scuttlebutt. News travels fast on movie sets, and I had a feeling Crystal was more than able and willing to dish the latest rumor.

"Speaking of foul play, guys," Tom said. "Last night I googled our friend Eddie Collins here and found out that he's a real-life private eye. Maybe just what we need."

Crystal stepped back and looked at me, her head once again cocked to one side. "Are you puttin' me on? You an honest-to-goodness private eye?'

"Guilty as charged."

"Well, don't that beat all? You gonna look into this here foul play stuff?"

"Count me out, Crystal. I'm not messing with the Burbank PD."

"Well, I don't blame you, honey." She chuckled and dabbed a little powder on my nose and forehead, then whisked it away with a soft brush. After a comb was run through my hair she pronounced me camera-ready. Randy did the same for Tom and the two of us offered our thanks and left the trailer.

I tossed my coffee cup into a nearby trash receptacle. "We got time for another one?"

"I haven't seen anybody looking for us," Tom said, and we started walking back to craft services. "I didn't mean to pull your cover in there, Eddie."

"How do you mean?"

"About you being a private eye."

"Nah, not a problem. I'm in the Yellow Pages."

"Insulin overdose? My sister's been a diabetic for as long as I can remember. There's no way she'd ever OD. If Gould was a diabetic, I find it hard to believe he'd make that kind of mistake."

"I agree," I said. We turned a corner and sidestepped a grip in a golf cart with a piece of scenery protruding from the rear end. I debated about how much I should tell Tom regarding the Gould death. I decided to keep the discovery of the Pandora key to myself, but I did share with him finding the Ken Thompson label on my costume. Also that I'd encountered Dreadlocks in my dressing room, and that he was later spotted coming out of Gould's trailer with lunch dishes. "Shortly after that Gould collapsed," I added. "Seems kind of suspicious to me."

We reached the coffee urns and filled fresh cups. "And you don't know who this dreadlocks guy is?" Tom said.

"Not a clue. Wardrobe says he's not on their crew. And there's no Ken Thompson on the cast list."

Tom poured some cream in his coffee and I picked up a donut and started nibbling. "Did the production put you in Gould's trailer?" I said.

"That's what they told me."

"Even though it might have been a crime scene? I mean, with the Dreadlocks guy coming out of there with Gould's lunch dishes?"

"Yeah, that AD…Steve's his name, I think?"

"Right. Steve Fischer."

"He told me that Burbank PD had been through it, and that they cleared it."

"Well, it's not that big. I guess it wouldn't take long to go through it." I sipped some coffee and an idea popped into my head. "Do you mind if I take a look in there, Tom? Maybe the cops missed something. Or transportation could have left something behind when they cleaned out Gould's stuff."

"Sure. Wanna do it now?"

"Yeah. While we've got time." The donut was in danger of assaulting my dental work so I flipped it into a trash bin, along with the tissues under my collar, and we started walking to Tom's trailer. "How's the business been treating you?" I said.

"Not too bad. I've got a little something going on the side, so I don't run into the wolf on the doorstep when I get my paper in the morning."

I had to chuckle at his assessment. "Oh, yeah? What are you into?"

"I'm an acting coach on the side. A partner and I run a little studio. We've got about ten young kids trying to break into the biz."

"Oh, man," I said, as I laughed and shook my head. "No offense, but I hope you're telling them to keep their day jobs."

"I hear you. We don't pull any punches about how tough this town is."

"And they're still determined?"

"Pretty much. We haven't run into a lot of desire approaching frenzy yet, so we cross our fingers and push on. Pragmatism is our motto. They seem to take it in stride."

"Well, more power to them. But I gotta tell you, Tom, I'm damn glad I hung out the PI shingle."

We shared a laugh as we walked up to his trailer. We stepped inside and set our coffee cups on a small table. The trailer was significantly larger than mine, but I assumed Tony Gould had wrangled better billing than Clay, Howard, and me, so Tom had inherited the bigger dressing room.

Despite more square footage, the trailer was pretty much like any other temporary home for actors on an extended contract. A beige, two-cushion sofa sat against one wall, a small TV in a corner of a shelf. Mini-fridge, sink, and a microwave made up the kitchenette, cupboards above and drawers below them. A small bedroom was at the end of a short hallway, with a bathroom on the right.

"I've gotta hid the head, Eddie. Poke around all you want."

As he squeezed himself into the bathroom, I opened several drawers next to the sink but didn't find anything, other than a sampling of silverware and kitchen utensils. The cupboards above the fridge and the sink contained just the rudiments for a home-away-from-home: two plates with matching cereal bowls and four glasses.

I walked down the hall into the bedroom, dominated by what amounted to a daybed. The cramped quarters made falling out of bed an impossibility. I slid open the door of a closet above the bed and found an extra pillow and a blanket. A tiny bedside table was shoved into one corner and had a lamp sitting on top of it. A single drawer was empty.

Behind me I heard the door of the bathroom slide open. "I'm back here, Tom."

"Find anything?"

"Nope. Pretty clean."

"They need some soap in that head," he said, as we walked to the other end of the trailer. He turned on the faucet, spritzed some soap from a pump onto his hands, then dried them with a paper towel. "I haven't dragged anything from home yet. Figured I'd get the lay of the land first. Whether or not I'd get along with you guys."

"And what's the verdict?"

"So far so good. Even better if I'd come up with an answer to that damn trivia question."

"Yeah, well, that's on me. I'm afraid I'm to blame for starting all that."

Tom picked up his coffee cup and stepped toward the sofa. His foot caught on a rug in front of it and he almost lost his balance. His cup jostled and some of the coffee spilled onto one of the cushions.

"Oh, crap." He set the cup down and pulled a couple of paper towels from the dispenser and dabbed at the spot. "This damn sure isn't going to come out."

"Just flip it over," I said.

"Good idea, boss." He pulled it off the sofa and soaked some more towels under the faucet.

The cushion had a zipper running along the rear side of it. It wasn't totally closed and I noticed a scrap of paper sticking out between the zipper's tracks. At first I thought it was just one of those tags like you see on mattresses and pillowcases, but when I bent over I saw that it was a slip of paper, much like a page from a small tablet. I pulled it out it as Tom started dabbing at the coffee stain with wet paper towels.

"Find something?" he said.

"Yeah. Not sure what it is, though." But as I looked more closely at the scrap of paper, it took on greater significance. Scrawled on one side and underscored was the word "keys." Below it, a list of names: Gould, Thompson, Forbes, and Benedetti.

I flipped the paper over. Two more names: Meredith Paulson and Barbara McAndrews. A daughter and her mother. A daughter who sued Pandora Productions and then disappeared.

12

As I stuck the slip of paper in my shirt pocket, Tom zipped up the sofa cushion and pushed it into place, coffee stain down.

"They're not going to send me a cleaning bill, are they?"

"Oh, hell no. Those Teamsters might not notice it for weeks."

"You're probably right, considering the fact that this cushion wasn't zipped up." He gave it a final shove and pushed it down flush with its companion. "Anything important on that slip of paper?"

"I don't think so. But I'll hand it off to that Burbank cop. Just in case." Of course, I had no intention of doing so. I still held the opinion that the Pandora key had nothing to do with Gould's death. I could be wrong, I told myself, but if so, I was determined my error was going to be mine, and mine alone.

Tom finished his coffee and threw the cup in the trash basket under the sink. "You think maybe we should head for the stage?"

"Probably better." I tossed the dregs of my coffee in the sink and deposited the cup where Tom had put his. We stepped out of the trailer and saw Debbie headed in our direction.

"Hey, guys, there you are," she said. "Been looking for you. They're ready to go."

"And we're ready for them," Tom said. "Right, Eddie?"

I nodded, silently agreeing with him. But as we followed Debbie, I had no doubt that my concentration on the scene before me was going to be compromised. Not by me being unprepared, but rather by puzzlement. Puzzlement as to why a simple scrap of paper, obviously placed where no one was expected to find it, should contain the names of four people linked to the key I'd found. And also, why were the names of Meredith Paulson and her mother on the same scrap of paper?

Questions, questions, as yet with no answers.

Tom and I were indeed ready, but I had a feeling we were the only ones. Walt Langley's camera operator wasn't having a good morning. At least two takes were ruined because he couldn't correctly make the right moves. Then the sound man contributed his miscues, and all in all, we weren't exactly creating reel magic. The technical problems gave me plenty of time to ponder what I'd discovered in Tom's trailer. In addition to being puzzled by the scrap of paper I'd found, I was also curious as to why I was able to find it in the first place. The quick turnaround from Gould's to Tom's occupancy of the trailer could no doubt have led to carelessness on the part of the transportation department. I'd give them the benefit of the doubt, but deep down I chided Meyerson's crime scene crew for neglecting to check the sofa cushions.

We finally got the scene after an hour and a half and were at the coffee urns with fresh cups when Langley walked up to us.

"Thanks for your patience, guys. Sometimes the magic works, and sometimes it doesn't, right?" he said, and the three of us shared a laugh. He looked at his watch. "It's eleven fifteen. I want to do a couple of establishing shots without the two of you, so I'm going to break you for lunch. Clay and Howard are called at one, and then we'll tackle a scene with the four of you. Sound good?"

We said it did, ditched our coffee cups and made our way to the roach coach. Considering I'd only had a bagel and a couple of bites from a stale donut, my fish tacos, dirty rice and salad disappeared pretty quickly. We bused our dishes, got more coffee and sat and hobnobbed about the Hollywood rat race. Despite my reservations, Tom persuaded me to come and talk to his students at a future class. I didn't think I had anything of importance to pass along to them, but he assured me they'd welcome the appearance of a working pro.

Clay showed up about ten minutes after noon, saw us and got in the lunch line. He set his tray on the table, straddled a chair and sat down.

"Nothing like a free lunch, right, Clay?" I said.

"You know it," he replied. "I've never known an actor to turn down chow that somebody else pays for." He started slicing off a piece of roast beef. "What'd you guys do this morning?"

"Mostly waited for the director to get his crew on the right track," Tom said.

"That doesn't surprise me," Clay replied. "I get the impression he's hired the B team."

"Got your trivia question, Clay," I said.

"And you're stumped, right?"

"Not really. I think I have an answer, but I'll wait for Howard before I ruin your lunch."

He chuckled and sopped up some gravy with a dinner roll, and then gestured to something behind us. "Speaking of the devil."

I turned around and saw Howard approaching, a bottle of Snapple in one hand and an apple in the other.

"Why didn't you get yourself some lunch, Howard?" Clay said.

"I slept late and the little woman made me steak and eggs."

"Lucky man," Tom said. "All I got was a groan and 'have a good day.'"

We watched Clay for a few moments as he dug into his lunch. When he noticed the three of us staring at him, he stopped eating and said, "What?"

"We're waiting for you to bring up your trivia question," Tom said.

"And I was waiting for you all to admit defeat," Clay replied. "All right, Collins, I'll give you first shot."

"Okay, Clay, here you go. The five movies first. *The Godfather*, *The Godfather: Part II*, *The Conversation*, *Dog Day Afternoon*, and *The Deer Hunter*." I paused, and looked at him, a forkful of roast beef on the way to his mouth.

"You son of a bitch, Collins. You know who it is, don't you?"

"I do. John Cazale."

He dropped his fork and leaned back in his chair. "Goddammit, you do need a hobby."

The three of us burst into laughter and Howard slapped the table. We patted Clay on the back, all of us trying to console him. He finally shook his head and said he'd come up with another one that would cause us all great embarrassment. Our taunts were interrupted when Debbie approached the table.

"Hi, guys. How was lunch?"

"It started out good," Clay said. "Then these three yahoos did their damnedest to spoil it."

In response to Debbie's raised eyebrows, I ran the trivia question by her. Not missing a beat, she immediately said John Cazale. It looked for a minute like Clay was going to choke on his lunch, so Tom, Howard and I eased up on him as we got rid of our dishes and followed Debbie into the soundstage.

For the better part of the next two hours, we three councilmen sat around a conference table in the city hall of our fictional town of Pine Bluff. Sleeves rolled up and ties askew, we debated with Tom Sanderson, our new Mayor Hessman. The argument stretched over two separate scenes. In between camera setups, I pulled out my cellphone and tried to unearth more information about Pandora Productions. I'd hoped that my surfing would run across the names Forbes and Benedetti, but no such luck. I finally gave up, after frustrating bouts with the small screen and big fingers that kept punching the wrong keys.

Our fearless director gave our conference room debates his blessing at four-thirty, and we were told we'd be wrapped for the day after two more set-ups. I poured a fresh cup of coffee and stepped outside. Cotton-ball clouds floated over Burbank and the Warner Bros. lot. The studio street in front of me was clogged with golf carts and people scurrying here and there, all of them giving the impression they were very important. And who knows, maybe they were.

My attention focused on two grips across the street wrestling a pair of Styrofoam pillars out of a soundstage to a waiting truck. They obviously had their hands full, especially the smaller of the two, who kept losing his grip on his end of the pillar. After dropping it a second time, they both bent over and burst into laughter before tackling it again.

I chuckled and lifted the coffee cup to my mouth, but stopped as I turned to my left and saw a man exit the adjacent soundstage. The guy was tall, dressed in jeans and an untucked plaid shirt. But what brought me up short was his hair. Long dreadlocks. The same color as those on the head of the guy who had snooped through my dressing trailer. He started walking down the street. I ditched my coffee in a trash barrel and followed him. He turned a corner. So did I, and was almost flattened by a golf cart pulling a small trailer. Dreadlocks walked up to a small door leading into another soundstage.

Before he could pull the door open I called out, "Excuse me, sir?"

He turned as I came up to him. "Help you?" he said.

It wasn't the same guy that had rifled through my costume. Trying not to look like I had just stepped in it, I blurted out, "Are you on the *Terms of Power* shoot?"

"Nope."

"You're not on the wardrobe crew?"

"No, I'm an electrician. I think you got the wrong person."

"Yeah, guess so," I said, as I gestured to his hair. "They've got someone on their crew with dreadlocks. I saw yours and jumped to a conclusion."

"No problem," he said.

"Do you know anybody on the lot with hair like yours?" I said.

"Can't say that I do. And believe me, I'd remember."

"Yeah, I reckon so. Sorry to bother you."

"No worries," he replied, and opened the door to the stage and disappeared. As I retraced my steps, I resisted the urge to tell myself I'd been foolish for following the guy. True, dreadlocks like those aren't all that rare in this day and age, but given the fact that I'd just recently seen someone sprouting a full set of them pawing through my costume without permission aroused my suspicions. When I rounded the corner I spotted Tom outside the *Terms of Power* stage.

"Hey, boss," he said. "They've been looking for you."

"Sorry. I was chasing down someone I thought I recognized," I said. He held the door open for me and we stepped into the dream factory in search of magic.

We created enough for the director to be true to his word. After two more set-ups, we wrapped for the day. That good news was compounded by the fact that I was told I was on hold for tomorrow, which, since it was Friday, gave me a long weekend. Plenty of time to switch hats and dig deeper into this puzzle I'd created for myself. A puzzle that now had two more pieces with the surnames Forbes and Benedetti.

13

On my way to the Warner Bros. parking structure I sent a text to Carla. She responded as I threaded my way through the Cahuenga Pass into Hollywood. Being the law-abiding driver that I am, I didn't look at it until a red light caught me. She said she was due to wrap her day's shooting at six o'clock and was dying for me to buy her dinner. I responded by saying that she'd read my mind. In turn, she texted back that she'd call me when she was through. The light changed and I glided through the intersection, wondering why in the hell we couldn't have simply used these damn things for they were meant: telephones. God help me if I ever develop arthritic fingers.

A garbage truck had to clear the alley behind my building before I could park my car and head for my office. Defying a total breakdown, the ancient elevator lurched to a halt and deposited me on the floor occupied by Collins Investigations. Mavis was long gone and had left no messages, only the mail in the middle of my desk. Surprisingly enough, I found three envelopes from SAG-AFTRA, denoting the arrival of money. Armed with a cold beer and a dollop of Mr. Beam, I sliced open the envelopes and was pleased to see the net amounted to just a shade over two hundred bucks. Well, now. Carla and I could dine a little higher on the hog tonight.

After writing a couple of checks for bills, I flipped open my laptop and saw that I had four emails. My face immediately lit up with a smile when I noticed one was from Kelly Robinson. There were two attachments. I opened the first and my smile broadened. A picture showed her among a group of girls surrounding a sign that read "Cincinnati city-wide champs."

The girls were in basketball uniforms. Below the photo were the words "Look at this, Eddie! We **are** the champions!"

I looked at the photo and thought back to last summer and the life-changing experience I'd had when I met this girl. Kelly Robinson is my daughter. She was given up for adoption a dozen years ago without my knowledge. I had never met her until she and her adoptive parents, Jim and Betty Robinson, had visited Los Angeles. Birth father and daughter took to each other right off the bat and I was pleased that the girl had now entered my life. I clicked on the second attachment and was greeted with a video clip of the rock band Queen and their hit "We Are the Champions." I replied with hearty congratulations and forwarded Kelly's email to Carla. The two of them had also hit it off when they'd met.

The clock in the corner of the laptop's screen revealed it was five-thirty. After a refill on my refreshments, I started poking around the Internet, trying to come up with a link between Ken Thompson, Tony Gould and two guys with the monikers Forbes and Benedetti. I poured over the IMDb's list of Gould's credits, seeing if either of those names came up on cast lists. No such luck. Then I did the same thing with Ken Thompson's credits.

Bingo.

Several years ago Thompson had worked on a film by the name of *Blind Instinct*. Halfway down the cast list was a character called Steve Jesperson. It was played by one Victor Benedetti. I clicked on the picture next to his name. The guy looked to be in his late forties, maybe early fifties. Thick, black hair. Full mustache. No hint of a smile, just dark eyes that demanded he be taken seriously. I pulled up his list of credits and saw that he apparently was still in the business. The most recent listing was just two years ago.

I started looking through the cast lists of Benedetti's credits. The guy had worked pretty steadily over the last decade, so it was time consuming. But the search finally paid off. Twelve years ago he'd appeared in something called *They Never Came Back*. The actor playing one Lionel Brewster had the name David Forbes. Clicking on his name revealed that he was also apparently still in the business, with recent television credits. His IMDb picture showed a man with sandy blond hair, thinning on top. He wore glasses, and looked like he'd be perfect for accountants, lawyers, completely different characteristics than those displayed by Victor Benedetti.

I leaned back in my chair and sipped on my liquid companions. Mavis would be proud of me for digging around on the Internet like this and getting results. Now granted, David Forbes and Victor Benedetti might not necessarily belong to the two surnames I'd found on the slip of paper I pulled from the cushion of the sofa in Tom Sanderson's trailer. However, it seemed obvious to me that these four men had crossed paths in some fashion.

I pulled the scrap of paper from my shirt pocket and looked at the word "keys" scrawled across one side of it, and underneath it the names "Gould, Thompson, Forbes, Benedetti." Did "keys" mean ones similar to the one I'd found in my costume? Did each of these four men have the same key? I didn't have an answer, and as I flipped over the scrap of paper and saw the names Meredith Paulson and Barbara McAndrews, another question surfaced. Why were the names of a mother and a daughter on the other side of this scrap of paper? A daughter who disappeared after losing a lawsuit to one of the four men.

Keys?

To what?

My reverie was interrupted by the chirp of my cellphone and a call from Carla.

"Hey, kiddo, are you all through?"

"I am. And I am starving. Where are you taking me, Shamus?"

"Dan Tana's."

"Are you serious?"

"As a heart attack. When's the last time you were there?"

"Are you kidding? Like never."

"Then no time like the present. Should I meet you there?"

"Okay. I won't have time to change. Is that all right?"

"California casual, baby." I gave her the address and said I'd meet her in a few minutes.

We disconnected, I closed the laptop and stuck the scrap of paper back in my shirt pocket. The puzzle of the keys was going to have to wait.

After handing off my car to a valet, I was shown to a four-top in a corner of the dining room. A young waiter with the obligatory Hollywood stubble covering his face laid two menus on the red-checkered tablecloth. He identified himself as Henry and promptly returned with two glasses of water.

Few are the times I've frequented this Hollywood landmark on Santa Monica Boulevard. It's been a favorite hangout of Tinseltown's great and near-great for fifty plus years, right up there with Musso and Frank, Spago, and the now-shuttered Chasen's. The walls were covered with plaques, newspaper articles and photos of dignitaries whom I assumed had frequented the place.

I looked up from the menu and saw Carla come through the front door. She had a brief word with the *maitre d'*, then pointed at me and ambled across the dining room. California casual fit her to a tee, but then I think anything Carla Rizzoli wears fits her to a tee, even given the fact that her previous line of work had required her to wear not much of anything.

She leaned over the table and planted a big sloppy kiss on me. "Did you hit the lottery or what?"

"Something like that. Three hefty residuals."

"Wahoo! Bring on the feed bag." She laughed and plopped down in a chair to my right. Something else that fits Carla to a tee is the French term *joie de vivre*. It's infectious, and always lifts my spirits. She set her purse on the chair next to her, pulled up the sleeves of the beige sweater she was wearing, then wrapped one arm around mine and leaned into me. "Thanks for forwarding that email from Kelly. That girl is beyond adorable."

"I couldn't agree with you more," I said.

"Do you know I've been thinking about you all day?"

"Really? I'm flattered. What about me?" She opened her mouth to answer my question, but stopped when she saw Henry appear.

"I'll save it for later," she whispered, as her hand slid up my thigh. *Joie de vivre* for adults only.

We ordered a bottle of red wine, whose name was unfamiliar to me, as most wines are. Henry vouched for its quality, and after sampling it, Carla agreed. We settled on calamari fritti for an appetizer and fresh French bread with olive oil for dipping. Henry drifted off and Carla gazed around at the various items hanging on the walls.

"So this is where the elite meet to eat?" she said.

"You think we fit in?"

"Well, we're here. They're going to have to make room." She reached over and squeezed my hand. "Thanks, Eddie." She raised her glass. "Here's to us."

I clinked glasses with her and we sipped the wine. Henry reappeared with the appetizer, French bread and a cruet with two bottles of olive oil. After setting the plates on the table, he asked if we were ready to order. We said yes. Carla settled on the veal cutlet Milanese, a la George Clooney. I looked at her with a lopsided grin.

"George is hot," she said, as she turned to me. "Almost as hot as you."

Henry suppressed a smile and said, "And for you, sir?"

"Well, he's not very hot, but I'll have the veal scaloppine, Karl Malden."

Carla broke into laughter as Henry picked up the menus. Before leaving, he leaned over and said, "Mr. Malden was a regular here for many years. A fine gentleman."

"Well, there ya go," I said. With a smile, he walked off and Carla and I clinked glasses. "To George and Karl," she said, and we dug into the calamari.

"How did your shoot go?" I said.

"Chaos, most of the day."

"How so?"

She went on to tell me that they'd been at the corner of La Brea and Hollywood Boulevard most of the time, a stone's throw from the iconic Gateway Sculpture. Since 1993, at the southeast corner of the intersection, silver statues of filmdom luminaries Mae West, Anna May Wong, Dolores Del Rio, and Dorothy Dandridge have supported a gazebo-like structure, almost as if they are sentinels at the western portal of the famed street. I suppose the fact that the artist depicted four distinct ethnicities pointed to the industry's efforts at diversity. However, I think the argument could be made that the jury is still out on that issue.

As Carla related, the location might have been a mistake. She said a young black woman had chained herself to Dandridge's likeness, after doing the same with three other young women representing their respective ethnicities. She then had a compatriot throw the keys to the locks down a sewer drain and thus began a protest. Needless to say, the shoot for *Three on a Beat* had been thoroughly disrupted.

Both of us had a good laugh and after we opened a second bottle of wine, Carla said, "And how was your day, Shamus?"

"Pretty good," I replied. Before I could continue, Henry arrived with our veal dishes, a la George Clooney and Karl Malden. We dug in and ate for a few moments, both of us oohing and aahing. I took a swallow of the red wine and pulled the scrap of paper from my shirt pocket. "Even though you and Mavis and Reggie have ganged up on me—"

"Oh, come on, we haven't ganged up on you."

"Well, let's just say the three of you aren't exactly on board about this damn key I found."

"Yeah, that's more like it," she said, and playfully punched my shoulder.

"Take a look at this," I said, as I handed her the piece of paper.

She looked at it for a minute. "Well, now. Interesting. Where did you get this?"

"Found it in Tony Gould's trailer."

"You think 'keys' refers to the one you found?"

"Not sure. But I've dug up a link to those four names, at least the surnames. They've all worked together."

"So where does that leave you?"

"Look at the other side of that paper."

She flipped it over. "More names. Who do they belong to?"

"Tony Gould's production company, Pandora, was hauled into court on a sexual harassment charge by Meredith Paulson. Barbara McAndrews is the girl's mother. Paulson lost the case and then vanished. Her disappearance has never been solved."

Her eyes lit up as I picked up the bottle of wine and refilled our glasses. "So, what do you think? Am I closer to getting an endorsement from you?"

She laid the scrap of paper on the table, sipped some wine and held the glass in front of her as she looked at me. "Maybe. Looks like you've raised some questions. But why do you want to continue digging, Eddie? I mean, it's a cold case, isn't it?"

"Yeah, but that still doesn't explain why I found that damn key, and why the guy with the dreadlocks was pawing through my costume." She nodded and we both concentrated on our veal for a few moments. "Besides, cold or not, the case involved sexual harassment. Maybe it's still going on. Doesn't that make you think differently?"

"Yeah, a little. But I still think you'd be better off letting someone else deal with it."

Her response didn't please me one damn bit, and I guess my displeasure made itself evident, since we were both silent for a few moments as we worked on our meals. The silence was deafening, and at one point she reached over and squeezed my hand.

"I don't mean to be a doubting Tomasina, Eddie. Maybe there's something there, but I'm worried that you're sticking your nose into something that could get you into trouble."

"I'm a big boy. I can take care of myself." My comment didn't sit well with her. Her eyes narrowed and she paused in the midst of chewing on a mouthful of food.

"I'm well aware of that, Eddie, but what happened in the past should probably stay there."

We glared at each other for a moment until I poured more wine. "Seems kind of strange that you would say that."

"Why?"

"Considering that asshole of a producer you've got. The one with wandering hands."

"Point taken. But I'm a big girl. I can take care of myself."

She said it almost defiantly, and I wiped my mouth with a napkin and took a sip of wine, then deliberately set the glass down. Her eyes didn't leave mine.

"*Touché*," I said. "Did you put a call into that union number I gave you?"

"Not yet. But I will." I sighed and shook my head. "I don't want to fight with you, Eddie."

"Me neither. Why haven't you made the call? That's what they're there for."

She looked down at her plate for a long moment. "Truth be told, I'm scared."

"Of what?"

"Putting me in jeopardy with the show."

"Carla, you can't think that way. It's exactly why that asshole behaves that way. Thinking you won't do anything about it." A slight frown appeared on her face, and I thought maybe I had overstepped a line. "I'm sorry, honey, I don't mean to sound like a nag, but you've got support with the Guild. Don't be afraid to reach out to them."

"I won't," she said, as she pushed her plate to the side. "He hasn't come near me since that one incident."

"That's good. Let's hope it stays that way."

I took a last bite of veal and also pushed my plate to the side. Carla stared off to her right, silent. I sipped from my wineglass and after a moment, reached over and squeezed her hand. "Hey, listen, kiddo, let's not squabble. We're both adults and know what we're doing. I'm just glad that you're concerned about me. I hope you feel the same with me."

"I do, Eddie."

She returned my squeeze of her hand. "Let's go back to my place and kiss and make up, okay?"

"You got a deal," I said, and signaled to Henry for the check.

Carla picked up the scrap of paper with the names on it and handed it to me. "You better not lose this. That's a lot of names to remember." She said it with a smile, giving me the sense that she might be on board with my key puzzle.

I settled the bill and we stood up to leave. "You got anything for dessert at your place?"

"Me," she said, as she walked toward the door.

I rolled my eyes and followed her, wondering how much *joie de vivre* a man could take.

14

I sat in Judith Quinn's casting office, not sure I was going to be successful in what I was attempting to do. Mavis was already in the office when I'd come in this morning, and yes, she'd been duly impressed with my Internet prowl of yesterday. I asked her to work her wizardry with the IMDb photos of Ken Thompson, David Forbes, and Victor Benedetti. Copies of each of them were in my shirt pocket as I sat and watched young hopefuls of both genders—or maybe more, in today's climate— parade through the office, picking up pages of dialogue and dropping off CDs, which one can assume were demo reels. Photos were left with the receptionist, and in one case a young man with a lean and hungry look left behind a bottle of wine.

Plying casting directors with gratuities of flowers, wine, candy, and such has never been my strong suit. I suppose that might have a direct effect on the amount of work I've landed over the years, but it's never been my thing. I'd rather rely on smiles and the attitude that they'd be crazy to not hire me. Sometimes it's worked, sometimes it hasn't.

The door to Judith's office burst open and she filled the portal. She leaned against one of the jambs, a hand cocked on the other hip. She was a tall woman and was anything but shy and soft-spoken. She had a shock of bright red hair, wore a long brown cardigan sweater over a soft red blouse and jeans. "Eddie Collins," she boomed. "Are you slumming or actually looking for work?"

"Not sure about the former, but definitely not the latter," I said, as I stood up and walked toward her. "How you doin', Judy?"

"As well as can be expected," she said, and enveloped me in a big bear hug, then pointed to my hat. "I see you're still upholding the tradition of the porkpie."

"Somebody has to."

She laughed and said, "Get your butt in here." She released me from the hug, told the receptionist to hold her calls, then yanked me into her office. "Can I get you anything? Coffee?"

"I'm good, thanks."

Judy Quinn has been one of the more respected and nicer casting directors in this town for a number of years. I've had the good fortune to have been the beneficiary of her largesse on several occasions, and I've always enjoyed auditioning for her. Part of that is because she can carry on a conversation about Spencer Tracy and Ingrid Bergman, which these days is a rarity among her younger colleagues, whose knowledge of the business goes back as far as the Kardashians and American Idol.

"Sorry I don't have flowers or candy for you, Judy, but I don't think they'd do any good anyway. Am I wrong?"

"Flowers make me sneeze and I'm on a perpetual diet, so those things are pretty much bullshit and a waste of money." She went behind her desk, which was overflowing with stacks of photos and bound pages of scripts. Movie one-sheets covered the walls of the office, projects she'd cast over the years, many of them familiar to me.

"So glad to get your call, Eddie. I haven't heard from you in donkey's years. You still with Morrie Howard?"

"Through thick and thin."

"Aw, he's an old sweetheart," she said, as she sank into her chair. "Give him a howdy from me."

"Will do."

"You sounded so damn mysterious over the phone. That gumshoe business getting to you?" She punctuated her question with a giggle and a slurp from a cup of coffee.

"I figured I had to be in order to get in the door."

"My door is always open for you, hon. What's cookin'?"

I pulled the photos from my shirt pocket and handed them over the desk. "These faces look familiar? The names are on the back."

She glanced at the pictures and names for several moments and handed them back to me. "I know Thompson and Benedetti, but I'm not sure about Forbes. I'd have to look through my files. They steal the crown jewels or something?"

"I'm working on something and their names popped up."

"Come on. Tell me it's something juicy. Murder? Mayhem?"

"Maybe nothing at all. Depends on whether or not I can locate them."

She lifted her coffee cup and sipped. "Thompson and Benedetti have been through here in the past, but nowadays, with everything going digital, I haven't run into them much."

Her reference to things going digital referred to a new twist in the casting business of late. Pretty much gone are the days when actors come in and physically audition for roles. Rather, they appear in home movies doing the material, then send it digitally to the casting director and hope for the best. I suppose that reality spares the hopeful from facing indifferent directors and producers, but at the same time it necessitates the actor investing in camera equipment and cajoling friends and loved ones to help them film the audition. So far I've been able to avail myself of my agent Morrie Howard and his camera, but I suspect the time will inevitably come when I'll have to buy some rudimentary movie equipment and rely on Carla and Mavis to feed me lines off-camera.

"When you get those digital submissions, do they come with addresses and phone numbers?"

"Just an email, but not generally their home address. They might give me a phone number in their email, but it's not required." She paused and sipped some coffee. "Why?"

"I need to talk to them, but I don't know where I can find them."

"Facebook? Google search? Nowadays, everybody seems to able to be found, Eddie. Did you try?"

"My secretary did just that, but came up short. You know how many Ken Thompsons there are?"

"I shudder to think," she said, and leaned back in her chair. "Generally speaking, I'd have to call their agents, and then make up some excuse for wanting their home addresses." She paused and said, "Is that what you're asking me to do?"

"In a nutshell, yeah."

She tapped a pencil on her desk and looked at me for a long moment. "I could ruffle some feathers with the Guild if anyone found out. You're aware of that, aren't you?"

"I am. And I wouldn't ask you if I didn't know that you've been around for a while and know the system like the back of your hand."

We sat and looked at each other, the only sound being that of traffic coming through an open window. Finally the jotted down the three names and said, "Okay, look, I'll see what I can find out. But if push comes to shove, I've never heard of you."

"And me likewise."

I stood. She came around from behind her desk and gently poked me in the chest. "And you owe me, Mister. Big time."

"Absolutely," I said, and turned to go. "What do you think of the Hollywood Bowl?"

"From what I remember, it's a kick. Why?"

"Bette Midler's there next month. I'll drop off two tickets for you."

She uttered a small chuckle and shook her head. "You goddamn actors. You're all alike, you know that?"

"Better than flowers or candy, right?"

She gave me another hug and walked to the door with me. "Have I got your cellphone number?"

"You should have."

"If I find anything, I'll shoot you a text. But do me a favor?"

"Name it."

"Put the addresses in your notebook. Then delete the damn text."

I nodded, tipped my hat to her and walked out of the office, making a mental note to myself to have Mavis get tickets to the Hollywood Bowl.

The communities of Sunland, Tujunga, and La Crescenta are collectively known as the Foothills, nestled as they are between the Verdugo and San Gabriel Mountains. The times I've had occasion to come up here have made me feel like I'm in a different world, divorced from the congestion and pace of Los Angeles proper and the Basin. One can see horses up here. And even a cow or two.

The address for Barbara McAndrews that Mavis had provided me was in Tujunga, on Helendale Avenue. My handy Thomas Guide map rode shotgun. Mavis's frequent attempts to persuade me to get a GPS certainly have merit, but I continue to drag my feet. I pulled into the parking lot of an El Pollo Loco, located the McAndrews address and jotted the directions onto a notebook page. But before setting out, a rumbling stomach and the pungent aroma of chicken on the grill made a two-piece combo irresistible. Actually, when I got inside the restaurant, a two-piece turned into a three-piece.

The front lawn of the house on Helendale was in complete shade from a huge elm tree. A driveway to the left of the front door consisted of a steep incline leading to a single-car garage, its door open to reveal a red VW bug. I climbed the stairs to a front porch and knocked on the door. No answer. On the other side of the driveway an elderly lady with a pair of pruning shears in her hand stopped what she was doing and looked at me suspiciously. I knocked again, and after a couple of moments started down the stairs.

"You looking for Barbara?" The neighbor had a floppy straw hat on her head, wore a pair of overalls, and peeled off her gloves as she walked to the fence separating the two properties.

"Yes, I am," I said. "Do you know if she's home?"

"She's in the backyard working in her garden. Climb up that damn hill there and go on back." She walked along the fence and hollered, "Barbara, there's someone here to see you."

"Who is it?" said a voice from the back of the house.

"Heck, I don't know. Come see for yourself."

"Thanks," I said, as I started up the incline.

"I like your hat, Mister. Don't see many of them anymore."

I tipped the porkpie to her and turned to see Barbara McAndrews come around the corner of the house. Her face was in shadow from another floppy straw hat. The knees of her jeans had pads on them, and an oversized plaid shirt draped over a soiled white tee shirt. In her gloved hands she carried a small trowel. She was a small woman and walked with a slight stoop.

"Barbara McAndrews?" I said.

She hesitated and gave me a long look before replying, "Yes. Can I help you?"

"My name's Eddie Collins," I said, and handed her one of my cards.

She brought it up close to her face and examined it. "Private Investigator? For heaven's sake, why do you want to talk to me?"

"I'm looking into the events surrounding the disappearance of your daughter, Meredith Paulson. She is your daughter, right?"

A look of sadness washed over her face at the mention of the girl's name. She slipped the card into a pocket of her shirt and peeled off her gloves.

"Everything all right?" her neighbor called out.

I turned to see the other woman leaning over the fence, her straw hat pushed back on her head.

"Yes, Dottie, it's okay."

"You sure?"

"Yes, for Pete's sake. You don't need to call the cops." She shook her head and smiled. "Don't pay Dottie no mind, Mr. Collins. She can be a bit of a snoop at times." Behind me, I could hear the neighbor muttering to herself as she walked back to her front yard. "Why don't you step out of the sun?" Barbara continued. She gestured for me to follow her.

A lemon tree occupied the far corner of the yard, ripe fruit on its branches. A small garden plot ran along a back fence. Spanning the width of the house was a concrete slab. An overhang jutted out from the rear wall, under which sat a glass-topped table and four plastic chairs. Next to the back door sat a washer and dryer.

When we stepped into the shade she turned to me. "Meredith's been gone for so many years now. What could you possibly want to know about her?"

"Her disappearance was never solved. Is that right?"

"Yes. As far as I'm concerned, the police just gave up."

"Like your daughter, I'm also an actor, Barbara." I went on to tell her of my discovery of the Pandora key and its possible connection to the cold case. She listened intently, and after I finished, said she had a pitcher of iced tea inside and would I like some. I said I would. She gestured for me to have a seat and went inside.

I sat down and saw Dottie the neighbor appear in her backyard on her way to a small shed in one corner. She glanced at me repeatedly, and when I raised my hand in greeting, she disappeared into the shed. Merely a nosy neighbor, or two elderly ladies committed to looking after each other? I had a feeling it was the latter.

My cell phone buzzed with a text. It was from Judy Quinn, and said she'd found an address for Victor Benedetti. *Working on Thompson*, the text continued. Bless the girl, I thought. As I pulled out my notebook, Barbara reappeared with a sweating pitcher of iced tea and two tall glasses with ice cubes in each of them. A clump of napkins stuck out from one of the pockets of her shirt. Clasped under her left arm was what looked to be a framed picture. She set the pitcher and glasses on the table, along with the picture, and took a seat. "I'd offer you a cookie or something, but I'm afraid there's nothing in the jar."

"No problem. I just had some El Pollo Loco."

"Oh, I love their chicken. Meredith and I used to go there all the time." She filled the glasses with tea and pulled the napkins from her shirt pocket. Then she picked up the picture, ran a napkin over the face of it and handed it to me. "This is Meredith."

"Do you mind if I take a photo of this?" I said.

"Not at all," she said, as she took it from me and set it on edge on the table while I zoomed in on it and snapped a picture.

Meredith Paulson was a beautiful young woman. Blonde hair framed a face with sparkling blue eyes and the trace of dimples in each of her cheeks. She wore a pale blue turtleneck sweater. A gold locket was on a chain around her neck. "A very pretty girl," I said. "I'm sorry she vanished."

"So am I," she said, as she took the picture from me. "She was my baby girl." She laid the frame on the table and flicked off a piece of the napkin. "Now what do you want to know about her?"

I took the photo of Ken Thompson out of my pocket and handed it to her. "This is Ken Thompson. I believe he was one of the defendants in your daughter's lawsuit. Is that right?"

A frown appeared on her brow as she looked at the picture. "Yes, that's him. Got off scot-free. Both him and that Gould character. God strike me dead if I ever see either one of those men again."

"Well, ironically enough, Tony Gould is dead. It looks like he might have been murdered a few days ago."

"Good," she snapped, and sipped some tea. "It's probably not right to speak ill of the dead, but I could give a rat's patootie."

I smiled, took out my notebook and flipped it open. "Can you tell me what happened? Why you brought a lawsuit against them?"

She set her glass down and looked off into the distance. "Oh, my, it's so long ago now, but it seems like only yesterday. Meredith was working on this movie..." She paused and ran a napkin over a drop of liquid on the table. "Well, doggone it, the name flew right out of my head."

"*Just In Time*?" I said.

"Yes, that's it. Well, anyway, Meredith had a nice part, but almost from the first day, she would call me and complain about how she was being treated." She picked up Thompson's photo and looked at it. "She said both Gould and this Thompson character kept hitting on her and making all sorts of...oh, I don't know, lewd remarks. Several times she said both of them even tried to get her to go to bed with them. Some of the things she told me were just..." She paused and drank some tea, then dabbed at the corner of one eye with a napkin. "I'm sorry, Mr. Collins, but bringing it up makes me so mad I could just spit."

"Understood," I said. "Did she finish making the movie?"

"No, after a week or so they fired her. When they started harassing her, she threatened to go to the authorities, and then, bang, all of a sudden she was fired. They said the reason was that she wasn't what they wanted for the part. Which of course was nonsense. When Meredith told them she was still going to lodge a complaint, they told her if she did, they'd see to it that she'd never work again." She paused and I made some notes. "Turns out they were right." She turned when we heard a phone ring from inside.

"You need to get that?"

"No, let the fool thing ring. Probably another telemarketer. They drive me nuts."

I took the photos of Benedetti and Forbes out of my pocket and handed them to her. "Do either one of these men look familiar to you? Their names are on the back."

Barbara held them up and then flipped them over. "Yes, they were both at the trial." She showed me Benedetti's picture. "This one testified. The defense attorney claimed he was a character witness for both Gould and Thompson. Another damn lie." She handed the photos back to me. "Are they still alive?"

"I think so. I'm going to try and find out for sure."

She nodded and sipped from her glass, then refilled mine. "Why are you getting involved in this, Mr. Collins? It's been a long time since Meredith disappeared. Every few years I call the police about her and they tell me they're still looking. I don't believe them for one damn minute. Doesn't seem like anything's ever going to be done about it."

I took a hit off my iced tea and proceeded to share with her my curiosity about the key, the dreadlocks guy going through my costume and all the information I'd dug up on the Internet. I admitted to her it was probably none of my business, but went on to say that my private eye nosiness made it difficult for me to let go. After I finished, she sat back in her chair and looked at me for a long moment as I finished off my glass of iced tea.

"Mr. Collins, I don't have a lot of money, but could I possibly hire you to find out what happened to Meredith?"

The question caught me by surprise. "Have the police told you for a fact that they've stopped the investigation?"

"Not in so many words. But I can sense that it's not much of a priority to them. Will the police let you look into it?"

"Not officially, but I do have a good friend on the force. He sometimes cuts red tape for me." While the prospect of landing another case appealed to me, the fact that I was tied up with *Terms of Power* made me wonder how effective I could be for her. "I'll tell you what, Barbara. I'm working on a movie right now, so I don't have a lot of time, but I could do some digging as time permits. How does that sound?"

"How much do you charge, Mr. Collins? As I said, I haven't got much. Maybe I can pay you a little at a time?"

I saw the sadness in her eyes. My past experience with finding a client's son, plus being reunited with my own biological daughter struck a nerve in me. "Okay, here's what we'll do. I'll charge you a retainer, which you can pay off in installments. And then, given the amount of time since Meredith's disappearance and my limited availability, I'll keep track of expenses, but won't bill you for them unless I produce results. How does that sound?"

"That would be just fine," she said, and started to get out of her chair. "Let me go and get my checkbook."

"No need for that right now. I'll have my secretary send you an invoice. That way, we'll have a record of it. All right?"

"Okay." She settled back into her chair. "My goodness, I've never even known a private investigator, let alone hired one. That'll put a bee in Dottie's bonnet." She laughed and poured herself a little more iced tea.

I put the three photos back in my shirt pocket. "Tell me about

Meredith's disappearance. When did it happen? Where? Anything you can remember."

She picked up the photo of her daughter and ran a finger around the edge of the frame. "It was two weeks after the trial. She went out with a group of her friends. Three girls she went to high school with. All of them were so proud of Meredith for getting her SAG card and landing some small roles in film and television. Anyway, they saw a movie in North Hollywood, and afterwards went to a bar. I don't remember what the name of it was. I guess they were there for a couple of hours. Meredith went back to her car. But she never showed up at her apartment."

"So she wasn't living with you?"

"No, she had her own place. On Magnolia in North Hollywood. Not far from the movie theaters."

"Do you remember the address?"

"Oh, yes." She gave it to me and I jotted it down in my notebook.

"Can you remember the names of the other three girls?" I said.

"Not offhand, but I have all that stuff in a box inside."

I asked her if she'd let me see it, and she said of course. I could take it with me. Barbara then went on to tell me details of LAPD's investigation. Who talked to her, and when. I filled several pages of my notebook. When I ran out of preliminary questions, she went inside and brought back a shoebox with all the material she had about the girl's disappearance. We exchanged phone numbers and I told her to give me a call anytime if she remembered anything else. I promised her I'd keep in constant touch with her, thanked her for the iced tea and she escorted me to the steep driveway leading to the street.

Dottie was on her knees digging under some rose bushes. When she heard us coming, she got to her feet and pushed her hat back on her head.

"Dottie, guess what?" Barbara said. "This is Mr. Collins. He's a private investigator. Can you believe it? He's going to look into Meredith's disappearance."

Dottie pulled off her gloves and walked up to the fence. She stuck out a hand and I gave it a shake. "Nice to meet you, Dottie."

"Likewise," she said. "You got the right hat." That provoked a laugh from the three of us. "It happened a long time ago. You think you can find out anything?"

"I'll sure give it a try," I said.

"Well, good luck. Lord knows Barbara here could use some good news about that whole mess."

I said goodbye to the two ladies and walked to my car. Another missing persons case, but this one with a trail that apparently had gone stone cold. I had my work cut out for me. However, as I pulled out my key ring, I spied the one with Pandora etched on it. I immediately flashed on the image of Barbara McAndrews' face and the sadness in her eyes over the loss of a daughter. I remembered an old man who'd hired me to find his son some months ago. And then I thought of the joy I've felt after reuniting with my own daughter.

Those thoughts alone were enough to convince me to jump into this case. Hopefully, I'd be successful.

15

So I had another case. One that presented more than a single challenge. Nine years after the fact is a long time to reopen a cold case, if indeed LAPD had ever closed the book on it. Plus, I still had more than a week left on my contract for *Terms of Power*. Multitasking taken to a new level. True, I had Reggie and Mavis to do some digging for me, but doors still needed to be knocked on, people interviewed, questions asked. Hopefully, the shoebox Barbara McAndrews had given me would provide some clues as to where and how to proceed.

As I headed down Sunland Boulevard to hook up with the I-5 south, my cell buzzed. The display indicated it was another text from Judy Quinn. I took a right at the next intersection and pulled to the curb next to—believe it or not—a small pasture with not one, but two cows in residence. They stood next to a wooden fence, chewing their cuds, totally indifferent to my presence. The text had an address for Ken Thompson and the words *Hope this is current. I'll keep looking for Forbes. I love Bette Midler!* I grinned and wrote the Benedetti and Thompson addresses in my notebook and then, per her request, deleted both texts. Bossie and Elsie continued to work on their cuds as I made a U-turn and got back on Sunland.

Mavis had a puzzled look on her face as I opened the door to Collins Investigations. She sat behind her desk, intently staring at her computer screen.

"Hi, Eddie."

"What's the matter? You look like you've forgotten your eBay password or something."

She grinned and looked up at me. "Nothing that simple. Some joker up in Bakersfield has a set of *The Wizard of Oz* coffee mugs for sale, but he doesn't want to sell the one with Dorothy and Toto on it."

"Oh, my God," I said, as I recoiled a step or two in mock horror.

"Smart ass. I mean, a set is a set, right?"

"Absolutely."

She gestured to the shoebox under my arm. "New shoes?"

"New case. Barbara McAndrews hired me to look into her daughter's disappearance. This is all the stuff she's held on to."

She looked at me for a long moment. A look I'd seen before. Skepticism.

"What do you think you're going to accomplish after nine years?"

"I'm not sure. But the look on her face when she started talking about her daughter practically screamed out for someone to care. She thinks LAPD has given up."

"Have they?"

"I don't know. That's a conversation I'll have to have with Lieutenant Rivers."

"Well, good luck with that. You know, Eddie, one of these times he's going to tell you to take a hike. To quit being a pest."

"Duly noted."

"Are you done with your movie?"

"Nope. And therein lies a possible problem."

"Maybe you should hire Reggie."

"Not a bad idea." I plopped down in one of the chairs in front of her desk and told her about Judy Quinn's discovery of the Thompson and Benedetti addresses.

She shook her head, pushed her chair back and walked into her little off-limits-to-Eddie alcove. "You're not going to let go of that key, are you?"

"Not when it keeps raising its ugly head and pointing to the possible involvement of Ken Thompson, Victor Benedetti, and David Forbes. Maybe I'll run across Dorothy and Toto while I'm at it."

She came back, twisting off the cap on a bottle of water. "You want me to write these one-liners down?"

"No, but what you can do is send Barbara McAndrews a contract for a retainer."

"Okay, boss man," she said, and pulled open a drawer in a filing cabinet.

I walked into my office and set the shoebox on the desk, then pawed my way through the beaded curtains into the Collins lair to answer a call of nature. Back at my desk with a cold libation, I pulled off the lid of the shoebox and was about to begin looking through its contents when another text arrived from Judy Quinn. *Bingo! A trifecta!* And then an address for David Forbes. I added it to my notebook and deleted the text.

The contents of the shoebox lacked any semblance of order. Barbara had saved all kinds of newspaper clippings, some more detailed than others. I managed to put them in some sort of chronological order by date. I jotted down the names of the presiding judge, and the names of both the defense attorney and counsel for the plaintiff, then called out to Mavis.

"You rang?" she said, as she filled the office doorway.

I handed her the slip of paper with the names. "See if you can find out if this judge is still on the bench and if these attorneys are still practicing."

"I'll give it a shot, but remember, it's nine years ago."

"So you keep reminding me." She turned to go. "Oh, and one more thing. See if you can get a couple of tickets for Bette Midler's concert next month at the Hollywood Bowl."

"I didn't know you liked Bette Midler."

"She's not bad. These are for Judy Quinn."

"More bribery?"

"Business expense."

"Yeah, right," she said, as she rolled her eyes and went back to her desk. "How much you want to spend?"

"Don't break me, but fairly close to the stage."

"Roger that."

I went back to the shoebox. Court proceedings lasted only three days. From what I could gather, the defendant had no shortage of character witnesses and denials of Meredith Paulson's alleged harassment. The jury deliberated for five hours and came back with a verdict finding for the defense. The attorney for Gould and Thompson said the jury basically determined that their conclusion was a "he said, she said" verdict. Yeah, right. I acknowledged that that was probable, but given the male dominance over women that has gone on in this town for decades, the jury's verdict made me suspicious. Whoever said justice is all the justice you can afford hit the nail on the head.

I gathered together the documents dealing with the trial, put a binder clip on them and set them aside. The initial *Los Angeles Times* item about Meredith Paulson's disappearance didn't warrant much ink. One column on page eight. A picture of her. The same one Barbara had shown me with the same turtle-neck sweater and necklace. As she had told me, the article said her daughter and three friends caught a movie, stopped for drinks, and that's the last Meredith Paulson was seen. More *Times* articles revealed the names of LAPD officers, but offered no conclusive evidence on what had happened to her. Barbara had made notes, and had stapled the business cards of two detectives to them. Her notes covered several ensuing months, but then abruptly stopped.

After a couple of hours I'd looked through almost everything in the shoebox, but didn't come away with any encouraging information. Maybe Charlie Rivers could shed some light on the case, if, however, I had the time to talk to him. Mavis stuck her head in the office with a notebook in her hand.

"Okay, here's what I've been able to dig up. The judge retired from the bench five years ago and moved to Arizona. The attorney for Gould and Thompson died two years after the trial."

"Crap," I said. "What about the girl's lawyer?"

"I tracked him down to a firm by the name of Carson, Wendt, and

Mosby up in North Hollywood. My call went to voice mail, and they haven't gotten back to me." She ripped the sheet of paper from the notebook and handed it to me. "Here's their address and number." Then she handed me another sheet of paper. "This is your receipt for the Bowl. Tenth row on the aisle good enough?"

"Terrific."

"They'll be at 'will call.'"

"Thanks."

"You need me for anything else? If not, I've gotta split. Hair appointment."

"Nope. You're good to go. Have a good weekend."

"Thanks. What are you up to?" she said.

"Not sure. I'll have to check in with Carla."

"All right. Try and stay out of trouble."

She went back to her desk and I started looking through some more of the shoebox. After a few minutes I heard her say goodbye and then the sound of the front door closing. I refilled my glass, put my feet up on the desk and went back to the documents. Ten minutes later my cell went off. Morrie Howard.

"Hey, Morrie, how they hangin'?"

"To the left, bubbeleh, always to the left." We shared a chuckle, which resulted in a husky cough on the other end of the line. "You're called at noon on Monday. Think you can make it?"

"I'll do my best." He told me to have a good weekend and signed off. I'd expected a much earlier call than that, but couldn't complain. I sent a text to Carla and went back to what the police had shared with Meredith Paulson's mother.

From what I could gather, the lead detectives on the case were Harlan Berenson and Mike Fogarty. They'd done extensive interviews with Paulson's three companions, people at the bar where they'd stopped for drinks after the movie, and residents of her apartment complex. Nothing conclusive. I had a momentary debate with myself, then picked up my cell phone and punched in a number.

Charlie Rivers answered after three rings. "Is this the same Eddie Collins who should maybe consider enrolling in the Police Academy, so as not to interfere with those of us committed to serving and protecting?"

"Jesus, it took you three rings to come up with that, Charlie? A simple hello would have sufficed."

"There's nothing simple with you, Collins. What's on your mind?"

"Cold cases. How long after a crime do they become cold?"

"Depends. Why?"

"I've got a client whose daughter disappeared nine years ago. LAPD's told her the case is more or less closed. Do you officially close them, or keep them open?"

"Once again, it depends."

"The leads on this one were Harlan Berenson and Mike Fogarty. You know them?"

"For crissakes, Eddie, nine years ago? I can't remember what I had for dinner last night." I could hear him talk to someone in the background before he came back on the line. "I'm in the middle of something here. Anything else?"

"Can a civilian look at a closed case file?"

"No."

"How about if said civilian knows a member of the department?"

There was a pause, followed by a deep sigh. "If said member of the department is cooperative with said civilian, there's a chance, yes. Is that where you're going with this?"

"You could say that."

Another pause, then, "Who's the victim, and where did she disappear from?"

"Meredith Paulson. She lived on Magnolia up in the Valley."

"Can't help you, Eddie. That's North Hollywood Division. Their jurisdiction."

"You know anybody up there?"

"Not well enough to go sticking my nose into something that doesn't concern me. I'm afraid you're on your own, detective."

"Fair enough," I said. "Let's get together some time and have a beer."

"If you're buying, I'm available," he said, and broke the connection.

Mavis had called it. He hadn't said so in so many words, but Charlie had basically told me to take a hike. While my disappointment stung, I had to admit that my relationship with Charlie over the years had more than yielded results. When my wife was murdered, he'd lent a sympathetic ear and helped me in my investigation into her death. It hadn't occurred to me that Meredith Paulson's disappearance might be another LAPD division's jurisdiction. I mentally kicked myself for that lapse, but came to the conclusion that it was a bump in the road, and probably wouldn't be the only one.

My reverie came to an end when my cell went off. The screen said it was Carla.

"You're not working?" she said.

"Today I'm wearing my PI hat. The movie put me on hold. What's up with you?"

"We're trying to cope with an inept director. Thank God the day's almost over. I'm in the mood for a couple of stiff drinks and some industrial-strength pasta. What say you?"

"I say bring it on. Call me when you're done."

"You got it," she said. "And, oh, by the way, the producers are throwing a party for cast and crew on Sunday. I'm in need of a date. Can you fix me up?"

"I know just the guy."

She giggled, made the sound of a kiss, and ended the call.

More *joie de vivre*? One could only hope

16

The party for the *Three on a Beat* cast and crew took place at the home of one of the show's producers, who happened to live in Pacific Palisades, an enclave through which Sunset Boulevard winds on its way to the blue Pacific. This particular Sunday was Southern California sunny; convertibles with tops down meandered along the street, their drivers hiding behind designer sunglasses and attitudes that screamed, "Don't blame me. I didn't ask for the trust- fund!"

I wore one of my gaudiest Hawaiian shirts, sported a fresh porkpie, and was doing my damnedest to be hip, slick, and cool. Carla, however, didn't have to try. She just *was*. She wore her hair up; sparkly earrings dangled from both lobes, and she wore sunglasses that could have doubled as a snorkel mask. A light blue blouse matched the miniskirt she wore. It drew attention to two of the most gorgeous legs a lucky fella like me could ever admire.

In fact, I was doing just that when a female trust-fund driver pulled up alongside and then abruptly cut in front of me and roared off, blond hair flying in the wind. I honked and flashed her a digital salute.

"You think that did any good?" Carla said.

"Probably not, but it's the gesture that counts."

"Maybe you should keep your eye on the road, Shamus."

I glanced at her, as her fingers walked themselves along my thigh. "Maybe you shouldn't distract your driver."

She laughed and tapped me on the shoulder. "Are you ready to do some meaningful mingling and schmoozing?"

"As long as it doesn't take me too far away from the bar." She shook her head and I slowed to navigate a turn. "You going to introduce me to your two co-stars? Whose names I've forgotten. Sorry."

"Marsha Bailey and Alison Jackson. And yes, as long as you behave yourself."

"I'll be a perfect gentleman. I suppose the creep with the wandering hands will be there, right? What the hell's his name again?"

"Artie Young. He'll be there. Just try and ignore him, okay?"

"If you say so," I said. In the back of my mind, however, I knew I might have difficulty doing so.

Carla held up the directions she'd written down and told me to take a left. We drove along a winding street with palatial mansions on both sides. Neatly-cropped lawns were splayed in front of them, and luxury cars sat in driveways. Carla pointed to a Spanish-style house on our right. I did a K-turn and parked on the other side of the street. We climbed out and walked across.

"Who's our host?" I said.

"Bert Addison. He's one of the executive producers."

"He's obviously doing well," I replied, as I gestured to a black Escalade and a light gray Mercedes convertible parked in the driveway, facing a double garage.

The house was a two-story with red adobe roofing. Rose bushes ran the length of the structure, both red and white in full bloom. Two clusters of multi-colored balloons were moored to a couple of metal uprights supporting a small balcony outside an upstairs room with glass doors.

Carla pushed a doorbell and after a few seconds it opened to reveal a tall, thin man dressed in cargo shorts, sandals, and an Hawaiian shirt. His hair was jet-black and his tanned face was wrinkle-free. I pegged him as being in his mid-forties.

"Carla!" Addison boomed, and then gave her a hug. "Good to see you. Come in, come in."

We did so, and stood in a foyer with a hardwood floor and a large beige area rug under our feet. A set of carpeted stairs led to the second floor. To the right sprawled a sunken living room and a dining room was on the left. Through a hallway in front of us I spied a swimming pool and heard music and people's laughter.

Addison thrust out a hand and said, "I'm Bert, and you must be Eddie Collins, the actor and private eye Carla's been telling us about."

"That's me," I replied, as I shook his hand. "How many lies has she been spreading?" We laughed and he started leading us through the hallway to the back yard.

"We better get you on the show," he said. "We could use some first-hand expertise."

"Well, my SAG dues are current," I said.

"Good to hear, Eddie. Let me work on that."

I'll try not to be on pins and needles, I thought, but instead said, "I like your shirt."

"Likewise," he replied.

We passed by a huge kitchen on our left where a slim, attractive brunette stood next to an island, washing her hands in a sink.

"This is my wife, Blanche," Addison said. "Honey, you know Carla, of course, and this is her partner Eddie Collins."

Blanche turned off the water, ripped a paper towel from a dispenser and walked up to us. "Hello, Carla. So nice to see you again." She stuck out a dry hand and said, "Eddie, pleased to meet you. Welcome."

We said our thanks and the Addisons ushered us through an open set of sliding glass doors into the backyard. There must have been twenty, twenty-five people milling about. Several kids splashed in the pool. A portable bar sat under a canvas awning, to which Bert directed us. Nearby stood a large grill, propane tank underneath and its hood raised, smoke drifting up from chicken, burgers and sausages being cooked. Close to the pool another awning covered a long table draped with white cloth. Cutlery, stacks of plates and napkins occupied one end. Huge overflowing bowls of salads were scattered along its length.

A young blond man in a white shirt and red vest asked us what we'd like to drink. I ordered a bottle of Heineken and Carla opted for a glass of white wine. I tossed a couple of singles in a tip jar and we began to meet and greet. Of course she knew everyone there, and I did my best to remember all the names.

She at one point led me to a couple standing next to a glass-topped table. The guy was a tall, muscular black man wearing designer jeans and a white polo shirt. The woman next to him was also black, and very attractive. She reminded me of a young Diana Ross.

"Marsha, this is Eddie," Carla said. "And this is Marsha Bailey, one third of *Three on a Beat*. She's the one that covers my butt when I mess up my lines."

Marsha poo-pooed the comment and introduced us to her boyfriend. He informed us he was a broker with a hedge fund in Beverly Hills. The four of us made small talk for a few minutes until Carla asked if Alison was there. Marsha looked around and spotted her on the far side of the pool. We excused ourselves and made our way to her other co-star.

Alison Jackson was a tiny, attractive blonde with an infectious, hearty laugh. We were introduced to her husband, a screenwriter. More small talk ensued and after ten minutes or so I spotted someone I knew. I excused myself and walked up to Wally Lambert, a director I'd worked with in the past.

"Wally Lambert, long time no see," I said, as I extended my hand.

"Oh, my God. Eddie. Great to see you, man." He shook and gestured to the people milling around. "How do you fit into this crowd?"

"Carla and I are together."

"Really? Oh, man, you are one lucky dude."

I agreed with him and we chatted, catching up. He told me was slated to direct the upcoming episode of the show. He went on to say that he'd directed one other episode and how impressed he was with Carla's work. I voiced more agreement and we moved to the bar to replace our drinks.

As we started to walk away, a man in a maroon silk shirt and pleated tan Dockers walked up to us. Aviator sunglasses dominated a face covered by Hollywood stubble. Dark hair was swept straight back, revealing the oh-so-subtle traces of nips and tucks. His silk shirt was unbuttoned almost to his navel. I wondered why he bothered, since the gap showed only a paltry display of chest hair. However, he made up for the lack with bling. Two gold chains hung around his neck, and bracelets and a Rolex encircled his wrists. He missed none of the accouterments for being hip, slick, and cool.

"Eddie, this is Artie Young, one of the producers on the show."

So, Artie Young, he of the wandering hands. My first impression was right on the mark. He projected the aura of somebody very impressed with himself, and had producer written all over him.

"Artie, meet Eddie Collins," Wally said. "He's Carla's...what?...partner, I guess, right?"

"Works for me," I said.

"How ya doin'?" Artie said, as he shook my hand with more firmness than I thought was necessary. "Carla is one damn fine actress," he continued. "We're lucky to have her."

A couple of double entendres welled up in my head as I listened to him prattle on about the show and the three actresses that were the glue of the whole enterprise. Our conversation went on for a couple of minutes and then gradually morphed into one between the two men about the show. Shop talk. I excused myself and wandered off, determined to corner Young when the opportunity presented itself.

Said opportunity happened about a half hour later. Carla and I had helped ourselves to plates of food and took a table with Alison, her boyfriend, and two writers on the show. The food was delicious, and the conversation pleasant. I kept glancing around the gathering, my eyes not losing sight of Artie Young. At one point I asked Carla if she wanted another glass of wine. She said she was good, and I got up to get another beer.

Artie stood at the bar waiting for the bartender to mix him a drink as I walked up behind him. "So I understand you're a producer on the show?" I said.

He turned and pushed his sunglasses up on his head. "Correct."

"I hear it's going very well."

"We couldn't be more pleased."

He picked up his drink and moved off a step or two. I reached for my fresh Heineken and got up close to him.

"I'm glad to hear that," I said. "But what I'm not glad to hear is you putting your hands on Carla."

He froze with his drink halfway to his mouth and backed up a step. "What the fuck are you talking about?"

"I'm told you made an inappropriate move on her."

He sidled back another step and I followed him. "Now, listen—"

"No, you listen. If you touch her again, I'm going to come looking for you, and you're going to hope I don't find you."

"Look, that was an accident."

"Not what I'm told. I know you think you're some hot-shot over-paid producer who thinks he can behave any damn way he pleases and nobody's going to do anything about it. I've been around guys like you for years, and you make me sick."

"Get the fuck away from me, man," he said, as he started to walk away. I grabbed his elbow and stopped him. "I don't know who the fuck you are, but you're way out of line."

"And you're skating on thin ice, pal." I stuck an index finger under his nose. "Keep your hands to yourself or I'm going rip off this goddamn dime store bling you've got hanging around your scrawny neck and feed it to you. Understood?" Defiance briefly flared in his eyes and then faded.

"Yeah, yeah, okay. Now get your fuckin' hands off me," he said. He slapped my hand away and slinked off, his face as red as his shirt.

I tilted my beer bottle up and looked around. My eyes locked on Carla, who had turned in her chair and was staring at me. I slowly walked back to the table and sat down.

"What did you say to him?" she said.

"Nothing. We were wondering how the Dodgers looked this season." I sipped from my beer and could see a look on her face that told me she didn't believe me one damn bit.

"I asked you to leave him alone, Eddie."

"I did. I just suggested that he might have been out of line. That's all."

"God, you're unbelievable," she said, and then got up and moved off.

The other people at the table looked like they wished they were someplace else. Their conversation continued, and I listened for a while, made a few innocuous comments, but finally excused myself and moved off.

Forty-five minutes elapsed and finally Carla cornered me and said she was ready to leave. We thanked the host and hostess, said our goodbyes and walked to the car.

The sun was still shining on the drive back into Hollywood, but given the atmosphere in the car, you could have fooled me. I told her I had heard all kinds of favorable comments about her work. She nodded, but didn't reply. Then I told her I had a conversation with Bert Addison where he again broached the subject of getting me on the show. She said that was nice, but said no more.

As we hit the western end of the Sunset Strip, I said, "Guess I'm in the doghouse, huh?"

She turned to me and after a moment said, "It pissed me off that you totally ignored my request to leave him alone, Eddie."

"Yeah, well, he had it coming."

"And what if he takes it out on me?"

"How?"

"By putting my job in jeopardy. Whether or not you believe it, the guy has clout with the producers. Stop and think for a minute, will you?"

"He's a punk. He probably runs errands and makes coffee."

"I can fight my own battles, Eddie."

I stopped for a light at Crescent Heights and Sunset and turned to her. "So, what do you want me to say, Carla? 'Jeez, honey, that's too bad. But maybe he won't do it again.' He's a creep, and the only language he understands is threats."

"Fine. Whatever you say."

That ended our discussion. When I pulled into the spare parking space in her building's garage, she said she had dialogue to work on for tomorrow's shooting, and would talk to me later. She leaned over, gave me a half-hearted kiss on the cheek and entered the building.

I drove off, wondering how long it would take for me to get my foot out of my mouth.

17

I was in a funk. A hell of a way to start the week.

Part of my funkiness I attributed to not sleeping worth a damn the previous night. And I suppose part of that was due to the dustup Carla and I had after the party. Since we've been together we've been pretty lucky in terms of getting along. Yes, there has been a disagreement or two, but nothing major. Nothing that had the potential of lasting beyond a few hours. I had a feeling this spat was different, and that bothered me.

But as I sat in an iHop toying with the scrambled eggs in front of me, I couldn't help but wonder what the hell her problem was. I'd been mulling over the way I'd gotten into Artie Young's face. Okay, maybe I'd been out of line, but guys like him—even though I didn't know him from Adam—push a button in me. Over the years I've come to easily recognize phoniness and pretension, both of which run rampant in this town and the "biz," as it were. And the fact of the matter was that the thought of a guy like him hitting on someone I'd come to care for an awful lot had set me off. If Carla expected me to look the other way and treat him as if he had merely flirted with her, excuse me, but I wasn't cool with that.

The waitress filled my coffee cup and I added more cream. Another element of my funk was the admission that Charlie Rivers' rebuff had kind of ruffled my feathers. I know. Stupid, right? Come on Collins, I kept thinking, you're the one who has the PI ticket. Quit with the feeling that you've always got to rely on someone else to get the job done. Nevertheless, my ego was smarting, which was fueling some uncertainty within me.

I nibbled on a strip of bacon and thought about Meredith Paulson and this case in front of me. At the root of her disappearance was an apparent incident of sexual misconduct. Another button to be pushed. Digging into an event that happened nine years ago was daunting, and maybe for the first time in a long while I felt a bit overwhelmed. Hopefully, making some reel magic this afternoon could help to put things in perspective.

I left a healthy tip and stepped outside. The onslaught of camera-toting tourists had already begun. Selfies being snapped over the stars on the Walk of Fame. Hollywood Boulevard was alive. Street performers romped and cavorted, all in an attempt to lure the gullible into an altogether too-brief taste of the celluloid circus. As I walked back to my office, metal doors rolled open to reveal every conceivable item of movie paraphernalia known to man. At times I've debated with myself whether or not I should flee this hoopla, but I always come to the conclusion that being in the center of the noise and confusion gives me a center, provides a charm, crazy as that may sound.

Nothing better illustrates that charm than running into one of my neighbors, Lenny Daye. He was inserting a key into his office door as I stepped off our prehistoric elevator. As usual, Lenny was sartorial splendor. The pattern of his shirt was just short of a nightmare, and if his turquoise trousers were any tighter, he'd be in danger of singing soprano.

"Morning, Lenny. Pretty early for you, isn't it?"

"Early bird gets the worm, Eddie. And believe me, I need a worm or two."

He pushed the door open a tad, then looked over his shoulder and gave me a grin and a wink, putting an emphasis on the double entendre that he hoped would register with me. It did. There's not much that's subtle with Lenny.

"You working, honey?" he said.

"Yup. A film over at Warners. And I picked up a case a couple of days ago."

"Well, look at you, Mr. Hollywood PI." From inside his office I heard the phone rang, and he pushed the door open. "I better get that. Catch ya later, gator." And with that, he disappeared into his office and I followed suit. Mavis stuck her head out from her alcove as I entered.

"Morning, Eddie."

"Hey," I said, as I sank down in one of the chairs in front of her desk. I took my hat off and absent-mindedly twirled it around a forefinger.

She appeared with a cup of coffee in one hand and a sheaf of papers in the other. "How was the weekend?"

"I've had better."

"Well, that's not exactly a ringing endorsement," she said, as she sat behind her desk. "Care to elaborate? Or should I consider it privileged information?"

I chuckled and told her about the party and the spat with Carla.

"Shoot. I'm sorry. Did you kiss and make up?"

"Not yet."

"Well, knowing the two of you, it'll happen. Fritz and I always let it simmer for a bit. Makes the kissin' and makin' up all the better. If you get my drift."

"Yeah, I get it, but I'm not sure she wants to."

"What makes you say that?"

"She couldn't wait to get out of the car when I dropped her off."

"What brought on the spat?"

"There's a producer on her show who put his hands on her a few days ago. He was there, and I got in his face and threatened him. For some reason, that pissed Carla off."

Mavis looked at me for a long moment over her coffee cup. "Maybe she wants to fight her own battles, Eddie."

"Yeah, maybe so, but I only did it for her benefit."

"I get that, boss man, but ever since I've gotten to know her, she's impressed me as a lady who can take care of herself. Look at it this way. When she was dancing at that place…what the heck was the name of it? Feline something?"

"Feline Follies."

"Right. From what she's shared with me, part of her job description was slapping hands and putting all kinds of creeps like that in their place. Seems to me she did pretty well."

I put my hat back on my head and looked at her, trying to stifle yet another opinion that disagreed with mine. "So, what should I have done? Plaster some deep furrows on my forehead, shrug my shoulders and go on about my own business?"

"Oh, come on, Eddie, I think you're over-simplifying the whole thing. For cryin' out loud, she's an adult, not some shrinking violet. Sure, she wants your concern and support, but maybe you crossed a line when you interfered with something job-related. Let her handle it. In the end, she'll thank you for it."

"I guess that remains to be seen," I said, in a tone of voice that provoked a look from her like I had just whined about putting on my galoshes before going out into the rain. After we glared at each for a couple of moments I said, "I got in touch with Charlie Rivers on Friday. You called it, kiddo."

"What did he say?"

"The Paulson girl's disappearance isn't in his jurisdiction. Pretty much slammed the door on me."

She sipped from her coffee. "When it rains, it pours, huh?"

"I guess."

"What about the movie? Are you called today?"

"Yeah, at noon."

"Well, that'll help you take your mind off it."

"Hopefully," I said, not really sure it would, but willing to give it the benefit of the doubt. I went back into my apartment, stripped, and stood under a hot shower. One of the reasons Mavis is an important cog in Collins Investigations is that she's always able to cut through the bullshit I sometimes find myself wallowing in. And she'd done it again. Carla had a solid gig going with *Three on a Beat*, something that was hard to come by in her profession, especially for a woman. Mavis was correct when she implied that I may have over-reacted. Yeah, okay, I probably should have bit my tongue and put a cap on my testosterone tube.

As I drove through the Warner Bros. gate and parked in the ramp, my Monday funk started to dissipate. For some strange reason, being on a movie lot always stirs within me a fascination for and appreciation of the business I'm in. On my way to the soundstage, I marveled that I was walking on the same streets as Bogie and Cagney had. By no means did I compare myself to them, but sharing the same space with them was still a kick.

I turned a corner and was jolted from the past into the present. The romanticism of those glory days of Warner Bros. tough-guy films gave way to a new reality. A group of Avengers, or X-Men, or some other superheroes of the week rehearsed a piece of choreography in front of one of the stages. I must admit to not being a big fan of these comic book characters and their increasing domination of the industry, but one couldn't begrudge their enthusiasm. I watched for a couple of minutes, until one of them costumed as a gigantic reptile of some sort lost his footing and almost knocked me on my ass.

"Sorry, man," the reptile said. "I'm pumped, you know?"

"I know," I said. "Happens to me all the time."

It laughed from somewhere inside its shell and clapped me on the shoulder. I continued walking and had to wonder why whoever was inside that shell wasn't irritated that no one was going to be able to see his face. Beyond my pay grade, I concluded.

I turned another corner and saw the *Terms of Power* soundstage. For a moment I thought I was in the wrong place. The tarp that normally covered the lunch tables was gone. So were the tables. The roach coach was still there, but its serving window was shuttered.

Something was up.

I walked to my trailer and grabbed the door handle. Locked.

I was sure Morrie had told me my call was noon. And he hadn't said anything about a location other than the Warner Bros. lot. Puzzled, I looked around and made my way to the door of the soundstage where I spotted Tom Sanderson approaching.

He held out his hands and then gestured to where the lunch tables normally were. "Hey, boss, what the hell's going on?"

"You tell me. Did you have a noon call?"

"Yeah. You know something I don't?"

"Beats me." We turned to enter the stage and almost ran into Steve Fischer.

"Hi, guys," he said. "There's some craft services inside. Help yourself and grab a seat."

"What's going on, Steve?" I said.

He shuffled his feet and ran a hand through his hair. "We've...uh...had a hiccup. The producer's gonna get everybody up to speed in a couple of minutes." He didn't reveal anything else and walked off. Tom and I looked at each other, blank looks on our faces, and walked into the soundstage.

Several round tables were scattered in one corner. A few crew members sat hunched over cups of coffee, carrying on whispered conversations. We spotted Clay and Howard at one of the tables, poured our coffee and joined them.

"What the hell's going on?" Tom said.

Clay finished a bite of a muffin and shook his head. "Damned if I know. I ran into Steve Fischer and he clammed up. Maybe they changed the location."

"Our agents would've called us if that was the case, right?" Howard said.

We agreed and tried to offer explanations but couldn't come up with any. After a few moments, Steve Fischer walked into the stage, along with Walt Langley, the director, and Howard Davidson, the producer. Attention shifted to them as they briefly huddled with each other and then Davidson broke away and stood in front of us.

"Hi, folks," he said. "I hate to throw the old adage at you, but I'm afraid

I've got some bad news and some good news. First, the bad news. Over the weekend we learned that our financing for *Terms of Power* dried up. Just disappeared and left town. We're still trying to figure out what the hell happened, but we can't locate anybody involved with the backers of our project. Faced with that, I'm afraid we're going to have put the production on hold."

Murmurs and confused looks traveled around the room. A crew member at the table next to us slammed his hand down and let fly with a mouthful of curses.

Davidson continued. "But fortunately, that leads to the good news. My co-producers and myself have been holed up all weekend looking for alternate financing. And the good news is that we're almost certain of a deal that will allow for filming to continue within a week or so. For you actors on SAG-AFTRA contracts, this necessitates putting you on hold. Now, we can't prevent you from accepting other employment, but we want to assure you that your contracts, at least to us, are still valid. We will be in close contact with your respective agents and will let them know immediately when and where production will resume. If there's renegotiation required, we'll enter in good faith. So that's it. I'll be glad to answer any questions."

Davidson called on a few people who had their hands up. Then the first AD told us if we had left any personal belongings in our trailers to let them know and they would provide access to the dressing rooms. The four of us didn't have any, and after apologies and encouragement from the director and producer, we stepped outside. Appropriately enough, the sun had disappeared behind a cloudbank. The four of us looked at each other as if we had wandered into a meeting of the Ladies Aid Society.

"There's another fine mess they've gotten us into," Tom said. "With apologies to Oliver Hardy, of course."

The four of us shared a laugh and Clay said, "Well, hell, I was hoping for a free lunch."

After a moment Howard said, "The Smoke House is right across the street."

"Good idea," Tom added. "Let's do it. I could use a cold beer...or maybe several."

Clay enlisted a passing production assistant to take a photo of the four of us outside the soundstage. We draped our arms around each other's shoulders and mugged for the camera. Clay said he'd email it to us, and we started toward the parking ramp.

The Smoke House is a venerable bistro literally across Barham Boulevard from the main gate of Warner Bros. It was dimly lit, cool, and served a good burger. The four of us placed our orders and raised our sweating mugs of beer.

"Here's to the reboot of *Terms of Power*," Clay said. "May it actually happen."

We echoed his toast and drank. After a moment, Howard said, "Man, I didn't see this coming."

"Me either," Tom said. "This ever happen to you guys?"

"Couple of times for me," I said.

"What happened?" Howard said.

I swallowed a mouthful of beer and licked the foam off my upper limb. "One worked out fine. The other one didn't. Still got my money, though. Thanks to a guild contract."

"Hear, hear," Clay said, and we all murmured agreement. I went on to elaborate on the occasions I'd mentioned. We turned, as a bit of an argument erupted from two men at the bar that was quickly quelled by the bartender.

Clay's phone buzzed and he looked at the screen. "How about this irony, guys? I've got an audition tomorrow."

"What? Your agent knew they were going to pull the rug out from under us?"

"I doubt it," Clay said. "But I gotta admit, this guy is on top of it. He'll submit me even if he knows I'm working."

"Life goes on, as some fool told me once," Howard said, and chuckles went around the table.

"I wonder what this does to that investigation into Gould's death?" Tom said.

"Good question," I replied. "Anybody see that Burbank cop around today?"

The three men shook their heads and leaned back from the table as the waiter walked up with our food. We dug in, and the conversation segued into our respective takes on the Hollywood not-so-fast lane.

When the check came, we all started to dig for money when Clay grabbed the bill and said, "Here's the deal, guys. Since I've got the audition tomorrow, let me get this."

The three of us dumped some good-natured jeers on him, but none of us argued. He settled up with the waiter and we stepped outside. We vowed to reassemble here when the movie resumed, if in fact it ever did.

Tom stuck out his hand. "Good to meet you, Eddie. Hope to see you in a few days."

"Likewise," I said, and took his hand.

"You still gonna keep poking around with that key you found?"

"Yeah. Matter of fact, I picked up a case in connection with it."

"Terrific. Good luck with it. And I meant it when I extended that invite to speak to my students."

"I'll give it some thought."

"Do that, boss. See you down the road."

He began to walk to his car, and I did the same, all of a sudden faced with the fact of having the time to devote to the Meredith Paulson case, a case I was unsure about.

Change hats, Collins, and soldier on.

18

The address Judy Quinn had given me for Ken Thompson was between Franklin and Hollywood Boulevards, just a little east of Gower. I sat in my car on a street that was T-boned by Thompson's. A black SUV was in his driveway, with a lime-green Kia parked behind it. I was on the proverbial PI stakeout. A cup of coffee sat within reach, and my Thomas Guide map was propped up on the steering wheel, giving one the impression I was lost.

Yesterday's funk had pretty much disappeared, having been replaced by the after-effects of too much time spent last night in the company of Mr. Jim Beam. Charlie Rivers' rejection, the spat with Carla, and the sudden cancellation of *Terms of Power* had propelled me to seek solace in the arms of alcohol. It hadn't worked. Visits to a couple of my favorite hangouts yielded nothing, save for a mindless conversation with a middle-aged food broker who was of the opinion that the Trump administration was eventually going to cause him to go postal.

I hadn't yet reached out to Carla. I suppose we were in a bit of a Mexican standoff, two stubborn people waiting for the other to make an overture. For a moment or two last night, while communing with my glass of whiskey, I thought about sending her a text, but didn't follow through. I didn't have a good reason for my hesitation, and by the time the food broker started his diatribe, I'd forgotten about it.

I sipped on my coffee and mulled over my next move with regard to Ken Thompson. Since he didn't know me, I could easily conjure up one of my fake IDs and just knock on his front door. As I fingered the Pandora key hanging from my keychain, I wondered if merely sticking it in his face would only make him clam up and slam the door on me.

Sudden movement down the street caught my attention.

The front door of Thompson's house opened and two men emerged. I picked up my digital camera, zoomed in on them and began taking photos. I'd been studying my picture of Ken Thompson enough so that his face was etched in my memory. The older of the two was definitely him. But his companion caught me completely by surprise.

The younger man was Dreadlocks, the guy who'd ransacked my dressing trailer looking for a key.

Sinking lower in the car seat, I continued snapping photos as the two men conversed on the front stoop. They shook hands and Dreadlocks walked to the green Kia, got in and backed out of the driveway. I now had confirmation of Thompson's address, and decided to follow the Kia and see where it led me.

Thompson stepped back inside as the Kia drove off. I fired up my car and followed, getting close enough to see a license plate. With one hand on the wheel, I used the other to jot down the number on a pad of paper next to me. He turned right on Hollywood, heading west, then took a left on La Brea and another right on Sunset Boulevard. The Kia looked like a tissue box on wheels. That, combined with its color, made the car easy to follow. It slowed and turned right into the parking lot of a two-storied open-air mall. The Kia waited for a car to back out and pulled into the vacant space.

Parking karma was on my side for a change. Brake lights of a car came on and it started to back up. I signaled that I wanted the space and waited for it to empty. I locked the car and saw Dreadlocks riding an exterior escalator to the second floor. Since he hadn't previously seen me with a porkpie on my head, I figured that the hat, along with sunglasses, wouldn't make it necessary to camouflage my presence. I stepped on the escalator and began the ascent.

Dreadlocks walked into a small bookstore. I watched him for a moment and then followed him, nodding to a uniformed mall guard who stood by the front door. Dreadlocks hovered over a table covered with paperbacks. He wore a lightweight blue windbreaker that was zippered up and cinched around his waist.

Pocketing my sunglasses, I moved behind a rack of mystery novels, pulled a Michael Connelly title out and flipped it open, all the while keeping an eye on him.

He glanced around the store, obviously looking for cameras, and, not seeing any, pulled the zipper of his windbreaker down a few inches and slipped a slim volume inside. He then ambled over to a magazine rack, picked one up, paged through it, then walked up to the cashier, paid for it and walked out into the mall.

As I went by the mall guard, he told me to have a good day, and I responded in kind. I looked to my left and saw Dreadlocks walk into a coffee shop. I leaned against a railing that overlooked the ground floor and watched him place his order. He tossed the magazine and the book on a table in one corner and sat down. While I waited for him to get his coffee order the guard ambled up to the railing a few feet to my left and leaned back against it. Maybe he thought I looked suspicious. I was tempted to tell him the guy with the dreadlocks was the one he should be watching, not me. However, I refrained.

When the barista called out Dreadlocks' order, he rose to get it, grabbed a couple of napkins from a dispenser and retook his seat.

Time to make my move.

I pushed myself off the railing and went into the coffee shop. There were a half a dozen other patrons besides Dreadlocks. I walked up to his table, pulled out a chair and sat down across from him.

He looked up and jerked back in his chair. His leg collided with the table and spilled some of his coffee. He patted the spillage with a napkin and said, "What the fuck, man! Who the hell are you?"

"You don't remember me?" I said. He stared at me, his face blank. "You were looking for a key the other day? In a dressing trailer you had no business being in?" His eyes narrowed, and I reached in my pocket, pulled out the Pandora key and dangled it in front of him. "This what you were looking for?"

His face turned pale and he picked up his magazine and paperback book, then pushed his chair back and stood. "I don't know who the fuck you are. I'm—"

"Just sit down, pal. You see that security guard there?" I said, as I pointed to the guard leaning against the railing. "I saw you steal that book. Now, if I were to tell him that, he'd probably want to see your receipt. And I don't think you've got one, do you?" He didn't say anything and just looked at the guard. "Now why don't you just sit down and let's talk."

He glared at me for a moment or two and finally sat down. Now that I had the opportunity to look at him up close without him running away, I pegged him to be in his late twenties, maybe early thirties. His eyes looked dead, and his face was dotted with scraggly chunks of a beard. The long brown dreadlocks cried out for some tender loving care. I had a feeling a controlled substance or two had passed his way on many occasions.

"What's your name?" I said.

"None of your damn business."

"I can find out, you know."

"Then go for it."

So, this is how he was going to play it. I laid my keychain on the table. "What's your relationship with Ken Thompson?"

"I don't know any Ken Thompson."

"You just came from his house. I followed you here."

He said nothing. Just lifted his coffee cup to his mouth and glared at me.

"What were you doing on the Warner Bros. lot the other day?"

"I've never been on the Warner Bros. lot."

"Come on, man, you and that rat's-nest hairdo of yours were in my trailer looking for this key. My costume had Ken Thompson's name on it, and you were seen coming out of Tony Gould's trailer with a tray full of dishes. Now, that same Tony Gould later keeled over from an apparent overdose of insulin. Tell me if I'm wrong, but I think you've got something to do with his death."

"Look, man, I ain't the only dude wearin' dreads in this city. You got me mistaken for someone else."

I picked up the metal disk attached to the Pandora key and dangled it in front of him. "Tell me about Pandora."

More glare.

"The names Victor Benedetti and David Forbes mean anything to you?"

He'd started to again raise his coffee cup, but paused when he heard the names. After a moment he took a swallow and set the cup down.

"I don't know what the fuck you're talking about, man, and we're done here." He grabbed his book and magazine, stood up and pushed his chair back.

"What about that book?" I said. "The guard is still out there. All I have to do is point you out to him."

He glanced outside, then tossed the book and the magazine on the table. "Take the fuckin' book. Knock yourself out."

With that, he stomped out of the coffee shop and bolted down the escalator. I picked up the book and saw that it was a graphic novel rendition of *The Handmaid's Tale*. The magazine was the latest edition of *Entertainment Weekly*. Book in hand, I walked up to the security guard. "Did you see that guy with the dreadlocks?"

"Yeah, what's his problem? He looked like he was in a hurry."

"He swiped this book from next door," I said, as I handed him the graphic novel. "I told him I was going to inform you, and he lit out. You want me to take it back to the store?"

The guard glanced over the railing, but Dreadlocks was already pulling out of his parking spot. "Ah, crap, he's history." He looked at the back cover of the book. "Fourteen ninety-five. Not worth the effort chasing him. I'll take it back. I saw you talking to him. What's the guy's name?"

"We didn't get that far. I told him I was going to rat him out, and that was it. He split."

"No harm, no foul, I guess," the guard said, after looking at me for a long moment. "Thanks for your help. No offense, but next time, you should maybe tell someone in authority before sticking your nose in. These days, you never know."

"You're right about that," I said. "Have a good one."

The guard walked back into the bookstore and I descended the escalator, wondering why a guy like that would seek out a graphic novel of *The Handmaid's Tale*. The novel was published years ago, but the recent streaming television show on Hulu had been a huge success. Maybe that sparked his interest. Curious as to why, when I reached the bottom of the escalator, I went back up, entered the bookstore and purchased a copy of the graphic novel. The mall guard had wandered down to the other end of the mall and didn't see me buying the book. No need to raise further scrutiny. As I again rode the down escalator, I felt secure in the knowledge that Dreadlocks had something to do with the Pandora key. My mention of Ken Thompson, Victor Benedetti and David Forbes spooked him.

Why, was the question.

Back in my car, I fished around in the glove compartment until I found Detective Meyerson's business card with his cellphone number. He picked up after three rings.

"Detective, this is Eddie Collins. From the *Terms of Power* set over at Warner Bros.?"

"Oh, yeah, right. I hear somebody sabotaged your movie. Ran away with the money or some shit?"

"That's what they told us."

"Well, hell, that's a bummer."

"We were told they're working on another deal. But in any case, what does that do to your investigation?"

"Doesn't help us a damn bit. You got anything for me, Collins?"

"I might have. I've got a quid pro quo deal to run by you."

There was a slight pause, as if he was weighing what I had to say. "Okay. Go on."

"Remember that guy with the dreadlocks I told you about? The one I found going through my dressing room looking for a key?"

"Yeah. And the same one who was also seen coming out of Gould's trailer with a tray full of dishes."

"That's the one. I've located him. Don't have a name for you, but I've got a plate you can run."

"Let's have it," Meyerson said.

"This is where the quid pro quo comes in. I need his name and his address."

Another pause, then: "Look, Collins, we've had this dance before. If you stick your nose into a police investigation, we're going to have a problem."

"I read you. This has got nothing to do with Gould's death. I need to find out why he was interested in getting that key."

"What's so damn important about that key?"

"I don't know, but I'll keep you in the loop if it has anything to do with the Gould death."

There was silence on the other end of the line, and I could hear subdued conversation in the background. After a moment he said, "All right, Collins, you got a deal. Give me the plate number."

I rattled off the digits and he said, "I'll call you back in a few minutes."

"Thanks, Detective," I said, and ended the call.

The open-air mall had a deli stuck in one corner. I ordered a pastrami sandwich and found a table in one corner. I took a bite and looked at my cellphone, I guess hoping that there might be a text from Carla. No such luck. After finishing the sandwich and maybe against my better judgment, I sent her a text. I relayed the information that my movie had been canceled, and then added, *Am I still in the doghouse? If I said I'm sorry, would that make you unlock the door?* My smart-ass attempts at humor have always worked with her in the past. Maybe this time I was pushing my luck. I wasn't sure.

I sipped on a glass of beer and watched the traffic in and out of the strip mall. I had to admit to a little reluctance in giving the information about Dreadlocks to Meyerson, but I still was of the belief that the death of Tony Gould and the discovery of the key, along with the disappearance of Meredith Paulson were two different arenas. Burbank PD needed to talk to this guy, and I didn't feel right about standing in the way of their investigation.

I went up to the counter and ordered another beer, then sat down and started paging through the book. I've never been a big fan of these graphic novels, but they've seemed to make an inroad into the publishing world. The blurb on the cover described a dystopian society where women are subjected to men. Not an unfamiliar trope, even in today's climate. Trying to conjure up a reason for Dreadlocks' interest in the subject matter baffled me. My bafflement was interrupted by my cell. The screen said Meyerson.

"Collins here."

"The guy's name is Roger Iverson. He lives in Studio City." Meyerson gave me the address, and I jotted it down in my notebook, next to the license plate of his Kia.

"Thanks, Detective. I'll let you know if I find out anything else about him."

"I'd appreciate it. And for what it's worth, Collins, you know we're on the same side."

"That we are. Talk to you later," I said, and broke the connection.

Roger Iverson. Joining the ranks of Ken Thompson, Victor Benedetti, and David Forbes. In what capacity was anybody's guess. I finished my beer and headed for my car. As I stuck my key in the ignition, the Pandora key and disc brushed against my knee. This seemingly innocuous talisman was starting to become more significant.

19

It was two o'clock by the time I got back to the office. The door was locked. Obviously, my Girl Friday wasn't in. A note stuck to the corner of Mavis' desk said she was out buying office supplies. I hung my hat on its peg for the day, sat behind my desk and started leafing through *The Handmaid's Tale* graphic novel. Graphic was an understatement. The art and adaptation were done by one Renee Nault. The book depicted a dystopian society where the handmaids wore voluminous red dresses, symbolic, I thought, of Nathaniel Hawthorne's Hester Prynne in *The Scarlet Letter*.

The story centered around a handmaid by the name of Offred, who was part of a class of women subjugated by domineering men. At one point she sees a doctor, who, in the course of examining her, forces himself upon her. The farther I got into the book, parallels started to emerge with the case of Meredith Paulson. She had made accusations of sexual harassment. They were rejected, and she then disappeared. The question was why. Retribution for her accusations? The more I thought about it, the more the possibility reared its ugly head. What baffled me, however, was Roger Iverson's interest in the book. And why steal it, as opposed to buying it? And what the hell was his connection to Ken Thompson?

I was forty pages in when my cellphone buzzed. It was Carla. Her text read, *"If" you said you're sorry?*

I looked at the screen for several long moments, trying to decide if I was going to be the first to blink. Her text implied it wouldn't be her. Okay, Collins, swallow your male pride. It's one word, five letters long. Saying it won't destroy your little corner of the world. I picked up the phone and replied. *Okay, here it comes: I'm sorry. Permission to plead my case in person?* I waited a few seconds, then came the reply. *I'll call you when I'm through shooting. A nice dinner with wine and candlelight works wonders.*

I grinned and replied with a "thumbs up" emoji, then walked into my office to answer nature's call and came back to the desk with a glass of cold beer. Buried somewhere in the notes Mavis had produced for me regarding the North Hollywood investigation of Meredith Paulson's disappearance were the names of the detectives on the case. Finally I found them: Harlan Berenson and Mike Fogarty. Granted, nine years ago made it conceivable that they might not even be on the force anymore. Only one way to find out. I located the phone number and dialed. A husky female voice answered.

"North Hollywood Community Police Center. How can I help you?"

"Yes, may I speak to Harlan Berenson please?"

A pause, then: "I don't show a Harlan Berenson on my directory."

"How about Mike Fogarty?"

After a moment she said, "Who's calling, and with regard to what, sir?"

"My name is Eddie Collins. I'm a licensed private investigator. I'd like to speak to Officer Fogarty regarding a case he worked on a few years ago."

"Please hold."

Three rings and the phone was answered with, "Mike Fogarty."

"Thanks for taking my call, Detective. My name's Eddie Collins."

"So I gather. The receptionist mentioned something about a case?"

"Right. Meredith Paulson. Disappeared nine years ago?"

There was a pause, and Fogarty said, "Yeah, right. I remember that one. My partner and I ran into a dead end. What's your interest?"

"I may have some information about it."

"What sort of information?"

"I'd rather come in and talk to you face to face. If you've got the time."

Another pause, and, "Okay, but I'm jammed up this afternoon. How about tomorrow morning. Say ten o'clock?"

"Perfect."

"Give me your phone number in case something comes up."

I gave him my cell number, thanked him for his time and hung up. I wasn't sure how relevant my information was. However, that scrap of paper I found in Gould's dressing room had on it the names of three men involved in a lawsuit involving Meredith Paulson. Furthermore, on the reverse side of that same scrap, her name and that of her mother appeared. Instinct told me there was some connection, and logic told me a cop would be interested. Hopefully, I wouldn't be wrong on both counts.

More pawing through Mavis' notes came up with the name of Frank Watson, the lead attorney who represented Meredith Paulson in her lawsuit against Pandora Productions. Watson's firm was Carson, Wendt, & Mosby in North Hollywood. My call was answered by a woman whose voice came close to sounding like Lily Tomlin's telephone operator Ernestine. I asked to speak to Frank Watson and was told that Mr. Watson was no longer with the firm. Then I asked to speak with someone connected to Paulson's lawsuit. My ersatz Ernestine took my name and number and said someone would get back to me. Yeah, right. I figured the chance of that happening would be the same as me appearing on center court at Wimbledon.

Tethered to my office awaiting callbacks was the perfect reason to get comfortable and do some reading. I found a smooth jazz station on my little boombox, turned on a fan to blow some dust around, then propped my feet up on the desk and got back into *The Handmaid's Tale*. At one point Offred had an audience with a character called "The Commander." What ensued was more sex with her against her will.

The entrance of Mavis put a stop to my reading.

"Eddie?"

"Yeah, back here."

I saw her carrying plastic bags from Staples into her little sanctuary, and after a moment she appeared in the doorway with a receipt in her hand. "We're still writing off some of these office expenses, aren't we?"

"So the accountant says, but who knows what the hell the Republicans will come up with next."

"What are you reading?" I held up the cover of the book and she took it out of my hand. "Good grief. Not exactly your cup of tea, is it?"

"Not normally, no, but remember that guy I told you about with the dreadlocks? The one I found going through my dressing room?"

"Yeah, what about him?"

"I ran across him this morning. His name is Roger Iverson. He swiped this book from a store out in Studio City."

"What the heck for?"

"Good question. Have you ever read this thing?"

"Nope. I started to watch the TV show, but it grossed me out."

"I can see why."

She handed me the book and went into her office. I read a few more pages, but put it aside and fetched another glass of beer. For the next hour and a half I sifted through more of the stuff in the shoebox Barbara McAndrews had given me. Mavis stuck her head back in the office and announced she was leaving for the day.

"Whatcha doin' tonight, boss man?"

"Having dinner with Carla."

Her eyebrows went up and a smile appeared on her face. "Are you going to kiss and make up?"

"We'll see. Hope springs eternal."

"Atta boy. Say hi for me."

I said I would, and she left the office.

Ten minutes later my laptop burped out a noise and when I flipped it open there was an invitation to a Skype call from Kelly Robinson, my daughter in Cincinnati. After finally meeting her and her adoptive parents several months back, she'd introduced me to Skype, and we'd been talking every few weeks or so. My lack of computer skills resulted in some trials and errors in connecting on my part, but thanks to her help it was now smooth sailing.

I made the connection and saw her sitting in her bedroom, cords from ear buds framing a face beaming with a huge smile.

"Hi Eddie."

"Hey, what's going on?"

"I've got great news."

"What?"

"I am now an actress. I'm playing Helen Keller in *The Miracle Worker*."

"Wow. Congratulations. That's quite a part."

"I know. Cool, right?"

She went on to tell me that a community theater there in Cincinnati was staging it, and that rehearsals had started just a few days ago.

"Did you ever do the play?"

"As a matter of fact, I did. Years ago. I played Captain Keller, her father."

"And I'll bet you were terrific. Mom and dad weren't quite sure I should do it, but now they're my biggest fans."

"That's great. And look at it this way, kiddo. You don't have to worry about not forgetting your lines."

A brief look of puzzlement crossed her face, and then she let loose with a giggle and bounced up and down in her chair.

"I know! I know! I've been practicing walking around with my eyes closed."

"Let me give you a tip," I said. "Do it with your eyes open, like she would have done. Just make sure you focus on one particular thing, and let your hands look like they're searching for something."

She thought about that for a moment and said, "Hey, that's good advice. Thanks."

"You're welcome. When does it open?"

"In a month. I wish you could be here."

"Well, let me think about that." I told her about the movie and what had happened. While I related it to her, the thought entered my head that it would be a real kick to fly back there and see her onstage.

"That would be so cool, Eddie." I could hear her cellphone go off. She picked it up, looked at it, then put it down. "Are you working on a case, or just being an actor?"

"I'm wearing both hats," I said, and briefly told her about the movie being put on hold, the key, and Meredith Paulson.

"Oh, yuck. I hope you find out what happened to her."

"I'll do my best."

"How's Carla?"

"She's fine. We're having dinner together tonight."

"Give her a big hug for me."

"Will do."

"Okay, I gotta scoot. Rehearsals, don't you know, dahling?" She cocked her head in the air, putting on her best 'actress' pose, which prompted a laugh from me. "Great to talk to you, Eddie. I miss you. And give Mavis a hug too."

"You got it. Miss you too. And good luck with the play."

"Thanks." She blew me a kiss and signed off.

I closed the laptop and looked at a picture of her sitting on the corner of my desk. Following in the footsteps of her birth father? I was proud of her, but at the same time couldn't help but harbor a dose of my innate skepticism about the business and the thought that she might want to pursue it at some time in the future. But it wasn't my call. James and Betty Robinson would have to steer her through those decisions.

I drove into the underground garage of Carla's building at seven o'clock. She opened her door after my knock and we stood and looked at each other for a moment, both of us, I suppose, wondering how this *detente* was going to conclude.

"Permission to enter the premises?" I said.

She grabbed me by the shirtfront and pulled me into the apartment. "You better. My neighbor across the way has this thing about strange men in the hallway." She shut the door and put her arms around me, then tilted her face up for a kiss, which I promptly delivered. We held it for a moment or two and she looked into my eyes. "How you doin', Shamus?"

"As well as can be expected."

"I've missed you."

"Me too. And before we go any further, I'm sorry about what happened on Sunday."

"Apology accepted. You want a beer?" she said, as she walked to the kitchen. "I'm having a glass of wine before we chow down."

"A beer would be great." I sank onto the sofa and she came back with a foamy glass of beer and the remains of the bottle. She sat down and we clinked glasses. It appeared that the *detente* was going well.

"Hey, look, I was out of line at the party. Despite what I think of Artie Young, my behavior was inappropriate."

She sipped some wine and set the glass on the coffee table. "Don't get me wrong, I know he's a creep and that he upsets you, but this show is very important to me and I don't want to do anything to jeopardize it."

"Understood. I just don't want to see you being taken advantage of."

"That's not going to happen. I had to put up with all kinds of Artie Youngs when I was dancing. What he did is small potatoes."

"But promise me if it happens again you'll go the Guild and let them deal with it."

"Done," she said, then leaned over and kissed me. "So what happened to your movie?"

"The money people took a powder."

"You're kidding."

"Nope. Slunk off into the night."

"But you still get paid, right?"

"Well, as a matter of fact, the producer told us they're very close to getting some alternative financing, so we're basically on hold and hoping for the best."

"Here's to that," she said, and we raised our glasses in a toast.

"By the way, I just got through with a Skype call from Kelly. She told me to give you a hug."

"Aw, that little charmer. How is she?"

"She's terrific. And get this. She's playing Helen Keller in a production of *The Miracle Worker.*"

"Oh, my god, that's wonderful. There, now, you see. The acorn doesn't fall far from the tree."

I went on to fill her in about my investigation and where I was at with it. She reciprocated by telling me how well her show was going. We finished our drinks and drove to a little out of the way bistro we'd discovered some months ago. There was candlelight. And good wine, with delicious food. Plus, good conversation with someone who I'd come to realize occupied a special place in my life. I acknowledged the fact that she made it easy for me to swallow my pride and admit that I'd been wrong in my confrontation with Artie Young.

The waiter cleared the remains of our chicken and fish entrees, brought us a third glass of wine and she reached out and squeezed my hand. "I hope your movie gets a reboot."

"Well, even if it doesn't, being hired by Barbara McAndrews will keep the wolf away from the door. But I'm beginning to wonder if I can do any good for her. I mean, nine years is a long time. The trail is pretty cold."

"Have you talked to the police?"

"I'm meeting with one of the North Hollywood cops tomorrow morning. Maybe he'll shed some light on it."

Carla's phone buzzed with a text. She looked at the screen and said, "Wahoo. They pushed my call time back an hour." She punched some keys in response, stuffed the phone in her bag and leaned across the table. "More time to...oh, I don't know...maybe fool around with my fella."

"Does that mean I'm out of the doghouse?"

"For the time being."

"Good. I'll throw away the flea powder."

She almost did a spit-take with her wine and tossed a wadded-up napkin at me.

"Hey, let me ask you something," I said. "Have you ever read *The Handmaid's Tale*?"

"No. I thought I'd like to watch the streaming version of it, but I don't have Hulu. Why?"

"Well, this morning I was about ready to talk to this Ken Thompson when he all of a sudden walked out of his house with the dreadlocks guy."

"The one who you caught going through your costume?"

"Right. Turns out his name is Roger Iverson. I followed him to a bookstore on Sunset. He swiped a graphic novel version of the book. I caught him at it, and then got curious as to what the hell he saw in the book and bought it."

"And?"

"I started reading it. Subjugation and victimization of women. The more I think about it, the more it relates to this Meredith Paulson case. A sexual harassment lawsuit. Which she loses, and then disappears. How come? So now I'm wondering if he's involved, and if he is, how."

Carla sipped from her wineglass and looked off to her left. "Wow. Sounds like that key you found—"

"Which everybody told me to forget about," I interrupted.

"—which everybody told you to forget about," she said. "Right. You've got a puzzle, Shamus. I'd advise you to stay on it." She had a smile on her face as she said it.

"Well, alert the media! Finally, an endorsement."

"I know, you poor tortured soul, you. And now you're out of the doghouse. Things are looking up." She laughed and pinched my cheek. "Let's get out of here. Take me home."

I did just that. But circumstances prevented me going any further.

20

M ike Fogarty had cop written all over him. About five minutes after I checked in at the front desk of LAPD's North Hollywood Station, he came down a hallway with a Robert Mitchum strut, full of confidence and authority. He didn't have Mitchum's height, though; I pegged him at five-six or so, stocky, barrel-chested, with a gray buzz-cut covering his head. He was in shirtsleeves and carried a half-inch thick manila folder in one hand. The other he outstretched in my direction.

"Mr. Collins? Mike Fogarty. Hope I haven't kept you waiting."

"Not at all," I replied, taking his firm handshake.

"Don't take this the wrong way, but could I see your license?"

"Sure thing," I said, as I reached for my wallet and handed him my ticket.

He looked at it, then handed it back. "Have to make sure you are who you say you are." He flashed me a lopsided grin and shrugged his shoulders. "Why, I'm not sure, but it is what it is."

"No problem."

"Follow me," he said, and we started walking back down the hallway. "I googled you after your call. You're an actor too, that right?"

"You got it."

"So the license helps pay the rent? That sort of deal?"

"That's the plan."

A uniformed cop walked by and Fogarty clapped him on the arm with the folder. "Hey, Rudy, how's it goin'?" The uniform tossed a reply over his shoulder and we pushed our way through a set of swinging doors into a squad room filled with cubicles, computers, and other trappings of a busy cop shop.

"Let's go in here," he said, opening a door into an interview room, which contained one gray metal table and three metal chairs. A single light hung over them. What was missing was the traditional two-way glass partition, through which we could be watched. I glanced up at the corners of the ceiling and Fogarty caught my look.

"No cameras, Mr. Collins. Just you and me." He pulled out one of the chairs and gestured for me to sit in the other one facing him. "You know, I had a couple of buddies at Rampart who put in their twenty and decided they were going to get into the movies. They worked as extras, but didn't last long. Too damn much sitting around."

"There is that," I said.

"One of them works security at the Beverly Center and the other moved to Idaho." He chuckled and took a small notepad out of the manila folder. "So, Collins, what can I do for you?"

"Meredith Paulson's mother hired me to look into her disappearance."

He opened the folder and flipped up a couple of pages. "Yeah, Paulson. Harley Berenson worked that one with me. Funny thing is, he retired and also moved up to Idaho." He looked up at me and a grin broke out on his face. "They must have some kind of jones for squirrels and acorns."

"Is the file still active?"

"Yeah, it's active, but I haven't turned up anything in…oh…Christ, four or five years now."

"Anything you can share with me?"

He leaned back in his chair and looked at me for a long moment. "Depends. You said you had something that might pertain to the case?"

"Could be," I said. "Just before she disappeared Paulson filed a lawsuit against a Pandora Productions, alleging sexual harassment."

"Yeah, I remember."

"A few days ago Tony Gould, the defendant in that case, died on the set of a movie at Warner Bros."

"Right. I saw that. Burbank PD is looking into it. Possible homicide."

"Correct. I worked on the film, but it went belly up. Before it did, another actor and myself were in his trailer and I found this." I took my notebook out of my shirt pocket, opened it and pulled out the scrap of paper I'd found in Gould's trailer, then slid it across the table. "It was stuck in a sofa cushion."

Fogarty picked up the scrap. "Ken Thompson and Victor Benedetti." He opened his folder and rifled through some pages. "They testified on Gould's behalf, right?"

"They did."

He gestured to the slip of paper. "But this David Forbes doesn't ring a bell."

"I did some poking around. All four men were connected to each at one time or another."

"So?"

"Look on the other side."

Fogarty turned over the scrap. "Meredith Paulson and Barbara McAndrews. Mother and daughter."

"Right," I said.

"Interesting." He turned the paper over. "What does this 'keys' refer to?"

"I'm not sure, but I found a guy by the name of Roger Iverson going through my costume. Ken Thompson had previously worn it. Iverson said he was looking for a key."

"To what?"

"That I don't know," I said, once again deliberately holding back the fact that I had the Pandora key in my possession. I suppose the argument could be made that I was withholding evidence, but I still wasn't convinced that the key pertained to Paulson's disappearance. And what's more, I still didn't have a clue as to what the damn key was for.

Fogarty turned the scrap over in his hands. "Mind if I make a copy of this?"

"Not at all."

He slid the manila folder to the center of the table and pushed his chair back. Before he stood, his eyes went from mine to the folder. "Be back in a minute."

Maybe Fogarty had some actor in him, I thought, as I watched him leave the room. He'd left the folder behind for a reason. I turned it around and opened it up. A quick scan of the file revealed where Paulson had gone after she and her friends left the movie. There were notes on interviews Fogarty and Berenson had made. I took out my cellphone and started taking pictures of the contents. The file wasn't all that thick, so I was able to take quite a few shots. I heard voices on the other side of the door and replaced the folder just before Fogarty came back in the room.

"Sorry. Some idiot jammed up the damn copy machine." He pulled out his chair and sat down, then handed me the scrap of paper. "You get what you need?"

I looked at him for several seconds and said, "I did. Thanks."

He chuckled and pulled the folder in front of him. "Every PI I know would be on that folder like an ant on a sugar cube. Glad to see you didn't disappoint."

"These cellphones come in handy," I said.

"The department frowns on sharing information with you private guys. Makes sense, I guess, but as far as I'm concerned, I didn't see anything. You know what I mean?"

"Exactly," I replied, and put the scrap of paper back in my notebook. "Did you talk to these guys?"

"Gould, we did, but I guess he's out of the picture now. The other three we didn't."

"I've got addresses for them."

"I'll take 'em," he said.

I gave him the whereabouts of Thompson, Benedetti, and Forbes. After he jotted down the information, he spent a few minutes giving me the broad outlines of where his investigation had gone, prefacing it by asking me to keep it confidential. I said I would, we shook hands and I walked back to my car.

Mike Fogarty hadn't really helped me all that much in my investigation of Meredith Paulson's disappearance, but I figured having a cop on my side couldn't hurt. Charlie Rivers, eat your heart out, I thought, as I grinned and pulled away from the police station.

Victor Benedetti's house sat on a cul-de-sac a few blocks north of Ventura Boulevard. There was nothing fancy about it, but the neighborhood had neatly trimmed front lawns and was tucked far enough away to escape the noise of the Valley's main drag. A small porch was to the left of the front door. A white railing ran around its edges. Several pieces of outdoor furniture were scattered around the floor. They were covered by an extension of the house's roof.

The driveway was empty. A copy of the *Los Angeles Times* lay in the middle of it. I picked it up and carried it with me as I walked to the front door. The paper was today's edition. I tossed it on a small wooden bench next to the front door and pushed the doorbell. Several minutes passed with no answer. I pushed it again. Same result. I turned around and started back down the driveway when a silver Mercedes pulled in and skidded to a stop. The driver's door flew open. Victor Benedetti climbed out and headed toward me. There was no mistaking him from the picture I'd found on the IMDb website. He was dressed in tan slacks, a blue shirt and had a full head of black, slicked-back hair. A scowl covered his face as he approached.

"Can I help you?" he said.

"Victor Benedetti?"

"Who's asking?"

"Eddie Collins. I'm a private investigator."

"What the hell do you want?"

"You were a friend of Tony Gould, right?"

His eyes narrowed as he stopped a couple feet from me. "I was. But that doesn't answer my question. What do you want with me?"

"You testified on his behalf in a lawsuit filed by Meredith Paulson."

The mention of the name caught him by surprise and he froze. "Yeah, so?"

"She lost the case and then disappeared. Got any idea as to why?"

"Look...what the fuck's your name again?"

I pulled a business card out of my shirt pocket and handed it to him. "Eddie Collins."

He glanced at it and stuffed it in a hip pocket. "Look, Collins, that was a long time ago and I have no idea what the fuck happened to her. So why don't you take a hike?"

"You worked with Gould, right?"

"I did."

"How about Ken Thompson?"

He paused and looked off to his right. "Maybe. I don't know. The name's familiar."

I took out my notebook and looked at one of its pages. "How about a film called *Blind Instinct*?"

"Oh yeah, a real hit."

"You know David Forbes?"

"Never heard of him."

I looked at the notebook again and said, "Looks like you worked with him on something called *They Never Came Back*."

Benedetti glared at me and I almost expected him to take a poke at me. "If you've got all the goddamn answers, Collins, you don't need anything from me. Now why don't you get your ass off my property before I call the cops?"

"Just a couple more questions, Vic. Can I call you Vic?"

After he moment he nodded and said, "Fine. But make it quick."

"I'm also an actor. I worked on Gould's last picture. I found a guy by the name of Roger Iverson going through my costume. It'd once been worn by Ken Thompson. Iverson said he was looking for a key." I reached in my pocket, pulled out my keychain and held it up by the Pandora disc. "I had a feeling he was looking for this."

When Benedetti caught sight of the Pandora key, he paled and the look of wariness in his eyes was unmistakable. "What the hell is that?"

"A key. Any idea what it's for?"

"I haven't got the slightest idea."

"Why do you suppose it's got the word 'Pandora' stamped on it?"

"Same answer."

"Those movies you did with Thompson and Forbes were produced by Pandora Productions. Kind of a coincidence, don't you think?" He just glared at me. "You have one of these, Vic?"

"I don't know what the fuck you're talking about." He reached in his pocket and pulled out a cellphone. "Now unless you want to stay and talk to the cops, we're done here. Got it?"

We stared at each other for a long moment, until I put my notebook back in my pocket. "Okay, Vic, give me a call if your memory comes back."

I walked to my car, got in and fired it up. As I pulled away from the curb, Benedetti still stood in the driveway. The scowl again covered his face as he watched me. He punched in a number on the cell and put it to his ear.

21

Vic Benedetti had a secret. One that involved a key and the word "Pandora." Of that I was sure. The question that remained was how it could be pried out of him. After I turned a corner I pulled over to the curb and jotted down the license plate of his Mercedes. Now, as I wound my way through the Cahuenga Pass into Hollywood I also got to wondering how my dreadlocks friend Roger Iverson figured into this puzzle. The information I'd gleaned from IMDb about Ken Thompson, Benedetti, and David Forbes led me to believe that all three of them were significantly older than Iverson. So, an apprentice? If so, to what? Maybe a relative? Of which one?

I pulled into the alley behind my building with no answers coming from Jerry Jeff Walker through the car's speakers. I scrolled through the photos I'd taken from the Meredith Paulson file as I waited for the elevator to limp downwards. A winsome young lass walked up next to me, obviously headed for one of my neighbors, the Elite Talent Agency.

"You're Mr. Collins, right?" she said.

"Guilty as charged. And you're...Allison?"

"Close. Alice."

"I knew that," I said, and we shared a chuckle.

"How's business?" she said.

"Not too bad. And yours?"

"Lousy." The elevator door creaked open and we stepped inside.

"Sorry to hear that," I said, not expecting her to elaborate, but she did anyway.

"My agent sent me on an interview for a job. The guy turned out to be a sleazeball. Wanted me to do a nude layout."

"Uh, oh. What did you do?"

"I threatened to kick him in the nuts. Then I threw a glass of water in his face and left."

"Good for you," I said, as I slowly placed my hands in front of my crotch.

She saw the move and burst into laughter. "Don't worry. Peggy has only good things to say about you."

"I'm glad to hear it," I said. Peggy was Peggy Stafford, owner of the Elite Agency.

"I'm on my way to tell her what happened. I don't want to get blackballed because of that creep." We continued to make small talk until the elevator lurched to a stop and the door creaked open.

"Good luck, Alice," I said, as I pushed my office door open. She said thanks and disappeared into the Elite Talent Agency.

Mavis was on the phone. I sank into one of the chairs in front of her desk and waited for her to finish the call. She finally did, and very deliberately replaced the receiver in its cradle. "Guess how many prompts I went through before I got to an actual, live person?"

"I'm afraid to ask."

"Eight. And then I couldn't understand a word the guy said." She shook her head, picked up a coffee cup, carried it into her private supply room, rinsed it out, then walked back to her desk. "So, what's up, boss man? How'd your meeting with the North Hollywood cop go?"

"Good." I handed her my phone with the pictures I'd taken from the Paulson file. "Can you print out these photos? Just regular paper?"

She swiped left with a finger. "There's ten here. All of them?"

"Yeah. Can do?"

"It'll take me a few minutes."

"Great," I said, as I stood up. "In the meantime, my stomach's in need of a burger. Can I bring you something?""

A double pumpkin spice Frappuccino would be terrific."

"You want coffee with that?"

"Enjoy your burger, smart aleck."

I did just that, after which I stood in line watching baristas create coffee concoctions that defied description. Mavis's face lit up like a Christmas tree when I handed her the clear-domed plastic container, its whipped cream badly in need of siphoning through a straw.

She handed me the pictures and then slurped. "How did you get these?"

"The cop left me alone with the Paulson file. An open invitation."

I looked through the pages. They had names and addresses of Meredith Paulson's friends, notes on interviews, and the name and address of the bar she and her companions had gone to after they left the movie theater.

"Hey, do me a favor, kiddo. Open up your map application and find this address." I gave her the numbers and she started clicking keys. "It should be a bar called 'The Short Stop.'"

"You want a street view, I assume?"

"That'd be great."

She stopped hitting the keys and turned the screen so I could see it. "Not 'The Short Stop' anymore."

I looked at the street view. The bar was now a Mexican restaurant. "Crap, that doesn't do me any good."

"Well, it's been nine years, Eddie."

"Yeah, yeah, don't remind me." I picked up the printouts and walked into my office. The more I heard that figure, the more I was beginning to think I should call Barbara McAndrews and tell her I couldn't do anything for her.

Instead, I looked through the file pages and found the names and phone numbers of the three people who were most likely the last to see Meredith Paulson. Amanda Rigby was first. A man answered and when I asked for her, he said there was no Amanda there. I asked him how long he'd had the number. Six years. I gave him my thanks and hung up.

Information didn't have a listing for Amanda Rigby. Dead end. The nine-year gap again raised its head.

The second number was for a Janice Williams. The call went to voicemail with a woman's message to leave my name and number. Even though I wasn't sure I'd reached Janice Williams herself, I dutifully left my name and number with a message saying I was interested in talking to her about Meredith Paulson. Cellphones might not have been as prevalent nine years ago as they are now, so I wasn't sure if the numbers from the file were cells or landlines.

"Hey, Mavis?"

"Hey, what?" came the reply, followed by her appearance in the doorway. "What can I do for you, Mr. Collins?"

I made note of her pursed lips and humbly said, "Mrs. Werner, do we by any chance have a cellphone directory?"

"That would be affirmative."

I jotted down the three numbers and handed them to her. "Would you see if any of these are cellphones, please?"

She smirked and returned to her desk as I answered nature's call back in my apartment. When I came back she was sitting in front of my desk.

"No cell listing for Amanda Rigby or Janice Williams. But the one you gave me for Peggy Turner is a cellphone."

"Thanks," I said, and dialed the number. It rang three times and a woman answered.

"Hello."

"May I speak to Peggy Turner, please?"

"This is she. Who is this?"

"My name is Eddie Collins. I'm a private investigator looking into the disappearance of Meredith Paulson." There was silence on the other end. "You were friends with her. Am I right?"

"Yes." More silence.

"Miss Turner? Are you still there?"

"Yes. Sorry. It's funny, but I was just thinking of her the other day."

"I'm wondering if we could meet. I'd like to ask you a few questions about that night you and two other friends went to the movies with her."

"Okay, but I'm at work right now." She paused, then said, "Tell you what. I'm due for lunch in an hour. If you want to come by here, we could talk."

"Great. Where is 'here'?"

She gave me the address of a bar and grill on Ventura Boulevard. "I'll see you there. Look for a guy wearing a porkpie." She broke the connection and I gathered up my notes, along with the Paulson pages, and slid them into a manilla folder. Hat *du jour* on my head, I walked to the front door.

"You found Peggy Turner?" Mavis said.

"I did. Let's hope her memory goes back nine years."

The address Peggy Turner gave me turned out to be a place called "The Back Nine." It was next door to a check-cashing outlet and a music store. The place was dimly lit. Overstuffed red booths ran along one wall. The bar was against the other wall. Several tables were scattered in the middle. Elevator music wafted from speakers in the corners of the ceiling. A television set hung behind the bar showing a golf game in progress. Reflecting the name of the place, pictures of golfers dotted the walls. Tiger Woods was prominent in several of them.

I found a stool at the L-shaped bar and ordered a Coke from a bartender whose florid face indicated he might have a tendency to sample the wares he served up. After a moment or two, a young woman pushed her way through a revolving door that led into the kitchen. She caught my eye and walked up. Peggy Turner looked to be in her thirties. She was attractive, tall, brunette, dressed in jeans and a tee shirt displaying the logo of the Los Angeles Lakers. A smile broke out on her face as she extended a hand.

"Mr. Collins?"

"That's right. Thanks for agreeing to meet with me."

"No problem. Why are you looking into Meredith's disappearance?"

"Her mother hired me."

"Gosh, that's been so long ago. I don't think the police are even looking for her anymore."

"They don't seem to be," I said.

She gestured to the front door. "There's a little deli on the corner. Why don't we get out of here?"

"Lead the way."

She turned to the bartender. "Lou, I'll be back in an hour."

"Roger," he replied.

The place Peggy referred to had four small round tables sitting outside. She went inside to order her lunch while I commandeered one of them. She came out carrying a bottle of Snapple and a little plastic basket filled with a tuna sandwich and a pickle. She straddled a chair and dug in.

"How did you find me?" she said.

"I'm a detective. That's what I do."

She saw the grin on my face. "Fair enough."

"I also tried to find Amanda Rigby and Janice Williams. They were with you and Meredith the night she disappeared, right?" She nodded and took a bite of the pickle. "You have any idea where they might be?"

"Amanda moved back to Florida. Unfortunately, Janice died in an automobile accident about...oh...five years ago now."

"Can you describe for me what the four of you did that night? Whatever you can remember."

She proceeded to tell me that the four of them had gone to see *Iron Man 2* at a multiplex in Burbank. They'd caught a screening that started a little after seven o'clock. Afterwards, they went to "The Short Stop." Meredith had driven by herself, as had Amanda. Peggy and Janice had ridden together in Janice's car. They stayed at the bar approximately two hours, and then had left at the same time.

"Were your cars parked close by?"

"Amanda had found a place across from the street. Janice and I had to walk a block. Meredith had further to walk and it was in the opposite direction of where we were. We asked her if she wanted a lift to her car, but she no, she'd be all right." She paused and swallowed some of the Snapple. She paused and I could tell she was fighting the urge to cry. "But obviously she wasn't. It was so stupid. We should have insisted on giving her a ride back to her car."

I jotted down some notes as she nibbled on her sandwich. "How about when you were in the bar? Any guys come on to her?"

"Well, there were four who tried, but they weren't serious. They were just horsing around. And besides, we knew them, so we kind of blew them off."

"Do you remember what time you left the bar?"

"Hmmmm, let me think. It had to be around eleven or so. We had jobs to get to the next morning."

"Meredith had filed a lawsuit against a movie company called Pandora Productions. Did the four of you ever discuss that?"

"Oh, yeah, many times. We were all pissed that she didn't win. She'd told us what those creeps had done to her. It was disgusting."

"Did you attend the trial at all?"

"Janice and I did a few times. For moral support, if nothing else."

She took a last bite of the sandwich and set the plastic basket on an adjoining table. I opened the file in front of me and pulled out the IMDb photos of Thompson, Benedetti, and Forbes.

"Let me show you some photos. A man by the name of Tony Gould was the head of Pandora Productions. These three men testified for him at the trial. Tell me if you remember seeing them in the courtroom."

I handed the photos to her and she looked at them for a long moment and then almost slammed the bottle of Snapple down on the table.

"Oh, my God!" she said.

"What? You recognize one of them?"

"All three of them."

"From the trial?"

"No. They've been in 'The Back Nine.' During my shift."

"Do you remember when?"

"Yeah, two days ago."

22

Peggy handed me the photos. Her eyes were wide open, almost in disbelief.

"Are you sure these are the guys?" I asked.

"Positively. Two friends of mine were in having drinks. They're regulars. One's a stockbroker and the other is an actress."

My radar went up. Another actress.

She pointed to the pictures of Thompson and Benedetti. "These two started hitting on them. They kept getting more obnoxious the more they drank. My friends finally left."

"Did the men follow them?"

"No. They were pretty loaded." She then pointed to the picture of Forbes. "This guy didn't say much. In fact, a few times he tried to get the other two to quit making assholes of themselves."

"Did the three men give any indication that they knew you? I mean, maybe recognized you from the trial?"

She shook her head. "In their condition I don't think they could have remembered anything from the day before, let alone nine years ago." She finished her bottle of Snapple. "Listen, I've got to get back."

"Thanks for your time, Peggy," I said, and handed her one of my business cards. "Give me a call if you think of anything else."

She slipped the card into a pocket. "You think these three have anything to do with Meredith's disappearance?"

"I'm not sure."

"Well, good luck, Mr. Collins. Meredith was a dear friend." She paused and her lips tightened up, as if she was fighting back tears. "She should still be here. If we hadn't..." She let the thought drop.

"Don't beat yourself up, Peggy. You had no way of knowing how things would turn out."

"Yeah, I know," she said. "Still..." After a moment she stood and placed her plastic basket into a bussing tray next to the door. "If they're involved, I hope you nail them."

I walked with her to The Back Nine. We shook hands and I headed for my car. I sat behind the wheel, key in the ignition, watching the metal Pandora disk slowly twirl in a ray of sunlight. What was it with these three guys and actresses? Tony Gould had been charged with sexual harassment. They'd testified on his behalf. Did Gould's acquittal give them license to think they could continue harassing?

I flicked the disk with my finger and fired up the car, more and more convinced that the purpose of this infernal key I'd found had some connection to the disappearance of Meredith Paulson.

David Forbes lived on a quiet residential street in Burbank, north of Warner Bros. Old trees hung over the pavement, making the drive down it feel like I was in a tunnel. It was late afternoon and the sun peeked through branches, creating somewhat of a mottled mosaic. On my left an elderly couple walked a Labradoodle. I passed a kid pushing a lawnmower in front of a two-story Tudor-like structure. Since he was barely tall enough to reach the push-bar, it wasn't going well.

The address for Forbes was on the right side of the street, four down from the struggling lawn mower. I parked a few houses beyond it and walked back. The house was modest in size, painted a light yellow, neatly trimmed lawn, rose bushes running along the front. A dark gray SUV sat in the driveway. I pulled out my notebook and jotted down the license number.

I walked up to the front door and rang the bell. After a moment or two, it was opened by a woman who stood about five foot, six inches. Dark hair with snatches of gray at her temples. She wore tan slacks and a light blue cardigan sweater over a white blouse. Soft wrinkles surrounded blue eyes.

"May I help you?"

"Could I speak with David Forbes, please? Do I have the right address?"

"You do. Why do you wish to speak with him?"

"I'm a private investigator. I'd like to talk to him about a trial from a few years ago."

Her eyes narrowed slightly and her chin rose a couple of inches. I had the feeling she thought this might be the beginning of a home invasion. She turned and called to the interior of the house. "David, someone here to speak with you." Then she opened the door wide and stepped back. "Come in."

I doffed my hat and crossed the threshold. As I did, Forbes came into view from the rear of the house. He appeared to be a little older than his IMDb photo. He had a bit of a paunch and his hair was tinged with gray and thinning on the top. He had a pair of reading glasses in his hand, which he slipped into a shirt pocket as he walked up.

"Yes, can I help you?" he said.

"He said he's a private investigator," his wife said. "What on earth does a private investigator want with you?"

"I have no idea," he replied.

I pulled out one of my cards and handed it to him. "My name is Eddie Collins. I'd like to talk to you about a trial from a few years ago. I believe you testified about a matter concerning Tony Gould and Pandora Productions?"

The comment resulted in a look on his face like he'd been caught shoplifting.

"Uh...yes? What about it? That was some time ago."

His wife closed the door and stood next to him. "David, what is this about?"

"I have no idea, Connie." He gestured to his right. "Why don't we go in here, Mr. Collins?"

Connie grabbed him by the forearm. "David?"

"It's okay, dear. I'm sure it's nothing."

After a moment, confusion washing over her face, she shook her head and walked to the rear of the house.

"In here, please," Forbes said, and led the way into a large living room bathed in what was left of the day's sun. Matching off-white sofas flanked a gas fireplace. He pointed to one of them and I sat. "Now, what's this all about?" he said, as he sank into the sofa opposite me.

"You testified on behalf of Tony Gould in a sexual harassment suit against him and Pandora Productions, right?"

"Yes, but as I said, it was some time ago, and Tony was acquitted. So, why are you bringing it up now?"

"Meredith Paulson, the plaintiff, disappeared shortly after the trial. She's never been found."

Another look crossed his face, this one giving the impression the previous shoplifting charge had been upgraded to grand larceny. "So, what does that have to do with me?"

I reached into my pocket, pulled out my keychain and held it up by the metal Pandora disk. "You may have heard that Tony Gould died a few days ago while working on a picture at Warner Bros. Something called *Terms of Power*?"

"Yes, I did. Very sad."

"I'm also an actor. I worked on that picture. I came into my dressing trailer and found a young guy with dreadlocks by the name of Roger Iverson going through my costume. He said he was looking for a key. That he'd been told to get it from a Ken Thompson, who had previously worn my costume on another film project. A little earlier in the day, I found this key in my costume." I paused and watched wariness wash over him, then flipped the keychain to him. The toss caught him off guard and he fumbled it. "Look at the metal disk." He did. "It says Pandora. Gould's production company. A company Thompson worked for. Do you have one of those, David?"

His face flushed and he laid the keychain on the glass-covered coffee table. "I've never seen anything like this."

"Are you sure?"

"Positively."

I picked up the keys by the disk and swung them back and forth, as if I was going to hypnotize him. "Later on, another actor and myself were in Tony Gould's dressing trailer where I found this." I pulled out the scrap of paper, which Mavis had by now wisely encased in a plastic sleeve. "It has the word 'keys' on it, and then the names Tony Gould, Ken Thompson, Vic Benedetti and you. Any idea why your names are listed together?"

He pulled out a handkerchief and dabbed at his upper lip. "I haven't the foggiest idea."

"You know Thompson and Benedetti, right? You've worked with them in the past, along with Gould, haven't you?"

"I don't know. I may have. I've worked with lots of actors."

"So have I," I said, as I turned the scrap over in my hand. "But that doesn't answer my question."

After a moment he said, "I don't recall the names."

I continued to swing the keychain in front of him. His eyes followed it for a moment until he dabbed at his upper lip again. "Then how do you explain the fact that the three of you were seen together out in the Valley at a place called The Back Nine just two nights ago?"

Slam dunk. Drop the mic. His eyes narrowed and beads of sweat appeared on his forehead, which quickly disappeared with another swipe of the handkerchief.

"Look Collins, I don't know what you're driving at. Yes, I was with them briefly, but I don't know why that's any of your business."

"Because IMDb tells me you also worked for Pandora Productions. As did Ken Thompson and Vic Benedetti. Thompson had one of these keys. I thought maybe you have one as well."

He stood up and took a step toward the door. "I think perhaps it's time we ended this conversation. I'd like for you to leave now."

"I will, but I've got just a couple more questions. Sit down, Forbes. I caught you lying red-handed. Why don't you see if you can redeem yourself?"

After a moment and a glance in the direction Connie had disappeared, he stuck the handkerchief in his shirt pocket and sat down. He didn't know what to do with hands, and finally wound up rubbing them together, as if he were washing them, ala Lady Macbeth.

"All right, Collins, what do you want to know? Let's make this quick. We have a dinner engagement." He pulled the handkerchief out of his pocket, but it snagged the reading glasses. He undid the snag, then slammed the glasses down on the coffee table and patted his upper lip. The room certainly wasn't warm; more likely Forbes had become very nervous.

"On the other side of this scrap of paper are the names of Meredith Paulson and Barbara McAndrews, the girl's mother." He stared at me, his eyes cold. "Now, I've tried my damnedest to figure out why their names should be on the same scrap of paper as yours. Three men who all worked for Pandora Pictures at one time. Any ideas?"

"You're the detective, Mr. Collins."

His nervousness didn't seem to affect his belligerence. "You're right," I said. "And you're the one who's lying."

"I'm not lying."

"Look, I don't know whether or not you're involved in the disappearance of the Paulson girl. But what I'm pretty sure of is that you've got one of these keys. The dread-locked kid I mentioned earlier, Roger Iverson, was seen coming out of Tony Gould's trailer shortly before he apparently overdosed on insulin. Gould had one of these keys. Iverson said he was looking for Thompson's in my trailer. That leaves Benedetti. He says he's never seen one like this, and now you say the same thing. It doesn't wash, Forbes. What does this key open?"

He folded his handkerchief and again dabbed at his forehead and upper lip. "You seem to have a nice narrative going, Collins, but there's only one problem. It isn't true. I've never seen a key like this. On a few occasions I get together with Thompson and Benedetti, but we're certainly not close friends. I know nothing about the disappearance of the Paulson girl, so you're barking up the wrong tree." He replaced his handkerchief in his pocket and again stood. "Now, at the risk of being rude, I'm asking you to leave. I'll show you to the door."

I'd reached an impasse. I put my hat back on my head and stood up. "Okay, thanks for your time."

I followed him to the front door. He opened it, but before I exited, I turned back to him. "I gave your name to both the LAPD and Burbank police. They'll probably be talking to you. I hope that doesn't spoil your dinner."

23

Wiser men than me have often opined that the eyes are the windows to the soul, which, by extension, is an indication if someone is telling you the truth or lying like a rug. I've done many a scene with actors over the years and have always felt that the most successful have been the ones where my fellow actor looks me in the eye and exudes nothing but honesty.

Vic Benedetti and David Forbes didn't pass muster.

As I sat in one of my favorite neighborhood watering holes nursing a beer and three fingers of Mr. Beam, I knew damn well that both of them had stonewalled me about whether or not they had one of the Pandora keys. After leaving Forbes' house, I had a strong urge to pitch the damn thing down the nearest storm drain. But I couldn't bring myself to do it. Finding the key in my costume, which had Ken Thompson's name stitched into it, and then having Roger Iverson show up and tell me he was looking for it threw coincidence right out the window. I was convinced the three men all possessed keys and that somehow they had something to do with Meredith Paulson's disappearance.

The pieces of this puzzle whirled around in my head, making me oblivious to Mick, the bartender, who had asked me a question.

"Hey, Eddie, what's the matter wit you? I'm talkin' to a wall here."

"Sorry, man, got something on my mind."

"You workin' on a case?"

"Yeah. What were you saying?"

"If a Democrat and a Republican are out in the woods, arguin', and a tree falls on one of 'em and kills him, will the other one still keep arguin'?"

"Yes. If the Republican is left standing, he'll blame it on Hillary and Obama."

Mick bent over in laughter and pounded his fist on the bar. "Yeah, you're probably right," he said, as he added another finger to my drink. "On the house."

I offered my thanks and raised the glass to my lips, but stopped when my cell went off. The screen said Reggie Benson.

"Hey, Reggie, how you doin'?"

"I'm okay, Eddie. Got some news."

"Yeah? What?"

"I got a raise."

"Terrific," I said.

"Yeah, ain't that something?" he continued. "Bernie is one heck of a guy."

"That he is."

"Hey, listen, Eddie, I want to celebrate and take you and Carla out for pizza."

"You don't have to do that."

"Yeah, I know, but I'm tired of you pickin' up the tab all the time. You guys free tonight?"

"Let me check with Carla and I'll get back to you."

"Okay. I ain't seen her in a while. Be good to catch up."

We arranged to talk again in a few minutes and he hung up. Hearing Reggie's news was a day brightener. He'd literally saved my life when we were both MPs in Korea some years back. When I reconnected with him a couple of years ago on the Santa Monica Pier I felt I owed him big time, and in addition to setting him up with Bernie, I'd come into some money and bought him a car. His gratitude sometimes got a little embarrassing, but I knew it was sincere.

I sent Carla a text with Reggie's proposal, and after a couple of minutes she called.

"Pizza with Reggie and my favorite shamus?" she said. "Count me in. Where and when?"

"Are you still working?"

"About ready to wrap. I'll meet you, okay?"

I gave her the name of a favorite pizza joint on Hillhurst in the Los Feliz district we'd frequented many times. She said she'd see us there. Reggie approved the choice, and I told him I'd pick him up.

Arrangements made, I sipped some bourbon and returned to my musings about the Pandora key and the lies I'd encountered all day. Getting past Benedetti's and Forbes' denial presented a problem. Unless I caught them red-handed with the key in their possession, there didn't seem to be a way of tripping them up. My quandary was interrupted by my cell phone. The screen said Harold Meyerson, the Burbank cop who'd gotten in my face on the Warners lot.

"This is Eddie Collins. What can I do for you, Detective?"

"Yeah, Collins. That guy with the dreadlocks you turned us onto? Roger Iverson?"

"What about him?"

"We brought him in and sweated him for a couple of hours, but we didn't get much. He admitted to being some kind of gofer for Gould, but says he was nowhere near the trailer that morning."

"He's lying. He was seen coming out of Gould's trailer with the guy's lunch dishes."

"By who?"

"Janice Wilkes. She's one of the actresses who was working on the film."

"You by any chance have a phone number for her?"

"Let me check." I put him on hold and scrolled through my contacts, but couldn't find her listed. "I don't have her number, Detective, but the movie's production company should have it."

"I thought it went belly up."

"It did, but they should still have an office. They've got to pay bills and close the books. Things like that."

"Thanks. I'll check it out. Anything happening on your end?"

"Nothing."

"You're still keeping me in the loop, right?"

"You got it, Detective." He rang off, leaving me with the knowledge of more lies. These from Roger Iverson. What the hell were these guys hiding? Having no answer, I finished off Mr. Beam and his buddy and left a healthy tip for Mick. As I pushed my way through the front door, he told me not to be a stranger.

I was pretty sure I'd have no trouble following his advice.

By the time Reggie and I arrived at the pizza place, Carla had a corner table and was on her phone with a mug of beer in front of her. When she spotted us, she jumped up and wrapped her arms around Reggie.

"Reggie, Reggie, how are you? I've missed you."

When she let him go, his face had turned a little red. "Good to see you too, Carla. How's your show going?"

"I'm having a ball. How's your job?"

"Great. I just got a raise."

"I know, I know. Eddie told me," she said, as she again enveloped him in a hug. "I am so happy for you."

After the hugging was over, I stuck out my hand to her. "Hi, I'm Eddie Collins."

After catching my mock sad face, she punched my arm and said, "You goof. Come here." She then wrapped her arms around me and planted a kiss on my lips. "There, Shamus, that make you feel better?"

"Infinitely," I said, glad to see both of them in such good spirits.

We sat down and looked over the menu, then agreed on a large pie with everything on it and anchovies on the side. Reggie and I went up to the counter and placed the order. He pulled out his wallet and handed a fifty-dollar bill to the girl at the register. He gave me a sidelong glance and a huge grin broke out on his face, like a kid bringing home a report card filled with nothing but As. I ordered a mug of beer for myself and another for Carla. Reggie asked for a Coke. I was pleased to see that his new-found largesse hadn't fueled a taste for booze. Lord knows the problem presents itself to those he'd left behind on the streets. Somehow I had the feeling that Reggie had completely turned his back on that taste.

Drinks in front of us, we spent a few minutes catching up. Reggie wanted to know all about Carla's TV show, and she, in turn, pumped him about his job. She found it fascinating when he described his duties. As I had done a few times in the past, I needled him about living among the dead, as it were. He took it in stride and directed a couple of good come-backs at me.

Our pizza arrived and we dug in. Carla and Reggie sampled the anchovies, but I abstained, giving her a look of mild displeasure.

"I've got a six o'clock call in the morning. That means I'll be sleeping alone, Shamus, so go ahead try some of these little suckers," she said, as she held the dish under my nose.

"Knock yourself out, kiddo."

She laughed and passed the anchovies to Reggie, who helped himself.

"What's goin' on with your case, Eddie?" he said. "You find out anything about that key?"

"Only that everybody's lying to me," I said, and went on to fill both of them in on what I'd been running into.

"Sounds like it's pretty much your word against theirs," Carla said.

"I agree. But then there's this." I took the plastic-coated scrap of paper out of my shirt pocket. "I found this in Tony Gould's trailer," I said, and handed it to them. They hunched over it as I continued. "Four names under the word 'keys.' One of them is dead and the other three don't know anything about the Pandora key I showed them."

"Maybe the names don't relate to the word 'keys,'" Carla said.

"That's possible. But then how does one explain Roger Iverson in my dressing trailer looking for a key? A key he said he was supposed to get from Ken Thompson. Whose name happened to be stitched into the lining of my costume."

They both looked at each other and sipped on their drinks. Carla picked up a slice and took a small bite. "I admit that's intriguing, Eddie, but you've been hired to look into that girl's disappearance, right?"

I nodded and sipped on my beer.

"How does the key figure in?"

"I'm not sure, but look at the other side of that paper."

Reggie flipped it over and Carla said, "Meredith Paulson. The name of the girl who disappeared, right?"

"You got it," I said.

"Who's the other one? Barbara McAndrews?" Reggie said.

"Her mother. And my client." I took a bite out of a slice and saw them glance at each other. "What do you think? More than coincidence?"

"Looks like it to me," Reggie said, as he looked at the scrap of paper. "What about this Ken Thompson? He sayin' the same thing?"

"I haven't talked to him yet. Figured on doing it tomorrow."

"The cops give you any help?" he said.

"Not much. I talked to a detective in the North Hollywood division who worked the case. It's been nine years since her disappearance and I think he's given up on it. I did get some facts from the file, but the length of time since she disappeared leaves the trail pretty cold."

Carla reached over and squeezed my shoulder. "Keep digging, Eddie. Something will turn up."

"I plan on it."

"If you need any help," Reggie said, "give me a shout."

"Thanks, pal."

We scarfed up the remnants of the pizza, finished our drinks, and walked out of the restaurant to the small parking lot in the rear. I'd parked my car next to Carla's. Before she unlocked her door, she wrapped her arms around me and looked up at me.

"This case bumming you out, Eddie?"

"Yeah, a little, but I stuck my nose into it. Now I've got to finish it."

She pulled my head down and kissed me. It went on for several moments, and finally she said, "I'd really like to be with you tonight, but I've got such a god-awful early call, and the stuff we're shooting tomorrow is pretty dialogue heavy, so I'd better be a good girl."

"Well, I don't know how, but I'll try and survive." I leaned down and kissed her again, this one lasting longer than previously.

Reggie stood on the other side of my car and suddenly cleared his throat. "Uh, maybe you two should get a room."

We broke apart and Carla laughed, then ran around the car and wrapped him in a bear hug. "Okay, smart aleck, that's enough out of you. But thanks for the pizza. Take care of yourself, you hear? Don't go wandering around your place of employment in the dark. You never know who you might run into."

"Yeah, yeah, Eddie keeps reminding me of that." She laughed and kissed him on the cheek, which caught him off guard and he broke into a sheepish grin.

She said goodnight and drove off. I unlocked the doors and we climbed into my car. Reggie's funeral home was on the other side of La Brea, so I headed west on Franklin. After a couple of blocks, I looked down at the dashboard and saw that I was running on empty.

"I gotta make a stop for gas. You in a hurry to get home?"

"Naw, nobody there waitin' up for me." We both broke into laughter and I punched him on the shoulder.

"You're a lucky guy, Eddie. Carla's a real nice girl."

"I keep reminding myself of that every day, buddy." We stopped for a red light and I turned to him. "What about you? You making eyes at any ladies?"

He ran his hand through his hair and shrugged. "Nope. I don't know if anyone's interested in somebody who lives in a funeral parlor. Not very attractive for inviting somebody over."

"Well, you can always follow your own advice."

"What's that?"

"Get a room."

He chuckled and nodded as we pulled into a gas station and convenience store where Vine runs into Franklin. I stuck my credit card into the pump and Reggie flipped open the gas tank door and inserted the nozzle. As the digits started to roll over and night bugs flitted around the lights over the pumps, I realized we weren't far away from Thompson's house. I wondered if Dreadlocks had scurried back to Thompson after our little dust-up in the bookstore. I had little doubt that he'd kept it to himself. He'd given me the impression that he'd be the kid who went into the principal's office and ratted everybody out.

As the numbers started to roll into the thirty-buck range, a motorcycle pulled into a parking space near the front door of the convenience store. The rider let loose with the obligatory blasts of the muffler before he shut down his hog, climbed off and lumbered toward the front door. He pulled it open and made a gesture for two people coming out to go in front of him.

Two people I recognized.

Roger Iverson and Ken Thompson.

Iverson carried a twelve-pack of beer and Thompson had a plastic bag dangling from one hand. I ducked behind the gas pump and gestured for Reggie to stop pumping. I put a finger to my lips and pointed toward the front of the store.

"What's up?" he whispered.

"Remember the guy with the dreadlocks I mentioned?"

He nodded and looked at Iverson and Thompson walking toward a car. Since I hadn't seen Iverson's green Kia, I assumed they were getting into Thompson's vehicle.

"Is that him?" Reggie said, and I nodded. He replaced the gas cap and hid behind another pump. "Who's the other guy?"

"Ken Thompson. He doesn't live far from here."

The two men crawled into the vehicle and it backed away from the curb. I motioned for Reggie to get in my car. I did the same and fired it up.

"Let's see where they go," I said, as I put the car in gear. "You all right with that?"

"No problem."

Thompson waited for traffic and pulled out onto Vine. Both men previously hadn't had an opportunity to see my car, and given the fact that it was dark, I wasn't too concerned about putting a tail on them. I followed a half block behind. We headed south on Vine and turned left on Sunset. Sure enough, his car turned onto his street. Just as he pulled into his driveway, I cut my headlights and glided up to where I'd staked him out yesterday. A streetlight revealed Iverson's car parked along the curb in front of the house. Another vehicle was parked ahead of it.

"That where Thompson lives?" Reggie said.

"Yeah. That's Iverson's green Kia under the streetlight."

"You recognize the one in front of it?"

"Nope. Benedetti drives a silver Mercedes, so it's not him."

"What do you want to do, Eddie?"

I thought about it for a minute. "I need to hear what they're talking about. Maybe there's a window left open."

"Pretty risky. If they catch you, you'll be busted for trespassing."

"If they catch me, that'll be the least of my worries."

"Man, I don't know. Maybe you need somebody to watch your back."

"You can do it from here. I'll mute my phone and leave the message app open. You do the same. If you see anybody else drive up, send me a text."

"Okay, but it's still pretty risky."

"I know. But I don't think I'll get another chance like this."

"Okay," he said, "but that shirt you're wearing sticks out like a sore thumb."

He was right. I had on a pale yellow shirt that screamed detection. "I've got a black sweatshirt in the trunk. When I tap on the lid you open it." I pointed down to where the trunk latch was.

"Roger that," he said.

I quickly opened the door and immediately shut it to prevent any more light coming on than necessary. I scooted to the rear of the car and knocked on the trunk. When it opened I grabbed the sweatshirt and closed the trunk, careful to make as little noise as possible. Reggie gave me a thumbs up and showed me his phone with the messages app lit up. I tapped the window and moved toward Thompson's house, not sure what the hell I was getting myself into.

24

Thompson's street was not a particularly long one. Iverson's Kia sat under the only streetlight, which was reinforced by several glowing lights above front stoops. I spotted the flickering of television sets through windows and heard the faint noises coming from them. Evening news, a reality show, perhaps a ballgame, all accompaniments to the family dinner. Besides Iverson's Kia and the car in front of it, I counted eight other vehicles parked along the street.

I'd managed to get only about ten yards down the sidewalk before I had to duck behind a hedge to my right. The driver's side door on the vehicle in front of Iverson's Kia opened and a man stepped out. He glanced up and down the street, then shut the door and headed for the front of Thompson's house. When he walked underneath the streetlight I recognized him.

It was David Forbes.

He rang the doorbell, and after a moment Thompson opened it and ushered Forbes inside. Three members of the liars club present and accounted for.

Even though I hadn't yet talked to Thompson, I had no doubt that he would feed me the same helping of malarkey the others had.

After checking to see if anyone was behind me, I stood and crept further down the walk. The houses on both sides of Thompson's were dark. The one on the near side had an empty driveway to the left of the front door leading to a single-car garage. A six-foot high wooden fence ran along the driveway, separating the two neighbors' properties. When I reached the edge of Thompson's lot, I again glanced behind me, then darted into the darkness between the two structures and plastered myself against the house.

In a moment or two my eyes adjusted to the dark and I glanced to my left. A heating/air conditioning unit sat about four feet away. Beyond that a cabinet protruded from the wall. It looked like it might be an upright storage locker for gardening tools. The neighbor's fence was about eight feet from Thompson's house.

A glow of light from the rear penetrated the darkness, revealing what appeared to be the deck of a patio jutting out from the house. There was a gap of maybe four feet between it and the fence, enough for a man pushing a power mower to get by. The deck was about four feet off the ground. What was probably plywood spanned the gap between ground and deck. Rising another three feet from the deck was a metal railing. A small plastic trash bin sat in the right angle formed by the railings. If I didn't blow it, getting to the bottom of that deck would give me a good vantage point to hear what the liars club was talking about.

Above the heating/air conditioning unit a sliver of light came through a window that was probably the front room. I bent down and moved to the bottom of it. Iron bars covered the opening, almost a necessity for living in today's Los Angeles. Inside, drapes covered the window, save for a gap of a couple of inches. I slowly raised my head and peeked through the window. Nobody was in the room. A solitary table lamp provided the only illumination.

Voices came from behind the house, but they were too faint to make out what was being said. Hugging the wall, I crept past another barred window and stopped when my cellphone buzzed. Reggie. His text read, *A silver Mercedes just pulled up.*

Vic Benedetti, the fourth member of the liars club.

I moved up next to the storage locker, powered down my phone, then put it in my hip pocket and waited. A doorbell rang and the conversation on the patio stopped.

I couldn't distinguish what the two men said as they walked through the house, but from the tone of Benedetti's voice, it sounded like he was angry.

The door to the patio opened and I heard Benedetti say in a loud voice, "But he had a key, Ken. How the hell did that happen?"

"Keep your voice down," Thompson replied. His voice had a deep resonance that reminded me of the venerable character actor John Carradine.

"Then why the hell are we sitting out here?"

"My wife's upstairs. She's already pissed at me."

"What about your neighbor?"

"She's eighty-two years old, Vic. She hasn't seen a sunset in twenty years."

"And the other one?"

"He's out of town. Relax. Let's just keep it down, all right?"

"Okay, okay," Benedetti said, his voice pitched lower. "But the question remains. How the fuck did this Collins character get a key?"

"I left mine in the costume I wore on the last shoot I did," Thompson said.

"And you didn't go looking for it?"

"I checked with the rental company. They couldn't find it."

"What? The key or the costume?"

"The key. And they rented the costume to the *Terms of Power* production. That's the shoot Gould was on. Roger checked with the wardrobe department and found out that Collins wound up with my costume. He went looking for it and Collins caught him at it."

"Well, that's great. That's just fucking great."

"Now calm down," Thompson said. "And let's figure out what the hell we're going to do. Have a beer. Cups are on the table."

I heard the sound of a can of beer being opened, and after a moment, the empty can flew through the air, destined for the trash bin. It missed its mark. I barely had time to duck behind the storage locker before Forbes appeared. He picked up the can and dropped it in the bin, then leaned back against the railing, a plastic cup in one hand. So much for getting closer without being seen.

"What's happened to Gould's key?" Benedetti said.

"I got it," Iverson said.

Again, Benedetti: "When?"

"The day before he...uh...you know."

"Dave," Benedetti said, "you've got yours?"

I peeked around the corner of the locker and saw Forbes holding up a key. "Right here, Vic. I told Collins I didn't know what the hell he was talking about."

"Yeah, so did I," Benedetti said. "But I'm not sure he believed me."

"Let him believe whatever he wants," Forbes said. "It's our word against his. How did it go with Gould, Roger? Any problems?"

"The cops talked to me, but I told them I was nowhere near Tony's trailer that morning."

"And they believed you?" Benedetti said.

"So far, so good," Iverson replied.

Obviously Dreadlocks didn't know that in the wake of my phone call with Meyerson he was going to get another visit from Burbank PD.

Before the men's conversation could continue, a scuffling came from next door, followed by the shrill bark of a dog. Forbes looked behind him as the dog scurried along the fence. It stopped opposite of where I stood, frozen, behind the storage locker. I could see the damn thing through a half-inch gap between the boards. It was a small dog and posed no physical threat, but its presence and yapping were the last things I needed. I watched it continue to bark and dig at the bottom of the fence. Then a door opened next door and a man with a flashlight came into view.

"Buster, shut up! Come here!" The beam of the flashlight traveled down the length of the fence and caught the dog throwing dirt behind him. "Buster, come on, boy." After a moment, the dog stopped, growled and snuffled, then trotted back to the guy with the flashlight.

Thompson had walked over to the railing and stood next to Forbes. "Thought you went fishing, Randy."

"I did. Got back this morning. Came home with a goddamn cold. Been in bed all day."

"Were they biting?" Thompson said.

"For everybody but me." Randy picked the dog up and stuck it under his arm. "Sorry for the interruption, Ken. I keep forgetting to lock that damn dog door."

"Hey, no problem." Randy dowsed his flashlight and headed for his back door as Thompson said, "Hope you feel better."

"Thanks," Randy replied, and disappeared into the house.

After a moment, Thompson pushed off the railing and said, "That goddamn dog's a royal pain in the ass. I'm hoping one day he disappears, if you get my drift." Both he and Forbes chuckled and moved away from the railing, out of my sight.

My suspicion that these guys had been lying to me about the Pandora key was true. But the question still remained as to what the hell the keys opened. Hoping to get more information, I got on my hands and knees and crawled to the point where deck and house met. The four men had gathered around what I could only assume was a picnic table. Getting closer was the right thing to do, since the men's conversation had become more subdued.

"So who the fuck is this Collins?" Benedetti asked.

"I googled him," Iverson said. "After he caught me in his trailer at Warners. Look at this. Here he is on the Internet Movie Data Base." He'd obviously handed his phone to Benedetti.

"He told me he was looking into the disappearance of that Paulson woman," Forbes said.

"You're kidding?" Thompson said. "That was...what? Ten years ago, for crissakes?"

"Nine," Forbes said.

There was a lull in the conversation, and I could hear a couple more beer cans being opened. One of them came flying toward the trash bin and again fell short. I flattened myself against the plywood facing of the deck, trying to make myself as invisible as possible. One of the men walked over, dropped the can in the bin and returned to the table.

"All right, guys, let's try and figure out this shit storm," Thompson said. "We've got three keys and Collins has one. Those are all of them, right?"

"I think so," Benedetti said. "At one point, Tony said he was going to have a couple more made, but then when he had his come to Jesus moment, he changed his mind."

"Come to Jesus moment my ass," Thompson said. "He started to fold when Paulson sued him and Pandora. She didn't make her case, but the guy got cold feet. Damn good thing he was diabetic. Made things much easier."

The sound of a siren pierced the night air, which set off a dog's howl from the lot behind Thompson's house.

After a moment, Benedetti said, "So, what now? Collins has tried to nail three of us about the goddamn key. What do we do with him?"

"Do we know where he lives?" Thompson said. "Where's his office?"

"His card only has a phone number," Forbes said.

"He's got a website," Iverson added. "Office on Hollywood Boulevard."

There was silence from the four men, save for the sound of another can of beer being opened. The smell of cigarette smoke wafted above me.

Finally Benedetti said, "We could put a tail on him. Pop him when he's not looking."

"Yeah, but the problem is," Iverson said, "after he talked to the three of us, he's going to be looking."

More silence from the picnic table. Across the street behind me a car door slammed. I heard the sound of another can of beer being opened, followed by steps to the garbage can and then back to the table.

After a moment Forbes said, "What do you think, Ken?"

"He's nosing around about the Paulson girl. That's not good. We have to deal with him. But I think what we need to do first is deal with the place up there."

"What do you mean?" Benedetti said.

"We've got to get rid of it. Clean it out."

"What the hell for?"

"Come on, Vic," Thompson said. "We haven't done anything up there in what…a year?"

"More like a year and a half," Forbes said.

"Exactly. And the way things are in this town right now, it's time to shut it down."

"There's a lot of crap in there," Benedetti said. "And there's only the four of us."

"So we'll do it in stages," Thompson said. "Starting tomorrow. Let's meet up there about one o'clock."

"I've got an audition at twelve-thirty," Benedetti said.

"Well, lah-de-dah, poor little you," Thompson said. "Glad to hear somebody's agent hasn't forgotten about them." Soft laughter floated around the table. "Okay, Vic, come when you can. Roger, I'll pick you up at noon. Questions?"

"You sure about this, Ken?" Forbes said.

"Look, guys, we've had a good run. Attitudes in the business have changed. There's more scrutiny, more ways for us to get tripped up. It's the right thing to do. Time to move on."

"What about Collins?" Iverson said.

"We'll take care of him once we get the place cleaned out," Thompson said. "Okay with everybody?"

There were murmurs of assent and I decided it was time to scram. I crawled back to the storage locker and got to my feet, then made tracks for the sidewalk and my car. Where the hell these guys were going tomorrow I didn't know, but what I did know was that they would have a tail on them.

Reggie cracked the door for me and I slid behind the wheel.

"Find out anything, Eddie?"

"Yeah, they're lying about the key. All four of them."

"They say what it's for?"

"No, but they referred to a 'place,' 'up there.'"

"That could be anywhere."

"Exactly. But they're going to meet 'up there' tomorrow at one, wherever the hell it is." I started the car and pulled away from the curb. "And then they're going to take care of me."

"That don't sound good."

"Yeah, I know. I'm going to have to start watching my back."

"Maybe it's time to go to the cops."

"Could be. But first I want to find out where the hell they're going tomorrow." I pulled up to a red light, looked to my left, and made a right turn. "What you got going in the morning?"

"Not much. Bernie's up in Sacramento. And the place is empty. Why?"

"I want to follow Thompson, wherever this 'up there' is. All right if we use your car?"

"No problem."

"I'm not sure if they know what mine looks like, so it might be better to use something that has less chance of being recognized."

"Good thinking."

"Iverson lives in Studio City. Thompson said he'll pick him up at noon. We should follow him from there. Okay?"

"Works for me."

"We probably should be at Iverson's by eleven-fifteen, eleven-thirty. Figuring for traffic, I'll be at your place at ten forty-five. Then we'll head for the Valley. Sound like a plan?"

"You're the man, Eddie." I pulled into the driveway of the funeral home. We bumped knuckles and I told him I'd see him in the morning and we'd find out where "up there" was.

25

Reggie lived on the second floor of Bernie Feldman's funeral parlor. His apartment was accessed by an exterior set of stairs at the rear. I parked my car in front of the building and grabbed a paper bag containing a couple pieces of pastry. Since Reggie didn't drink coffee, I was able to negotiate the bag and a cup of coffee I'd picked up on the way. Shifting the coffee to the hand with the bag, I popped the trunk and draped a pair of binoculars around my neck. If surveillance was part of our job description I figured they might come in handy. Reluctantly, I also opened the metal lockbox and reached in for my firearm. I don't normally carry it, despite having a permit, but considering the fact that we didn't really know what we were getting into, I decided it might be prudent to have it with me, so I clipped it to my belt and closed the trunk.

Reggie's red Subaru was parked in front of the two-car garage at the end of the driveway. He sat at the top of the stairs.

"Mornin', Eddie."

"Good morning," I replied, and watched him bound down the stairs. He wore sneakers, camo cargo pants, and a dark blue zippered hoodie. A baseball cap sat on his head and he also had binoculars around his neck. "You ready to go?"

"You bet."

"Did you get any breakfast?"

"A banana and some Wheaties. Breakfast of Champions."

I chuckled, always tickled by his seeming innocence and the sunny disposition that came with it. In the months since I'd helped him get off the streets, Reggie had blossomed and his optimism had become a welcome antidote to my innate cynicism.

"How about you?" he said.

I held up the bag. "Couple of elephant ears in here."

He pointed to the binoculars around my neck. "I had the same idea. Got mine at a sidewalk sale on Hollywood Boulevard. Might come in handy, huh?"

I agreed with him, pulled back my jacket to show him the firearm on my belt, then we crawled into the Subaru and he backed down the driveway. I told him to get on the Hollywood Freeway and head through the Cahuenga Pass into the Valley. I sipped my coffee and watched him negotiate the morning traffic with no apparent trepidation.

"Car working okay for you?" I said.

"Like a top. How's my driving?"

"Your Wheaties are working for you, Champ."

He grinned and accelerated as we headed up the Franklin ramp onto the Hollywood Freeway. Traffic was light, so Reggie didn't show much evidence of white-knuckling as we swung onto the Ventura westbound. It didn't take us long to get into Studio City. We exited at Colfax and I directed him to Iverson's street, which was a mixture of single-dwelling structures and several apartment buildings. The address I had for him was one of the latter. His green Kia was parked in front of the building.

We found a space on the opposite side of the street. I looked at my watch. We were early. I pulled one of the elephant ears from the bag and held it out to Reggie. "Here you go. I've got two of them."

"I'm good," he said, and rolled his window down. "Those guys said they were meeting at one o'clock, right?"

"Right," I replied, and sunk my teeth into the pastry.

He looked at his watch. "Wherever they're meeting must be out of the city. Maybe an hour or so, huh?"

"Yeah, could be," I said. "But maybe they figured on traffic slowing them down."

"Yup, there is that. Man, I sometimes get real tired of the darn traffic in this town."

"Welcome to Los Angeles, pal."

He laughed and adjusted his rearview mirror. A UPS truck came around a corner and headed toward us. It stopped a few yards ahead. The hazard lights came on, and after a moment, the man in the brown shorts with a package under one arm and an electronic receipt book in his other hand darted to a house across the street. Delivery made, the truck rumbled past us, leaving a trace of exhaust behind.

"So, what else did those guys talk about last night?" Reggie said.

"Thompson admitted that the key I found in my costume belonged to him. That's what Iverson was looking for."

"Did they say anything about that guy Gould? The one that might have been murdered?"

"They did, briefly. Thompson said that it was a good thing Gould was diabetic. Said something to the effect that it made things easier."

"And the cops said they thought he died of an insulin overdose, right?"

"Right. I told the Burbank detective that Iverson was seen coming out of Gould's trailer the morning before he collapsed. I don't think he knows he's going to get squeezed some more."

"Man, that sounds like they had something to do with it."

"That's what I'm thinking," I said. I sipped on my coffee and put the bag containing the other elephant ear on the floor in front of me.

"You ever think you should maybe tell the cops about what you heard last night?"

"Yeah, I did. After I dropped you off, that thought rattled around in my head. But I don't know how much good it would do, Reggie, at least right now. It's only hearsay, and wouldn't hold up in court." I took a sip of coffee and glanced at a woman to my right walking a cocker spaniel. The dog stopped to do its business, and after she filled a plastic glove with the deposit, she looked at me as if to seek my approval. I nodded, tipped my hat to her and she and her pooch shuffled off. "Let's see what we learn today," I continued. "Maybe I'll change my mind." I took another swallow of coffee and pointed across the street. "There's our guy."

Iverson had come out of his apartment building and was leaning against his car. I needn't have worried about being seen because his phone had come out of his pocket and he was zeroed in on the screen.

"Man, those are some dreads," Reggie said. "How the heck do you clean those things?"

"Very carefully. Or else you hire somebody. Like pest control."

He laughed and shook his head. "How do you think he figures in with those other guys? I mean, from the pictures you showed me, he looks like he's younger."

"You're right. I'm not sure how he fits in. He supposedly worked for Gould as a gofer, assistant, something. I have a feeling he might have more of a link to Thompson."

We watched Iverson on his phone for several minutes. At one point, Reggie glanced at his side mirror and then tapped me on the arm. "SUV behind us," he said. "Drivin' pretty slow."

I scrunched down in my seat as the vehicle came alongside us. Thompson was behind the wheel. He stopped across from Iverson, who stuffed his phone in his pocket and got into the SUV. As it moved off, Reggie started his car. When Thompson got to the corner and turned right, Reggie pulled out and followed him.

"You gotta give me some help, Eddie. Not sure how good I am at this tailin' stuff."

"Just keep him in sight. With all the damn traffic in this town, he's probably not even looking behind him."

"Hope you're right," he said, as he turned the corner.

Reggie's driving passed muster. Thompson made a right on Colfax, heading north, and then made another right on Moorpark. We came to the juncture of the Ventura and Hollywood freeways. Thompson signaled a left turn. Reggie did the same. We got on the freeway and I expected

Thompson to head west on the Ventura, but he surprised me and stayed on the Hollywood Freeway heading north.

"Where's this gonna take us, Eddie?"

"Not sure," I said. We crossed Vanowen and Sherman Way. Thompson stayed in the center lanes, his speed about sixty-five. Logic would assume that traffic should be light leaving Los Angeles proper, but no dice. In this town, rush hour is indifferent to the clock. Thompson carefully moved into the slow lane and Reggie did the same. We merged onto I-5, the Golden State Freeway, then passed the city of San Fernando and the 118, otherwise known as the Ronald Reagan Freeway.

"Where the heck do you think they're going?" Reggie said.

"Beats me. The one-eighteen would take us into Simi Valley. Looks like he's heading over the hill into Santa Clarita."

And that's exactly what he did. A patch of roadwork slowed us down just after we passed the 14, leading to the high desert and the Antelope Valley. Yellow cones siphoned traffic into two lanes. Thompson was four cars ahead of us.

Once through the construction, we passed Six Flags Magic Mountain on our left. I was reminded of a time months ago when I'd done some extra work on a film shooting behind the amusement park. Carla had hired me to find her brother and she'd disappeared while working on that same picture. Fortunately, I eventually found both her and her brother Frankie.

My reverie stopped when I saw Thompson signal he was getting off the freeway. At the bottom of the ramp we followed him as he turned left, crossed under the I-5 and headed west on Route 126 toward the communities of Piru, Fillmore, and Santa Paula.

"This beats the hell out of me," I said. "I don't know what he's going to find up here." Orchards and vineyards filled fields on both sides of the highway. "You better drop back a little. We've only got one lane and there's less traffic."

"Roger that," he said, and slowed to where Thompson's SUV was about a half mile ahead of us. "You ever been up here?"

"Couple of times. I worked on a film once around here someplace. Nice change of pace from LA."

We slowed down as Thompson entered the city limits of Piru. My watch told me it was 12:40. "Their meeting is in twenty minutes. Wherever the hell they're going, it has to be close." Piru's main drag was similar to any small town I'd been in: storefronts, a bar or two, a hardware store, bank, and cafe.

Ahead of us, Thompson's vehicle took a right in front of an automotive garage. "Pull over, Reggie. Let him get ahead."

We pulled over and sat next to a curb for a couple of minutes, then eased around the garage where they'd turned off. The road wasn't paved and we could see a trail of dust hanging in the still air half a mile ahead. Orchards and vineyards gave way to woods and black sticks of trees, grim reminders of forest fires that had plagued the terrain in preceding months.

"How far have we gone?" I said.

"Just under five miles. Wherever the heck they're going, it's in the boondocks."

We followed at a snail's pace and saw the dust curl around a bend to the left. We went around the bend and I told Reggie to pull over and stop. He put the car in park and we looked at what lay ahead of us.

To our left was a ridge covered with scrub brush and skeletons of blackened trees. Off to the right about a half mile ahead was a wooden structure that resembled some sort of warehouse or large storage space. We put our binoculars up to our eyes. The lot was barren and my guess was a couple acres in size. The wooden structure was probably seventy-five yards from the road. The whole lot was surrounded by a wire cyclone fence with a gate twenty feet from the road. Rows of barbed wire angled inward on the top of the fence. Next to the gate sat a small wooden shed that looked like it might have been a guardhouse of some sort at one time.

With its rear hatch open, Thompson's SUV was parked close to a door in the wooden structure. Next to it sat what I was sure was Forbes' car. To the right of the vehicles was another larger door, its wooden panels open and flattened against the side of the building. We dropped our binoculars and sat in silence.

"What do you make of it, Eddie?"

"Damned if I know. Warehouse? Somebody's abandoned plant of some kind?"

"There's a lot of orchards around here. Could be some kind of fruit processing deal or something."

"Maybe, but I don't see the necessity of barbed wire on top of that fence," I said, as I put the glasses to my eyes again. The building was squat, maybe thirty or thirty-five yards square. It was in bad need of a paint job. No windows were visible, and the roof had spots where shingles were missing.

My eyes shifted to the larger door, where Iverson and Forbes came through, each carrying a cardboard box. They placed them in the back of Thompson's SUV and went back into the building.

"Did you see that?" I said.

"Yeah. Dreadlocks. Who's the other guy?"

"Forbes," I said, as I used my shirt tail to wipe away a smudge on my glasses. "Let's get closer. Park up by that shed."

Reggie drove up to the driveway leading to the gate and backed in next to the shed, saying that it might be easier to get away in a hurry, if need be. Once again, I admired his instincts. We got out of the car and I examined the gate. A short length of chain was wound between it and the fence. A "no trespassing" sign had been wired into fence's links. An unlocked padlock hung from one of them. On impulse, I tried to stick my Pandora key into it, but it didn't fit.

We again trained our glasses on the front of the building. There was no movement for several minutes when we heard the sound of a car coming around the bend. Reggie turned to his right as it approached.

"Heads up, Eddie. It's a silver Mercedes."

I focused my glasses on the car. It had to be Benedetti's. I flashed back to his saying last night that he'd be late for the liars club hookup, but I hadn't expected him to get here this quickly.

"Get behind the shed," Reggie said. "I'll deal with him."

I scooted to the other side of the makeshift guard shack and hugged the wall. I heard the Mercedes pull onto the graveled driveway and a door open.

"What are you doing here, pal?" Benedetti said. "This is private property."

"Yes, sir, I know. I was just out doing some birding. Saw a bald eagle across the road there and stopped to see if I could get a better look at him."

"Well, you'd better move on. You're trespassing."

"Will do, sir. I didn't mean to."

I heard Benedetti wrestle with the chain on the gate, then the sound of it creaking open. The Mercedes drove through, then a door opened again, and the gate creaked closed and the chain was put back in place.

"That some kind of produce processing plant?" Reggie said. "Lots of orchards around here."

"That's none of your damn business," Benedetti said. "Now get a move on."

"Yes, sir," Reggie replied.

I peered around the corner of the shed and watched Benedetti's Mercedes drive toward the other two vehicles. He parked, got out of the car, glanced in our direction, then pulled open the smaller door and entered the building.

After a moment, I went around to the passenger door of the Subaru. I leaned on the roof and looked at Reggie as he opened his door. "Bird watching?" I said.

He grinned and said, "Good thing I thought of the binoculars."

"Do you even know what a bald eagle looks like?"

"Yeah, I watch National Geographic." He laughed, took off his cap and ran his hand through his hair. "I guess we better mosey, huh?"

"Let's at least get around that bend," I said, as I opened the car door and crawled inside.

26

When we got around the bend and out of sight of the warehouse, shed, or whatever the hell it was, I told Reggie to make a right onto a dirt road leading up the ridge into the woods. After about fifty yards we stopped. He put the car in park and turned to me.

"What's up?" he said.

"We've got to get inside that place."

"How we gonna do that?"

"Wait until they leave."

"But we can't let them see us."

"Exactly." I sat and thought for a minute. "Let's follow this road. See where it leads us."

Reggie put the car in gear and we slowly drove deeper into the woods. It was probably a logging trail of some sort and was full of ruts. We bounced along for a quarter mile or so until we came to a turn-out on our right. Extensive woods greeted us as we crawled out of the car.

"You think we dare leave it here?" I said.

"I'll lock it up. It should be all right."

"Let's double back and see what they're up to," I said. We started off through the woods in the direction of the gravel road. The terrain was uphill for about fifty yards, then leveled off as we reached the top of the ridge. I leaned over and put my hands on my knees, trying to get my wind back. Reggie, however, looked like he'd been out for a stroll to the corner store.

"You all right?" he said.

196 • CLIVE ROSENGREN

"Yeah, just give me a minute."

"Maybe Carla should give you a membership to a gym for your birthday."

"Maybe you shouldn't make fun of your elders," I replied, trying to ignore the trace of a smirk on his face.

"Yes, sir," he said. He gave me a mock salute and ran his hand over his mouth, figuratively wiping away the smirk.

I finally straightened up and looked at our surroundings. Despite blackened remnants of pine and oak trees, there were still plenty of unscathed ones all around us. Along with new growth and underbrush, we found ourselves in serious woods. A slight breeze brought the faint smell of charred wood. We scrambled down the other side of the ridge and hunkered behind a fallen tree that was partially scarred by fire.

The warehouse lay directly in front of us across the gravel road. I put the glasses up to my eyes. The four men were outside, clustered around Thompson's SUV. Benedetti pulled his cellphone from a pocket and walked off a few paces to take a call. The rear of the SUV was full of cardboard boxes of various sizes. After a few minutes, Benedetti pocketed his phone and followed the other three men back into the shed.

There was no further movement. Shadows started to appear as the sun began dipping behind the ridge. Reggie poked my arm and gestured behind us. I turned and saw a deer staring at us. Satisfied that we didn't present any danger, it wandered off. I turned back to look where the vehicles were parked. Still no movement. I panned the binoculars to my left and saw the shadows had deepened.

"I don't suppose you have a flashlight in your car, do you?"

"Nah, I don't. But that's probably something I should get."

"I don't know how long those guys are going to be in there. The sun's starting to sink and we don't know for sure if there's even electricity in the damn place."

Reggie focused his binoculars on the warehouse and said, "There's a pole behind. And one wire running from it to another pole by the gate."

I raised my glasses and saw what he was talking about. "All right, let's do this. You remember seeing that hardware store back in Piru?"

"Yeah, with a lumberyard next to it."

"Right. Why don't you go back to your car and go get us a couple of good, sturdy flashlights?"

"Okay. I'll get extra batteries too."

"Good idea. Can you find your way back here?"

"Yeah, no problem. What if they leave and lock the place up?"

"This may be wishful thinking, but I'm hoping if there's a padlock on that door my Pandora key is going to fit it."

Reggie focused his binoculars on the warehouse. "Look at the two sides of that bigger door."

I did so.

"See those u-shaped brackets on the inside?"

"Yeah. You drop a two-by-six between them and that locks it."

"Which means they've probably put a padlock on the smaller door."

"I hope you're right," I said. "But we've got another problem."

"What?"

"How the hell are we going to get over that fence? I'm not too keen on tangling with barbed wire."

Reggie dropped his binoculars and after a moment said, "We could cut it." I turned to look at him. "I'll get us a bolt cutter. Cut a hole through it. Away from the gate, so it's less noticeable. We don't want to cut that padlock on the gate. If they come back, we're up you know where without a paddle."

We looked at each other for a moment and once again I couldn't help but marvel at his ability to assess the situation in front of us. He'd once told me he had logged a little time at the San Diego Police Academy. It must have rubbed off, because he had good instincts.

"Okay, pardner, you're on. Let me give you some money," I said, as I started to dig into my pocket for my money clip.

"We'll figure it out later. Hold down the fort and I'll be back in a flash." He popped me on the shoulder and started for his car.

"Be careful."

"Always am," he replied, and disappeared over the crest of the ridge.

I turned back to look at the warehouse. There still was no movement. So here I was, deep in the woods, lying on my belly, surrounded by pine needles and dead leaves. I've been on my share of stakeouts, but never one where I was kept company by flora and fauna.

On the heels of that thought, a squirrel appeared ten feet to my right. Nose twitching, it made tentative, jerky advances on me. I had to admire its bravery. An acorn lay in front of me on the other side of the downed log. That was its objective. With furtive sideways glances at me, it finally pounced on the nut and scampered off, victory in its teeth.

Entertainment over, I pulled my cellphone from my pocket. Fortunately, there was service, and not wanting to send up an alarm with a phone call, I sent a text to Carla, informing her of my whereabouts. No immediate response, so I muted it, replaced the phone and focused my attention on the warehouse in front of me.

While I had no way of knowing for sure, my hunch told me the Pandora key I'd come upon accidentally would gain me entry into this ramshackle structure on the other side of the road. Its contents and what connection they had to these four men remained unknown, but no less intriguing.

Forty-five minutes elapsed with a minimum of movement from the liars club. A couple more squirrels paid me a visit and had a short game of tag, then stopped and scampered off when their noses told them there was no food to be had from the strange clod lying behind the log.

Just as my cell chirped with a text from Carla, there was movement across the road. Forbes swung shut the two flaps of the bigger door, and after a moment, all four of them came out of the smaller one. Thompson locked it, but his back was to me, so I couldn't tell whether or not a padlock was used.

Forbes and Benedetti climbed into their cars and drove toward the gate. Thompson and Iverson followed. I focused the glasses on the smaller door, and sure enough, a padlock dangled from a hasp. Benedetti got out of his car and swung the gate open, then crawled back in his car and drove off. Forbes followed, and when Thompson's SUV cleared the gate, he stopped and Iverson jumped out and locked it behind them. All three vehicles disappeared around the bend and I hoped they wouldn't encounter Reggie's car on his way back.

I glanced at the text from Carla. *You know, if you wanted to commune with nature, we have Griffith Park.* She referred, of course, to the four thousand-plus acres in the center of Los Angeles. I responded. *Yeah, but no helicopters up here.* With a couple of exchanges, I told her where I was and what I was up to. She told me to be careful and we signed off just as Reggie came down the slope with his hands full.

"They're gone, huh?" he said.

"Did you run into them on your way back?"

"They were coming around the bend just as I turned off on the dirt road." He handed me one of the black flashlights and two size D batteries. "These should do the trick," he added, and held up a bolt cutter about two feet long. "And this bad boy is gonna make short work of that fence."

I unscrewed the bottom of the flashlight and slipped in the batteries. "There's a padlock on that smaller door."

"And I'm willing to bet your Pandora key unlocks it, right?"

"Let's find out," I said, as we got to our feet and started to make our way down the slope to the gravel road. No traffic greeted us as we crossed over and approached the cyclone fence fifty yards or so to the left of the gate.

Reggie unlocked the bolt cutter and started snipping the wire links. He'd managed to make just a few cuts when we heard the sound of a vehicle coming over a rise in the gravel road. Reggie tossed the bolt cutter into the grass and positioned himself in front of the hole he was creating. Once again, acting on instinct, he cued me and we focused our binoculars on the trees across the road.

A beat-up pickup approached, slowed, and when the grizzled old man behind the wheel saw what were probably two guys bird-watching, he shook his head and continued on his way into Piru. When the truck disappeared around the bend, we looked at each other and burst into laughter.

"The Audubon Society rocks!" I said. We bumped knuckles and Reggie picked up the bolt cutter and went back to work. He cut two sides of a square about a yard in length. We pulled the bottom of the fence out of the dirt, then bent back the sides of our makeshift door and Reggie crawled through. I got down on my belly and followed him through the opening. We pushed the sides back to camouflage the cuts, and satisfied, started walking back to the warehouse.

The sun had dipped below a ridge to the west of us as we approached the door. I pulled my key chain out of my pocket, put the Pandora key between my fingers and stuck it into the padlock.

Bingo!

The key turned and the padlock snapped open.

I pushed the door in and entered the warehouse. Reggie squeezed through the gap, then shoved the door closed behind him. If we'd harbored any notion that this structure was once some kind of fruit or vegetable enterprise, we were disappointed. The smell that greeted us was one of decay, dust and death. I turned my flashlight on and looked for a light switch. Above us a string dangled from a light bulb. I pulled it and a dim light came on.

What it illuminated was unlike anything I'd ever seen.

27

The pool of light from the single dim bulb barely revealed a concrete walkway down the center of the building. Four rooms, or stalls, flanked the center strip, two on each side. All of them had a four-foot gap in the side adjacent to the slab of concrete in the center. They made me think of spaces for gates. My first impression of the interior of this structure reminded me of a barn back in the Midwest where my cousins milked the cows on their farm. I was the city kid and they had a tendency to tease and pick on me. My visits always resulted in them spraying me with warm milk straight from the udders. Great fun for them, and ultimately became part of the fascination the place had for me.

Stepping into this environment erased all those memories.

Gloom pervaded the space, along with the odors of dust, mildew, and a faint trace of gasoline. On my right was the double door we had seen from across the road. It was now closed, with a two-by-six spanning the metal brackets Reggie had pointed out. A wooden table jutted out from the exterior wall. A few empty cardboard boxes and some electrical cables lay on top.

Reggie stood to my left. He shined his flashlight to his side of the building and then followed its beam. "There's a toilet here," he said.

I walked over to him and saw a small two-sided enclosure in the corner with a door hanging askew from its hinges. Deep gouges were cut into the wood around the doorknob. Inside was a single commode. Another string hung from a lightbulb in the ceiling. When I pulled on it dim light filled the space and roaches scurried into gaps in the floor.

The commode was filthy and gave off a stench that almost made my eyes water. Two rolls of toilet paper smudged with dirt and dust hung from nails embedded in the wall.

"Man, I think I'd resort to the green latrine before using this thing," Reggie said.

"I'm with you," I replied.

Against the exterior wall next to the toilet was a long metal trough with two faucets. A roll of dirty paper towels hung from another nail in the wall. A plastic bucket sat under the trough. I turned the handle on one of the faucets. After a shudder of pipes and some clanging, brown liquid dribbled into the trough and I quickly turned it off.

Reggie and his flashlight went back to the center walkway and moved toward the rear of the building. He found another string, pulled it, and one more dim bulb came alive at the end of the concrete walk.

"You smell gas, Eddie?"

"Yeah, a little," I said, as I shined my light into the first stall to the left of the concrete walkway. The four sides of the space were covered with dark green blankets. Sheets of half-inch plywood constituted the floor. Next to me sat a small footlocker, not unlike the one that occupied the foot of my bunk when I was in the employ of Uncle Sam. In two of the corners stood klieg lights, smaller versions of those found on most movie sets. Wires dangled from them. Their throw was focused on a mattress and box spring on the floor, covered by a tattered and soiled sheet. Revulsion bubbled up in me as the realization sunk in that these guys had been shooting movies. And from the looks of the surroundings, they weren't the kind you'd find at your local multiplex.

I heard a creak from the rear of the building. Reggie had found another door and had swung open both flaps of it. He stood in the opening, flashlight trained on something in front of him.

"What did you find?" I said.

"There's a generator back here," he replied. "That's why we're smelling gas."

I walked to the rear and for the first time noticed electrical cables that filled a small trench the length of the concrete walkway. If indeed this had been a barn at one time, the trench would be where animals deposited what would then have to be mucked out periodically. I remembered my cousins saddling me with that task many times.

The cables were plugged into a large surge protector on the floor. Its cable ran through a hole in the rear wall. I stepped outside and saw that it connected to the generator. A red jerry gasoline can sat next to it. I turned my light on the expanse behind the structure. About fifty feet away the deepening twilight revealed a pile of lumber and debris. Perched on top was a small turkey vulture. My light caught the glint of its eyes and it promptly took flight.

Back inside, the beam of my flashlight found a similar trench on the other side of the center walkway, also filled with cables that were plugged into another surge protector.

We explored the three other stalls with our flashlights. Like the one where I'd discovered the footlocker, they all had dark blankets tacked up on the four sides, creating flimsy walls. Each of them had plywood flooring and klieg lights that were focused on mattresses and box springs. Linens that covered them were soiled. I kicked one of them and dust flew up. We stood in the center of the building, letting the reality of what we were seeing sink in.

"Christ, are you thinkin' what I'm thinkin'?" Reggie said.

"I am."

"Damn." He took off his cap and slapped it against his leg. "You think they mighta brought that Paulson girl here?"

"There'd have to be some solid proof, but that thought had crossed my mind."

Reggie went to take another look at the generator as I walked back to the stall where I'd found the footlocker. I lifted the lid and saw further evidence of the depravity that had apparently taken place in this ramshackle building. Inside the locker was an assortment of clothing.

Women's clothing. Skimpy pieces of lingerie. Among them were pairs of handcuffs, leather neck-collars, further indications that Thompson, Iverson, Benedetti, and Forbes were sick men. If Meredith Paulson's disappearance had any connection to this smut factory, I didn't hold out much hope that she'd ever be found alive.

"Hey, Eddie, come here and take a look at this."

Reggie was on the other side of the center walkway in the room next to the rear wall. "What did you find?" I said, as my light caught him on his knees next to a footlocker similar to the one I'd come upon.

"Look at this stuff," he said.

I squatted next to him. "I found another one of these lockers up front."

"Yeah, I think there's one in every room."

I focused my flashlight on the contents of the locker. Among similar remnants of clothing were pieces of jewelry. Bracelets, necklaces, more handcuffs and paraphernalia used in bondage/discipline pornography. Nestled in one corner of the locker was a small metal tin that contained smaller pieces of jewelry—rings and earrings. I poked a finger through them and stopped when I saw something familiar.

I picked up a necklace and held it in the beam of my flashlight. "Look at this. Maybe we're closer to that proof we need."

"Whatcha got?"

I pulled my cell from my shirt pocket and opened the photos app. I found the picture of Meredith Paulson I'd taken when I'd first spoken to her mother. The photo revealed a very distinctive pendant in the shape of a heart that hung from a necklace draped around her neck.

"This look like the one in the photo?" I asked.

Reggie shined his light on the pendant and then the photo. "Yeah, it does, but that don't necessarily mean it's the same one."

"That's true," I said, as I pocketed both the pendant and my cell. "But what do you think the odds are they're one and the same?"

My question went unanswered as we froze when we heard the crunch of gravel from a vehicle pulling up in front of the building.

"Dammit, they're back!" I said. "We have to scram."

"Where the hell we gonna go?"

"There's a pile of wood and debris behind the place. We'll be out of sight."

Reggie slammed down the lid of the footlocker. I darted to the front and doused the dim light bulb. Reggie did the same to the one at the rear, and with flashlights bobbing in the dark, we scooted through the rear door.

"We're not gonna be able to lock it," Reggie said.

"Yeah, I know," I said, as we went through the opening and closed the two flaps of the door behind us. "Push on the doors and maybe they'll stick in the dirt." We did, and the panels caught in the ground, leaving a slight gap at the top of the door.

"Close enough," I said. "Follow me."

We ran to the pile of debris, ducked behind it and flattened ourselves in the dirt. Reggie took his cap off and slapped at a rat that had burrowed into the pile. We doused our flashlights and settled in, just in time to hear loud voices from inside the building.

28

Something had definitely died in that pile of debris, which explained the presence of the rat and subsequently the turkey vulture I'd scared off. But the smell was the farthest thing from my mind as we lay in the dirt and listened to loud, angry voices coming from inside the smut factory.

"You recognize them?" Reggie whispered.

"Sounds like Thompson and Iverson."

After a few minutes of arguing and yelling from inside, my suspicions were proven right when the rear door apparently was thrown open and the voices became more distinguishable.

"How the fuck can you manage to leave both doors unlocked?" Thompson said.

"Goddammit, I didn't!" Iverson shouted in return. "I distinctly remember slapping the two-by-six into this door."

"And what about the padlock?"

"I locked it. I know I did."

"You sure? Sometimes you have to push it hard for it to catch."

"I know, I know, and that's what I did," Iverson said.

There was a pause in their conversation. Crickets chirped as Reggie and I lay frozen in position. I heard footsteps in the gravel behind the building and had a moment of panic, wondering what the hell we would do if either Thompson or Iverson decided to investigate the pile of debris.

The footsteps stopped and Thompson said, "All right, humor me for a minute. For the sake of argument, let's say you're right. But the fact remains that the padlock was opened. With a key. There's one key we don't have. Now tell me who the hell has it?"

After a moment Iverson replied, "That PI. Collins."

"Exactly."

"I get your point, Ken, but how the hell would he know about this place?"

"We could have been followed. Do you know what his car looks like?"

"No."

More silence. Beads of sweat trickled down the back of my neck. I heard the hoot of an owl and glanced over at Reggie. His eyes were wide open and he also had a look of panic on his face. I grabbed his arm and leaned over to whisper in his ear.

"If one of them comes over here, jump up and we'll come at him from both sides."

"What about the other one?" he said.

"I'll handle him."

"What if he has a gun?"

"Then I'll shoot the son of a bitch."

I squeezed his arm and a smile broke out on his face. His apparent relief was welcome; I needed Reggie's mojo. I thought back to a long-ago night in a Korean village when he single-handedly dispatched a drugged-up sergeant who was determined to kill me. A guy with that kind of confidence was good to have next to me.

A cell phone went off and Thompson answered. After a moment he said, "Yeah, we're here, but we've got a problem. The front and back doors were unlocked." Pause. "He swears he locked them." Another pause. "Hell, Vic, I don't know. I've got no reason not to believe him." Another beat. "Yeah, okay, we'll be there in a few."

The call ended and Iverson said, "What about that guy Vic saw? The bird watcher? Maybe he was Collins."

"Nah, Vic talked to him the other day. He sure as hell would remember what he looked like. He said the bird watcher was a scrawny little guy."

Reggie shook his head and whispered, "Asshole."

I grinned in spite of myself.

"All right, look," Thompson said. "We'll get a different padlock. In the meantime, let's get some of the stuff from downstairs. Vic and Dave are at the motel. I need a good steak and several stiff drinks."

Reggie grabbed my forearm and whispered, "Downstairs? Did we miss something?"

"We must have," I replied.

Our attention suddenly shifted to the rear of the building as the generator roared to life. We could hear the men talking, but the sound of the motor prevented us from making out what was being said. Their conversation stopped and we continued to lay low, trying to ignore the stench coming from the pile of debris around us. After half an hour the generator shut down and we heard the two halves of the rear door close and the thud of the two-by-six sliding into place.

"I think we dodged a bullet," Reggie whispered.

"Maybe. Let's wait until they drive away."

After a minute or two a vehicle started up and we heard the sound of it driving off. We waited a few more minutes, then stood and dusted ourselves off. Reggie moved to his right and kicked at something in the pile.

"Hey, Eddie, look at this."

"What?" I said, as I walked over to him.

He pointed to some empty paper bags wedged between pieces of broken lumber. "What the heck are those?"

I squatted down and shined my flashlight on them, then picked up a shard of wood and dislodged a bag from the pile.

"Quicklime," I said. "What the hell do they need that crap for?"

"Maybe rodents," Reggie said. "That was one big-assed rat I shooed away."

"Yeah, maybe," I said, as I continued to poke around the pile. Then a thought crept into my head. "You know what else that stuff has been used for, don't you?" I was near enough to him to see the thought wash over his face.

"Oh, Christ, yeah," he said. "Bodies. You think that's what they did?"

"I'm beginning to think they could be capable of anything."

Reggie squatted down and used another shard of wood to poke into the pile as I walked off a few paces, shining my light over scraggly patches of weeds and tufts of grass. Twenty feet further on I stopped and focused the light on a slightly raised mound of earth. It wasn't freshly-turned dirt, but new enough to where it wasn't covered with weeds.

"Reggie, look at this."

He followed the beam of his flashlight and stood next to me. "Oh, my God," he said. "That could be a grave."

"Yeah."

"Should I find something to dig with?"

"No, leave it be. We've found enough to convince the cops to get a warrant and dig it up. But I want to get another look at that damn place. Let's go back inside." We turned around and skirted the pile of debris. "You take one side," I said. "In case one of them stayed behind. I'll meet you in front." I wasn't sure all the stealth was necessary, but if either Thompson or Iverson had stayed back, they'd have to deal with us coming at them from different directions. I drew my gun and peeked around the rear corner of the building, saw the coast was clear, then crept toward the front.

No vehicle. And no Thompson or Iverson.

Reggie came around the corner of the other side of the building and joined me at the front door. I holstered my gun, pulled out the Pandora key and stuck it in the lock.

"If they get a different padlock, we're sunk," Reggie said, as he pulled the door open.

"All the more reason to find out what the hell Thompson meant by 'downstairs.'"

I pulled the string on the light bulb and started examining the floors of the stalls on the right-hand side of the concrete walkway. After closing the door, Reggie did the same on the other side. The first enclosure didn't reveal anything out of the ordinary. The floor of the second one, however, struck me as odd. One of the plywood flooring sheets was askew, revealing electric cables running underground.

"Reggie, come over here."

He came alongside me and his flashlight caught the slab of plywood laying at an angle. We each grabbed one end of it, lifted, and laid it aside. Underneath, sunk into the dirt, was a trapdoor made of two-by-six boards with metal strips spanning them. Recessed metal rings were embedded in every corner. We each grabbed two of them, grunted with the weight, and lifted. More stench greeted us: mildew, dust, and a pervasive odor of something that had died. We laid the trapdoor on top of the piece of plywood flooring and directed the beams of our flashlights into the hole. A wooden staircase led down, its steps so rickety they could collapse at any time. I stuck my flashlight under one arm, turned around and started to back into the hole.

After I got three rungs down I grabbed my flashlight and used the other hand to hold onto the side of the staircase. "Keep your light on me until I get to the bottom," I said. "And be careful. These steps are pretty damn narrow."

I reached the bottom and directed my light up at Reggie. "Okay, come on ahead."

"Maybe I better stay up here," he said.

"Why? You claustrophobic?"

"Nah, nothing like that. But the thought occurred to me that we should maybe be on the lookout in case those guys decide to come back. If we're both down there and they show up, we're sitting ducks."

"Good thinking," I replied.

I ran the beam of my light around the interior of what could have been a root or wine cellar, although that didn't seem feasible. Nobody in their right mind would store wine in this kind of environment. The space was about twenty feet square. Its walls were concrete blocks, not set in cement, but just staggered on top of each other. Heavy planks spanned them, forming a ceiling. The floor was dirt. Whoever fashioned this basement had had one hell of a job on their hands. Lowering this many blocks and planks down here was no simple feat.

My light revealed a battery-operated lamp hanging from a hook in one of the planks. I found the switch and turned it on. Two fluorescent rods lit up, but not with enough light to reach into the corners of the enclosure. However, they did reveal another, smaller surge protector secured to one of the concrete blocks. Its male plug was connected to the cable snaking down from the stall above. A coil of electrical cable lay on the ground beneath it.

"There's juice down there?" Reggie said from his perch at the top of the stairs.

"Just a battery-powered lamp," I said. "That generator has to provide anything else."

"What's the place look like?"

"Concrete blocks for walls, planks for ceiling. The floor is dirt. Damp as hell."

I went back to probing the interior with my flashlight. Another smaller mattress was propped on one end in a corner. A soiled sheet lay on top of a small wooden table next to it. Underneath the opposite block wall was an oblong mound of dirt, a shovel and an empty bag of quicklime in the corner.

"Looks like there's another grave down here," I called up to Reggie.

"Crap," he muttered in response.

In another corner stood a tall metal cabinet, much like an athletic locker. The door was ajar. I swung it open.

Empty plastic jewel cases occupied the top shelf. I picked up one of them and saw the name "Betty" scrawled on it with a Magic Marker. Every one of the cases had names on them. "Julie," "Cate," "Fran," and on and on. Near the bottom of the pile was a case with "Meredith" on the label.

"There's a stack of empty DVD cases here. Names on every one of them."

"Oh, man," Reggie said. "Is there one with…you know?"

"Yeah, you got it. Meredith."

"Damn," he said. "You better bring it up with you."

"Will do."

The shelf below the one with the jewel cases contained three cardboard boxes, one of them larger than the other two. I pulled it out to catch the beam of my flashlight. Inside were more instruments of restraint: fur-lined cuffs, collars, chains. Disgusted, I threw it back into the cabinet and pulled out one of the smaller boxes.

This one contained at least a dozen empty pill bottles, all of them some variation of pain killers and opioids. I put it back and grabbed the second box. Inside were numerous small plastic bags, all of them empty. I pried one open and stuck my index finger inside, then rubbed it against my thumb. It felt like a powder. My guess was most likely cocaine. Maybe even heroin. Ammunition to sedate helpless women while these four dirtbags had their disgusting fun.

"Lots of empty nickel and dime bags too," I said.

There was no response from Reggie.

"You hear what I said?"

Silence.

"Reggie?"

After a moment he said, "Eddie, you better come up here."

"What's the matter?"

"You just better come back up."

I stuck the jewel case with Meredith's name on it down the small of my back and walked over to the foot of the staircase. "You all right?" I said, as I shined my flashlight up to the top of the stairs. He was seated on the top step.

Looming over each of Reggie's shoulders were Ken Thompson and Vic Benedetti. Both of them had guns in their hands.

29

Thompson took Reggie's flashlight from him and shined it right in my eyes. I put my hand up to block the beam and had a brief thought of reaching for my firearm, but with two guns pointing at me and Reggie in the line of fire, the thought quickly disappeared.

"I didn't hear them, Eddie."

"It's okay," I said.

"Dowse your light, Collins," Thompson said. "Then grab that lantern and very slowly come up the steps."

"How about taking that damn thing out of my eyes?" I said, as I turned my flashlight off. He shifted the throw of light to my feet. I reached up, took the lantern off its hook and started to climb.

"On your feet, Birdman," Benedetti said. He grabbed Reggie by the collar of his shirt and yanked on it.

"Yeah, yeah, okay. Dammit, I ain't crippled." As he stood up, he swung back with his left fist and connected with Benedetti's kneecap. Benedetti lashed out with the barrel of his gun and clipped Reggie on his forehead, causing him to stagger back a couple of steps.

"Shut the fuck up," Benedetti snarled.

When I reached the top of the stairs, Thompson had retreated a pace or two, but still had his gun and Reggie's light pointed at me. Benedetti reached out, took my flashlight and slid it into a side pocket of the safari jacket he wore. "Set the lantern on the ground."

I did so, and locked eyes with Reggie. He put his hand to his forehead and touched the trickle of blood that had formed. The previous look of panic he'd had back behind the woodpile was now replaced by one of intense anger and resolve.

"Now pull back your jacket," Benedetti said. "Let me see if you're carrying." I opened it to reveal the gun holstered at my hip. "Very slowly unclip it and toss it over here," he continued. I had no choice but to do what he said. The holstered gun hit the concrete in front of him. He kept his gun on Reggie as he bent down and picked it up and put it in another pocket of his jacket.

"Both of you get in that stall," Thompson said, as he gestured to one of the enclosures on the other side of the center concrete walkway. As I walked in front of him I got my first close-up look. Last night on his patio I remembered thinking he sounded like the actor John Carradine. His appearance bore that out. He was about my height, but lankier. A lantern jaw dominated his face, which was grooved by deep wrinkles running down his cheeks on both sides of his mouth.

He gestured with his gun and I crossed to the other side of the building. Benedetti picked up the lantern and motioned for Reggie to follow me. We entered the makeshift room and were told to back up against the far wall. Both men followed us and Benedetti set the lantern on the plywood flooring, then pulled my flashlight from his pocket, turned it on and shined it right in my face. Thompson did the same to Reggie with the light he'd taken from him.

"Now your cellphones," Thompson said. "Put them on the ground and slide 'em over here."

I glanced at Reggie, hoping to see any semblance of defiance on his face, but, like me, the two guns aimed at us made it plain we had no option. I fished out my phone, laid it on the plywood and shoved it toward Thompson's feet. Reggie did the same. Benedetti picked them up and deposited them into yet another pocket of his safari jacket.

No sooner had he done that when Thompson's phone went off. He looked at the screen and put it to his ear. "Yeah?" A pause, then: "We figured right. They were here."

While he continued his conversation, Benedetti moved to Reggie's left, gripped the green blanket covering the wall behind us and yanked it down, revealing 2x4 studs with 1x3 slats spanning the gaps between them. The studs and the slats had seen better days. The wood was old; cracks in the grains were plentiful.

Thompson finished his call and ripped down the blanket to my right, unveiling more decrepit framework. "That was Dave. He and Roger are on their way." He tossed the blanket in a corner and said, "Have a seat, you two." He gestured with the flashlight and Reggie and I sat down, his gun still aimed at us.

Benedetti walked over to the footlocker I'd examined earlier. He grabbed it by a handle and dragged it to the center of the stall, opened it, then shined his flashlight into it and began rummaging around inside.

Thompson fished a pack of cigarettes from a pocket, clicked open a Zippo, lit up, and exhaled a cloud of smoke while looking down at us. "I understand we wore the same costume, Collins."

"That's right," I said. "You better be more careful about leaving stuff in the pockets."

"I guess so. Speaking of which, why don't you do me a favor and give me that key you found?"

"What key would that be?" I said.

"Oh, come on, you're not in a position to start being an asshole. Vic here has zero tolerance for assholes." Benedetti stopped what he was doing and looked at me with a shit-eating grin. "Let's have your keys," Thompson continued.

I dug into a jacket pocket, pulled out my key ring and held it up.

"Take the Pandora key off and toss it over here."

"Take it off yourself," I said, and tossed the key ring in his direction, purposely throwing it wide. He lunged for it and at the same time I started to get to my feet, but stopped when Benedetti fired a round into the wall behind me. I cringed and fell back. My ears screamed with the sound of the shot in the enclosed space.

"Next time I won't miss," Benedetti said. He went back to rummaging in the footlocker as Thompson let loose with another cloud of smoke and picked up my key ring.

He put the cigarette in one corner of his mouth and separated the Pandora key. "You know, Collins, hindsight is twenty-twenty. You'd have saved yourself a lot of trouble if you'd just given this thing back to wardrobe."

"But then I wouldn't have had the pleasure of meeting your dreadlocked friend," I said. "Did Iverson mess with Gould's insulin?" He didn't answer, just put my key ring in his pocket, took a deep drag off his cigarette and glared at me. "What happened, Ken? Gould wanted to pull the plug on your little enterprise here?"

"You've got a vivid imagination, Collins. I think you watch too many movies."

"Maybe so, but I overheard you guys last night on your patio. Sounded like Gould got cold feet. You afraid he was going to flip on the four of you?" My comment caught him by surprise and he glanced at Benedetti.

After he exchanged a look with Thompson, Benedetti stood up and pushed the footlocker against the far wall. He held two sets of metal handcuffs. "Tony Gould was a pussy. He got what he deserved." He tucked his gun into a trouser pocket and said, "Cover me, Ken. These cuffs are the only ones I found, but they'll do nicely."

The cuffs were separated by a four-inch chain. He inserted two small keys and opened both sets, then dropped the keys into his shirt pocket and moved next to me. "Put one of these on your right wrist. And make sure we hear the click loud and clear." I circled my wrist with the cuff and closed it. The ratcheting sound seemed to drown out the ringing in my ears. He pulled the binoculars from around my neck and said, "Lose the watch. Time ain't gonna matter much to you anymore." I slid my watch off my left wrist and handed it to him. He tossed it in the open footlocker and then did the same with the binoculars. "Raise your hands up to that one-by-three." He draped my right hand over the board, then snapped the other cuff on my left wrist, leaving me with my arms in the air, snuggled up against one of the studs. He then moved to Reggie and repeated the process.

"Both the Burbank and North Hollywood cops know about the four of you," I said. "You're going to need to keep looking over your shoulders."

"I'll take that into consideration," Thompson said. "But I can't tell them anything they'd be interested in."

"They know you both testified on Gould's behalf in that suit Meredith Paulson filed against Pandora."

"Yeah, so what?" Benedetti said, as he closed the footlocker's lid and shoved it against the far wall.

"After she lost the case she disappeared. You guys know what happened to her?"

"Haven't a clue," Thompson said.

"Come on, Ken," I said. "Now you're the one being an asshole. I found a piece of jewelry in one of those footlockers that's exactly like one her mother gave her. There's a stack of empty jewel cases down in that dungeon of yours. Her name is on one of them. What happened to the disc? You sell it? Like you did with all the others? Filmed your little pornographic movies with the girls and then made sure they disappeared?"

"You're full of shit, Collins, and I'm tired of listening," Benedetti said.

"So am I," Thompson said. "Let's take care of that generator. By then, Dave and Roger will be here and we can deal with these two. I'll bring the car around back."

He dropped his cigarette on the plywood flooring, ground it out with his foot, then walked toward the front door and went outside. Benedetti took his flashlight out of his jacket and shined it on Reggie and me.

"Well, Birdman, looks like you've seen your last bald eagle," he said, as he kicked one of Reggie's feet.

"I wouldn't count on it."

"Oh, I would," Benedetti replied.

I heard Thompson's SUV come to life and listened as it moved to the back of the building. "What was it with you guys? Couldn't get it at home so you had to prey on young women?"

"Sorry to disappoint you, Collins, but I've never had a problem." As some sort of punctuation to his remark, he kicked my left knee, cackled and walked to the rear door of the building. As he walked under it, he pulled the chain on the other light above the concrete walkway. Reggie and I were left in the glow of the battery-operated lantern and the two dim bulbs in the ceiling of the structure.

When we heard the two men's voices coming from the rear, Reggie turned to me and said, "You all right?"

I flexed my knee and replied, "Yeah, I'm good."

"They're not going to let us out of here, are they?"

"It doesn't sound like it." I pulled on the handcuffs and winced when they cut into my wrists. "You got any ideas?"

He got to his knees and yanked on his cuffs. "Good thing they didn't cuff us to those studs. These one-by-threes are pretty old. They might give."

I twisted around and got on my knees. The one Benedetti had kicked was a little tender, but in light of what was facing us, the pain didn't faze me. I pulled on the cuffs, but couldn't sense any give in the board.

"Grab the ends of the chain," he said. "Take the pressure off your wrists."

From the rear of the building, we heard Thompson and Benedetti grunting and cursing. They obviously were attempting to lift the generator into the back of the SUV.

I did as Reggie suggested. The pain in my wrists was less, but didn't result in any give in the 1x3.

"Maybe this will help," Reggie said, as he put one foot against the 2x4 stud and the other against the exterior wall of the building. He gave another yank on the cuffs' chain. The 1x3 cracked and came a little bit loose from the stud.

I heard the hatchback on the SUV slam. From the rear door of the building Benedetti said, "I still think we should burn the goddamn place down."

I wasn't sure what Thompson's muffled reply was, but the SUV came to life and I heard it start to move.

Benedetti was back in the building and was coming toward us, muttering as he walked.

Following Reggie's lead, I put one foot against another 2x4 stud and gave the chain a good pull. Maybe it was my imagination, but it felt like the slat loosened a bit.

I glanced over at Reggie. His pulls on the cuffs were getting results. With one final yank, his slat came loose from the stud, taking two nails with it. He pried the other end loose, slid his cuffs off and got to his feet.

Just as he did so Benedetti appeared in the opening of the stall.

"All right, you two—" He stopped when he saw Reggie free himself. With a shout, he jumped on his back. Reggie snapped his head back and caught Benedetti in the face. He fell back, got to his knees and began to dig for his gun. Reggie picked up the loose 1x3 with the protruding nails and swung at Benedetti's head. The nails caught him in the face. He screamed and his hands came up to one of his eyes. A second swing hit him on the forehead. Reggie pounced on him and wrapped the chain of his cuffs around Benedetti's neck. He tightened the garrote and Benedetti squirmed and kicked. He put his bloodied hands to the chain, trying to pry himself loose.

With one last yank, I pulled the 1x3 loose from the stud and slid my cuffs off the freed end. Just as I did so I heard Thompson's SUV come to rest in the front of the building. The engine shut down, and after a moment, I heard the vehicle's door open, then slam shut.

Benedetti's struggles had diminished as Reggie's garotte tightened. Thompson was still armed. I had to get the drop on him. Remembering which jacket pocket Benedetti had stashed my gun, I kneeled on his legs and pulled the holster out and freed the gun. Just as I scampered to the opening of the stall and raised my cuffed hands with the firearm between them, Thompson came through the front door, taking a puff off a cigarette.

"That's far enough, Ken. Drop the butt and put your hands behind your head."

Thompson froze for a moment, then flicked the lit cigarette in my direction and made a move for his gun. I fired a round over his head and he stopped.

"The next one's going to be lower. Put your hands behind your head. Do it now."

Thompson raised his arms and followed my instructions. "You're forgetting about Forbes and Iverson, Collins. They're on their way."

"So they are. Where did you stash your gun?"

After a moment he said, "Right trouser pocket."

"Very slowly, pull it out, put it on the ground and kick it over to me."

I moved two steps toward him. The dim lightbulb above our heads made visibility poor, but I was close enough to put a round into center mass if I had to. Thompson dropped his right arm and gingerly put his hand into his pocket and pulled out his gun. "Are you sure about this, Collins? You've got nothing on me."

"Don't bet on it. I'm going to be singing like a canary. Now drop the goddamn gun and kick it over here."

He did so. I pocketed it and glanced over my shoulder. Benedetti had stopped squirming. Blood covered his left eye socket. "Is he out, Reggie?"

"Like a light."

"Let up on the chain and get those cuff keys out of his shirt pocket."

"After a moment he said, "Got 'em."

"Cuff him to one of those studs."

Behind me I heard the click of one of Reggie's cufflinks going around one of Benedetti's wrists. Then the sound of his body being dragged and finally the click of cufflinks being closed.

"Done," Reggie said.

"Great. Now get over here and get me out of mine." I kept my gun on Thompson as Reggie unlocked my cuffs. He hadn't moved a muscle. I gestured to his gun on the ground in front of me and Reggie picked it up. "Get next to your buddy Vic. On your ass up against the wall."

With his hands locked behind his head, Thompson moved into the stall and sat down next to Benedetti. He looked at the bloodied face and said, "You blinded the guy," he said. "Are you nuts?"

"Give me a goddamn break," I said. "With all the carnage you guys created in this place, you should be used to it. Cuff him to one of those studs, Reggie."

Thompson wouldn't show his hands, but changed his mind when Reggie slapped his head. He continued to whine as the cuffs went on one wrist and then onto the other after his hands were wrapped around one of the studs.

"See if you can find something in that footlocker to gag these assholes with," I said.

Reggie flipped open the lid and held the lantern above the inside. He put his binoculars around his neck and tossed mine to me, along with my watch. After rummaging around for a few seconds, he let loose with a gleeful shout and held up two ball gags, standard equipment in kinky sexual escapades.

"Hey, look at these. How 'bout givin' 'em a little taste of their own medicine?" He set the lantern down next to Benedetti, pried open his mouth, stuck the ball in, and then strapped the gag to his head. Benedetti didn't stir. When Reggie knelt next to Thompson and told him to open his mouth, he responded by spitting in his face.

"Get that fuckin' thing away from me," Thompson snarled.

Now I was the one who reached out and slapped him. "Open your goddamn mouth," I said. He just glared at me, so I pinched his nose shut and after a few seconds, he opened up and Reggie stuck the ball in and strapped the gag around his head.

Mission accomplished.

We sat back on our heels and looked at our two captives. Two pitiful predators who were now trussed up like hostages. Which indeed they were.

"Time to call the cops?" Reggie said.

I started going through pockets to retrieve the stuff taken from me: keychain from Thompson and phones from Benedetti's safari jacket. "We've still got Forbes and Iverson to deal with," I said, as I handed Reggie his cell. "We better wait until after they get here. You ride herd on these two, and I'll watch the front door. Check Benedetti's pulse while you're at it."

"Roger," he said, as I moved to the front door and focused my attention on the road.

"It's weak, but he's got one," Reggie said.

About fifteen minutes elapsed before I saw a vehicle approaching the front gate. Thompson and Benedetti had left it open so Forbes drove straight through and came toward the barn. I got Reggie's attention and he moved to one side of the door, with me on the other.

The car crunched over gravel and parked next to Thompson's SUV. Two doors slammed and footsteps approached the door. Iverson came through first, Forbes right behind him. "Yo, we're here," Iverson said.

When they cleared the doorway Reggie and I stepped away from the wall and trained our guns on them. "Hands behind your heads, fellas, fingers laced together," I said. After a couple of moments, they followed instructions and Reggie frisked both of them.

"They're clean," he said.

"Where's Ken and Vic?" Forbes said.

"Right over here," I said.

We pushed both men into the stall. When Thompson saw them, he struggled against the cuffs and kept trying to talk around the ball gag in his mouth, but all he could do was grunt and whine. Benedetti didn't do either. I ripped another blanket down, revealing more slats and studs. While I kept them covered, Reggie rummaged through the other footlockers and came up with two more sets of handcuffs. He cuffed Forbes and Iverson to more studs, then we both stood and took a good long look at the four of them.

Reggie let out a huge sigh and said, "I really feel like stomping all over these assholes."

"Me too," I said. "But this place has seen enough violence. I think we're better off not adding to it."

"Yeah, you're probably right"

Reggie kept watch over them as I stepped outside and called 911. I couldn't give the dispatcher a location, but did provide my name, along with Reggie's, and briefly told her what the police could expect and that she should call for an ambulance as well. The lady on the other end of the line initially sounded confused, but I told her I would leave my phone on and they could trace my location.

Which they did, and after a half hour or so, the welcome sound of sirens and the sight of flashing lights approached. Reggie and I stood next to Thompson's and Forbes' vehicles, our hands raised, ready to spill our guts about what had transpired with the liars club and their final meeting.

30

When I'd powered up my phone to call 911 I'd seen that there were two texts and two missed calls from Carla. A glance at my watch revealed that it was only 7:45. Time had elapsed in slow motion since Reggie and I had entered this dilapidated barn behind us and encountered the depravity that had taken place inside it.

I called Carla's number and she picked up after only one ring.

"Eddie? Are you all right? I've been calling and texting you. Where are you?"

"Still up north of Piru. Reggie and I ran into a mess, but we're both okay."

"Oh, my God, you had me worried. What the hell happened?"

I recapped everything. She periodically interrupted with outbursts of disgust and anger. I told her we were waiting for the authorities to show up and that I would call her after they were done with us.

"No matter how late, okay? I've got a late call tomorrow."

"No matter how late," I said. She heaved a huge sigh and then told me she loved me. I reciprocated and we ended the call.

The cavalcade of sirens and lights belonged to units from the Ventura County Sheriff's office. Three patrol cars and an ambulance wheeled into the lot and skidded to a stop. Doors flew open and headlights flooded Reggie and me with our hands in the air. Three deputies, weapons drawn, approached us.

"Who placed the nine-one-one call?" one of them said.

"I did, sir," I replied. "My name's Eddie Collins. I'm a licensed private detective and this is Reggie Benson, my associate."

"I need to see some identification," the deputy said.

"My license is in my right hip pocket. Along with my permit to carry a firearm."

"Are you carrying that firearm now, sir?"

"Yes. It's clipped to my belt."

"And you, Mr. Benson?"

"I'm unarmed. Just have a flashlight."

"What's in your right trouser pocket, Mr. Collins?"

"I also have a flashlight."

"Both of you remove them please."

Reggie and I took our flashlights from our pockets and again raised our hands.

The deputy turned to his right. "Hank, get the firearm and frisk the other guy."

The deputy named Hank approached me, still with his weapon drawn. His name tag read Jacobson. He reached around me, found the holstered gun and pulled it off my belt. He patted Reggie down and said, "He's clean, Mel," then walked back to one of the cars and smelled the barrel. "It's been fired."

Mel turned to me. "Mr. Collins?"

"I fired one round. I'll show you when we get inside."

"You gentlemen can lower your arms," Mel said. He approached us and I saw the name Carter on his name tag. "Your identification, sir?"

I pulled my wallet out and handed him my driver's license and those for my firearm and private eye ticket. He looked at them, handed them back, then asked for Reggie's ID.

Satisfied, he said, "Who's the ambulance for?"

"There's four handcuffed men in there," I said, gesturing to the building behind me. "One of them needs medical attention."

He signaled to two EMTs and they hustled into the barn with a gurney.

Carter holstered his firearm and said, "Okay. What do we have here?"

Reggie and I turned and he followed us inside. When we cleared the doorway, one of the EMTs kneeling over Benedetti said, "Mel, we've gotta get the cuffs off this guy."

Reggie pulled the key from his shirt pocket and unlocked Benedetti's cuffs. I shined my flashlight above the door and located the bullet hole. "There's where my round landed," I said. Then I swept the floor with the light and pointed to the single shell casing. "And here's the brass."

Carter pulled on a pair of gloves, took a plastic bag from a hip pocket and put the casing inside. He asked me the reason for the round being fired and I told him it was to scare one of the four men who attempted to draw his weapon.

Reggie and I shined our lights down the center concrete walkway and I described what we thought had apparently been going on inside this place. We entered the stall where the four men were handcuffed to the 2x4 studs. I identified Thompson as the one who attempted to draw his weapon, then gave Carter the names of the other three. Benedetti was being placed on a gurney.

"What's the cause of his injuries?" Carter asked.

Reggie gave him the lowdown on our being handcuffed, our breaking free, and his subsequent scuffle with Benedetti.

"And what's with the gag?" the deputy said, as he gestured for one of the EMTs to remove the ball gag from Benedetti's mouth.

We explained that Thompson and Benedetti had arrived separately and of our desire to gag them so as to not alert Forbes and Iverson. We drew his attention to the footlocker and the paraphernalia inside.

Carter looked inside and shook his head in disgust. "I've read and heard about this sort of crap, but never thought I'd see it up close." He stood over the three handcuffed men and gestured for Reggie to remove the gag from Thompson's mouth.

He spit out the gag and erupted. "This is bullshit, Sheriff! The fuckin' guy's making stuff up."

Carter nodded and called for his two deputies to bring in an extra set of handcuffs. Jacobs and the other deputy whose name was Williams entered and replaced the three sets of cuffs with department-issued hardware.

Carter pulled his own set off his belt and handed it to deputy Williams. "Cuff him to the gurney, Jack." Then he handed the key to one of the EMTs and they wheeled Benedetti out to the ambulance. He said he would be taken to a hospital in nearby Fillmore.

Carter looked down at the three men, told them they were under arrest and then Mirandized them. "Put the mop-head in your unit, Hank. Jack, you take the other two." With weapons drawn, the two deputies escorted the three men out of the barn. If looks could kill, Reggie and I were dead men from the glares we received as they left.

Carter turned to Reggie and me and said, "Okay, gentlemen, how about the rest of the cook's tour?"

We showed him the dungeon with its probable grave and the empty jewel cases and drug baggies. Our flashlights led him to the mound of earth behind the barn and the empty bag of quicklime. He took copious notes and seemed overwhelmed by what we told him. He indicated forensics would have to pore over the place when daylight arrived. If the quicklime hadn't taken care of everything, DNA would be extracted. Also, if possible, dental records would be sought.

It took Reggie and me a good half hour to lay everything out for Carter. We were told we needed to be taken to the sheriff's station in Fillmore for further questioning. He got on his phone and gave orders for another unit to come to the scene, put out the yellow tape and remain to guard the location. Two tow trucks were also ordered to haul away Thompson's and Forbes' vehicles.

Before we got into Carter's patrol unit, Reggie told him where his car was located. With assurances that Reggie would follow, the two of us climbed into the backseat of the car and drove off. Neither one of us bothered to give a last look at the ramshackle palace of pornography behind us.

With me in the rear seat and Reggie following in his car, Carter's patrol unit picked its way through the woods and onto the gravel road leading back to Piru.

"One thing I can't figure, Collins."

"What's that?"

"Why didn't you go to the authorities from the get-go?"

It was a question that Carla, Mavis, and even Reggie had posed. "I didn't think I had anything concrete to offer police," I responded. "True, I overheard them talking on Thompson's patio, but what I heard didn't seem to be all that relevant. Beyond that, chalk it up to private eye curiosity and the girl's mother needing some answers."

"Makes sense, I guess, but I need to do some more unpacking."

"I read you," I said.

We spent another three hours at the sheriff's station, going over and over every minute detail of my investigation and where it had led. When the deputies finished with us, my gun was returned to me. Before we left the sheriff's station, our contact information was taken, and firm instructions were given to not leave the area. We assured Carter we had no intention of doing so.

It was nearly midnight before we piled into Reggie's car and headed for Los Angeles. Both of us were silent as we slowly glided through Piru on our way to the I-5.

"A hell of a night," Reggie said.

"One for the books," I replied.

"What do you think? Is there enough there to convict them?"

"Christ, I hope so. But we better count on being called to testify."

"Yeah, I figured that," he said. "Maybe I'm wrong, but what you heard from Thompson's patio should be pretty incriminating, right?"

"I would think so, but you can rest assured I'll be fodder for some hot-shot lawyer."

He nodded and we headed up the ramp to the freeway. Traffic was practically non-existent as we headed south.

"Let me ask you this, Eddie. They'll most likely make bail, right?"

"That's a possibility."

"You think they'll come after us?"

I pondered his question as we slowed for traffic cones and night construction. "If they have any hope of beating the rap, they'd be stupid if they did." On its face, I believed what I said, but the nagging inward truth made me wonder. With the inhumanity those four had displayed, I guess anything was possible.

Reggie parked his car in front of the garage and we climbed out, weariness seeping into both of us.

"Thanks for your help. I was glad you were there," I said, as I hugged him.

"So am I, man. Get some rest."

"You too. Talk to you soon."

I started my car and dialed Carla's number. "Back from Piru. You still up?"

"And waiting for your call. Have you had anything to eat?"

"An elephant ear this morning."

"Good grief. Get your buns over here."

I couldn't think of a better invitation, so I put the car in gear and drove off.

31

Sleeping late is a luxury I rarely indulge in, but on this particular Friday morning I basked in the pleasure, aided, of course, by the presence of Carla next to me. Last night, after Reggie dropped me off, I went over to her place and we talked into the early hours. Her company and the comfort of her arms around me did wonders in wiping out the memories of the depravity that Reggie and I had confronted up in Ventura County.

After a light brunch of fruit and yogurt, she went off to her television show and I to my office. Mavis looked up from her computer when I pushed the door open.

"Hi, Eddie. What's new?"

"You really want to know?"

"Lay it on me, boss man."

Which I did, and after hearing the whole story, she leaned back in her chair and looked at me for a long moment. "Well, I'm glad your fixation on that key finally paid off," she said, "and, more important, that you're all right. Too bad the results were so disgusting. Do you think the Paulson girl was one of the victims?"

I pulled from my pocket the necklace I'd found in one of the footlockers. "I don't know for sure, but I found this in that barn up in Piru," I said, as I handed it to her. "It's exactly like the one she wore in the picture I have of her."

"Shouldn't you have given this to those deputies?" she said. "I mean, it's evidence, isn't it?"

"Yeah, you're right, but the pain I saw in Barbara's face when I talked to her the other day makes me think it's more important for her to have this reminder of her daughter. There's plenty more evidence in that damn place to implicate those four creeps."

"Okay by me," she said. "Just saying."

"Point taken. Sometimes you gotta do what you gotta do." She handed the necklace back. "You going to turn me in?"

"I haven't yet. My lips are sealed." She grinned and tossed a paperclip at me.

"But I don't relish the conversation I'll have to have with her."

"You'd better call her anyway."

"Yeah, good idea."

As I started for my office her phone rang. She picked it up and said, "Just a moment." With her hand over the receiver she said, "It's for you. Somebody from the Ventura County District Attorney's office."

I sat behind my desk and picked up the receiver. "This is Eddie Collins."

"Mr. Collins, this is Phil Ainsley calling. I'm with the Ventura County District Attorney's office."

"Yes, sir."

"The sheriff's office has informed us of the circumstances surrounding the arrests they made last night. Glad to hear that you and Mr. Benson are all right."

"Thank you."

"Pursuant to obtaining the facts, we're going to issue a subpoena for you to appear as a prosecution witness before a grand jury Monday morning. We realize this is short notice, but will that be possible?"

"Absolutely."

"Fine. You can expect an officer to present you with the subpoena shortly. Time and location will be provided."

"All right."

"Thank you for your cooperation, sir. Looking forward to seeing you on Monday."

I hung up and looked at Mavis standing in the doorway. "They're not wasting any time. Monday morning. The subpoena is on its way."

"Good. Go and nail those sick puppies."

I called Reggie and told him to expect a subpoena. Two hours later mine arrived with the appearance of a Ventura County Sheriff's Deputy. When I asked him if he'd served Reggie with his, he told me he was on the way. Reggie called me later in the afternoon to report that he'd been served. We made arrangements for me to pick him up Monday morning for our trip up to Ventura, the county seat.

I have been on a witness stand before on a couple of occasions and have always been somewhat intimidated by the inherent confrontational aspect of a trial. On this Monday morning there was none of that. The jury room was cool from air conditioning and comfortable with soft lighting. A court reporter, Ainsley from the DA's office, the panel and me were the only people in the room. The grand jury itself was comprised of eight men and seven women, of various ages and ethnicities, and all very serious and intent on the testimony I provided. Once again, I related in detail my investigation and where it led me. I was asked several questions, after which they thanked me and I went outside. Reggie stood and came up to me.

"How'd it go?" he said.

"Fine. They listened to everything I said."

"Gotta admit, Eddie, I'm a little nervous."

"You were there, buddy," I said, and clapped him on the shoulder. "Just tell them what happened."

"Okay," he said, and turned as Ainsley opened the door to the jury room and called his name. I gave him a thumbs-up and found a seat.

After ten minutes or so Deputy Mel Carter appeared, along with his fellow officers Hank Jacobs and Jack Williams. We all exchanged handshakes and Carter told me that crime scene technicians had started their work at daybreak Friday morning. Their first task had been digging up the mound of earth behind the wood pile and the one in the dungeon. What they discovered prompted the district attorney's office to quickly jump on its presentation before the grand jury.

The remains of four bodies were buried behind the pile of wood. An additional five in the dungeon. Whichever one of those four creeps had emptied the bags of quicklime was either careless or in a hurry: enough bones were left intact for DNA to be obtained. Also, in three cases, partial dental records could be accessed.

Reggie came out of the jury room and before Carter went inside, I asked him to keep me informed of further developments. He assured me he would, and he told me if the grand jury handed down an indictment, both Reggie and I would no doubt be called to testify.

An indictment was indeed handed down. However, a surprise entered the picture at the four men's arraignment. I remembered telling Thompson that I was going to sing like a canary. But what I didn't expect was that David Forbes would beat me at my own game; he flipped on his three compadres, admitting guilt and agreeing to a plea agreement.

32

As they generally do, a couple of days passed. About ten o'clock on Wednesday morning, just as I finished my first cup of coffee, Morrie Howard called. As per usual, his conversation began with a cough that sounded like a death rattle.

"Morrie, you've got to quit smoking those damn cigarettes."

"Yeah, yeah. Anybody can quit smoking, bubbeleh, but it takes a hell of a man to stand up to lung cancer."

I had to grin in spite of myself. "What's up?"

"Good news. Your *Terms of Power* gig has got new life. They found the money, and you've got a start date for next week. Wednesday. Location to be determined. Seems like Warner Bros. gave their space to somebody else. So stay tuned. I assume you're available?"

"Right as always, Morrie. Thanks for the news."

"You bet. I'll be in touch."

I slapped the desk with both hands and said, "Well, all right!"

Mavis stuck her around the corner. "What's up?"

"*Terms of Power* is back on."

"Terrific. When?"

"Wednesday of next week."

She gave me a thumbs up and I pawed my way through the beaded curtain into my apartment for another cup of thinly disguised coffee. I no sooner sat down behind my desk when my cell went off. The screen said Clay Dawson.

"Did you get the news?" I said.

"I sure did."

"But I suppose you've got another job, right?"

"Are you kidding? I can't get arrested." We both laughed and he continued. "So, listen, I was thinking we'd better convene the Four Horseman before we start. What say you?"

"I say let's do it."

"How about Friday at the Smokehouse? Twelve-thirty?"

"Sounds good. You want me to call Howard and Tom?"

"I already did. They're both on board."

"Great. See you then," I said, and ended the call.

A few scattered raindrops sprinkled my windshield as I handed the keys to the valet outside the Smokehouse on Friday. Inside, I spotted Clay, Howard, and Tom at a four-top in the back near a window. After handshakes all around, I took the remaining seat and unfolded my napkin.

"Good to see you guys," I said. "The Four Horsemen ride again."

"Damn straight," Clay said. "Anybody get any job offers while we were in limbo?"

The three of us shook our heads and Howard said, "My agent told me we're not on the Warner Bros. lot. Yours tell you the same?"

"Apparently they lost the studio space to someone else," I said.

A waiter appeared, identified himself as Brad, and took our drink orders. After he walked off, we looked at our menus. I opted for a grilled chicken sandwich and fries; the other three went with burgers. Glasses of beer appeared. We ordered and raised our drinks in a toast.

"To the reboot," Clay said.

We all agreed and took healthy pulls from our frosted steins.

"I gotta admit that I didn't think it was going to happen," Tom said.

"Oh, hell, Tom," Clay said. "I heard when they saw the dailies and your electrifying performance, they had no choice but to find more money. They couldn't deprive the movie-going public of your brilliance."

"I wish I'd worn my boots, because you are so full of shit," Tom said. "However, I did hear there was talk of replacing you."

"*Touché,*" Chad said, as Brad walked up with a basket of rolls and cups of butter.

"Hey, Eddie," Tom said. "Any developments on that case you were working on?"

I split a roll, dabbed some butter on half of it and told the three of them what had gone down on the Meredith Paulson case. They listened intently and shook their heads when I finished.

"Goddammit," Clay said. "Schmucks like those should lose their *cojones.*"

"If they're convicted, they won't need them," Howard said.

Balancing a huge tray, our waiter reappeared, set up a foldable table for it, then distributed the plates. We ordered another round of beer and dug in.

After several minutes of nothing but slurping and chowing down, Tom wiped his mouth on his napkin and said, "All right, guys, we can't let this lunch go by without some trivia. I've got one for the three of you."

"Oh, my God, here we go," Clay said. "Lay it on us, man."

Tom sipped from his beer stein and leaned on the table. "Okay. The year is nineteen fifty-five. The film is *Bad Day at black Rock.*"

"Gotcha," I said.

"Yeah, Spencer Tracy," Clay added.

"Internet Movie Data Base lists fifteen principals," Tom continued. "Among those fifteen how many Oscars are there?"

"Only fifteen principals?" Howard said. "Can't be that many."

"The question is who were the winners and for which films?" Tom said.

"Well, Tracy won two," Clay said.

"What are the movies?" Tom said.

"That's a no-brainer. *Captains Courageous* and *Boys Town.*"

"I gotta admit, Clay, you're good. That's two."

I took a bite of my sandwich and exchanged glances with Howard. I'd seen the movie in question, but it had been some time. Tracy played a one-armed WWII vet who drops into this small desert town to bestow a medal on the Japanese father of a soldier who'd saved his life, only to run into a nest of bigotry. I pictured the movie in my head and it came to me.

"Lee Marvin," I said, "for *Cat Ballou.*"

"And Ernie Borgnine for *Marty*," Howard added.

"That's four," Tom said.

We paused for a moment and concentrated on our food.

"Wait a minute," Clay said. "Walter Brennan was in that damn thing. There's three more right there. He won three out of the first five supporting actor Oscars."

"And they were?" Tom said.

"Oh, boy," Clay said. "Come on you guys, help me out."

For some inexplicable reason I knew this. "*The Westerner*," "*Kentucky*," and "*Come and Get It*," I said.

"Damn, Eddie, pretty good," Tom said, as I exchanged high-fives with Clay and Howard.

"Seven Oscars?" Howard said. "Man, that's amazing."

"Not so fast," Tom said. "There's one more."

"Jesus," Clay said, his face blank. "Who the hell else?"

The three of us were silent and looked at Tom with the trace of a smug smile on his face. Brad walked up and I signaled for another round of beer. The table was quiet.

"No hint?" Clay said.

Tom took a pull from his beer glass. "All right. He played the sheriff."

"I thought Brennan played the sheriff," Clay said.

"Nope," Tom said, and leaned back as Brad showed up with four more steins of beer.

More silence from the three of us. I couldn't remember. After a moment, Clay and Howard both said they had no idea.

"Dean Jagger," Tom said.

"For what?" Howard said.

"Supporting actor for *Twelve O'Clock High*," Tom replied.

Clay rapped the table with his hand. "Damn, that's right. He was a drunken pilot, right?"

"Yeah," Tom said. "And he was a drunken sheriff in *Bad Day at Black Rock*."

"Christ, I hope he sobered up before he died," Howard said.

Laughter floated around the table and we offered our congratulations to Tom for his question. Clay vowed to have more trivia for us when we reassembled on the movie, and I told them I'd also contribute. With what, I wasn't sure, but assured them I'd add to the game. We finished our sandwiches, dallied over another beer, and parted ways. As I drove along Barham over the freeway into Hollywood, I had to admit that these three compadres were a joy to be around and would be welcome as we continued with *Terms of Power*.

Two days later, Carla and I were enjoying a fine Sunday afternoon on the Santa Monica Pier having fish tacos. Her show had wrapped its latest episode and was on hiatus for the next week. The sun was warm, a light breeze came off the ocean, and the tacos were especially tasty. I took a bite out of one of them and watched two elderly men fishing off the pier, disregarding repeated warnings about eating what they pulled out of the Santa Monica Bay.

"Penny for your thoughts, Shamus."

I gestured to the fishermen. "Do you think they'll make fish tacos out of what they catch?"

"Good God, I hope not!" She laughed and then looked suspiciously at the food in front of her. "You had to go and say that, didn't you? Should I be worried?"

"Oh, hell, no, I've been ordering these out here for years."

"I'll take your word for it." She took another bite and looked at me as she chewed. "You've been pretty quiet today. What's on your mind?"

"I was just thinking that it's only been a little over a week since that nightmare up at Piru."

"Yeah," she said, as she squeezed my hand. We were silent for a moment or two. I tossed a morsel to a gull strutting next to our outdoor table.

"Then I got to thinking about that Skype call I had with Kelly. She was so hyped about being in that play, and I…well…I don't know."

"What? You're proud of her, aren't you?"

"I am, yes. But I began to wonder if she'd ever be serious about carrying on with that. You know, studying it, and some day…" I trailed off and sent another French fry in the gull's direction.

"Following in her father's footsteps, you mean?"

"Yeah. And then right away I'm reminded of those four animals and… well, it doesn't sound all that wise."

"Don't forget, Eddie, those four guys aren't the norm. And they're going to pay for what they did. Big time."

"You're right." I took a pull off my bottle of Corona. "Hell, I don't know. Maybe she'll grow out of it."

"Could be," Carla said. "But I'll bet if she doesn't, the Robinsons will come to you for advice. All you can do is wait and see."

"I guess so," I said, and bit into a taco. A morsel fell into the plastic basket and I pitched it to the bird. We turned at the sound of a shriek coming from two young girls looking at one of their cellphones. They kept giggling as they skipped off toward the shore.

After a moment Carla said, "And you know, I've been thinking."

"Uh, oh."

She wrapped my knuckles with a fork. "No, seriously. That day you got into Artie Young's face at the party?" She paused and sipped from her glass of beer.

"Yeah? What about it?"

"Given what you and Reggie went through up there with those four assholes, I…well…I probably over-reacted."

"So did I, Carla. But he pushed a button. I was in the middle of trying to prove the suspicions I had about those guys, and I might have let it get in my way." The seagull wouldn't give up. I broke off a piece of a French fry and tossed it on the wooden flooring, where it promptly disappeared into the bird's beak. "The thing is, over the years I've seen so many young women come into this town, full of dreams, only to see them vanish at the hands of guys like those Pandora slime balls. What happened to Meredith Paulson was the worst possible way those dreams could be shattered, and it scared me that a guy like Artie Young could do the same to someone who's close to me."

She stopped eating and looked at me for a long moment. Her huge snorkel-like sunglasses prevented me from seeing her eyes, but when she slid a corner of her napkin behind one of the lenses, I realized what she was doing.

"Are you crying? There's no crying on the Santa Monica Pier!"

She burst into laughter and leaned over and kissed me. "I love you, Shamus, and just so you know, you push my buttons."

I returned her kiss and we clinked our bottles of beer. Our toast was interrupted by my phone ringing. The screen revealed a number with an 805 area code.

"This is Eddie Collins."

"Mel Carter from Ventura sheriff's, Mr. Collins. Sorry to bother you on a Sunday."

"No problem, sir. Any news?"

"We received dental records on those three victims."

"And?"

"You'll probably want to have a talk with your client."

Barbara McAndrews sipped from a glass of iced tea as we sat at a table on her back patio. Dottie, her neighbor, had again scrutinized me as I'd climbed the front steps and knocked on the door. She set her glass on a coaster and picked up the necklace.

"And they're sure Meredith was one of them?" she said, as she twined the chain through her fingers.

"I'm afraid so," I said.

She put on a pair of reading glasses and held the necklace up to her face. "Well, they're probably right. Look at the back of this."

She handed the necklace to me and I put it up close to my eyes.

"See that scratch in the center of it?"

"I do."

"I remember exactly how that happened. She was...oh, I guess maybe fifteen. She and a friend of hers were riding their bikes on that Hansen Dam causeway over in Lake View Terrace. Some young tough forced her off the path and she took a fall. Jammed it into one of the rocks. She told me later she threw a rock at the kid and hit him in the back of the head." She chuckled, removed her glasses and took a swipe at a tear in the corner of one eye. "What will they do with her remains, Mr. Collins?"

"You'll hear from the authorities up in Ventura County. Should be soon."

After a long pause she said, "Oh, my, all that cruelty. She was such a good girl. Why would anyone want to do something like that?"

I watched a scrub jay land a few feet from me, looking for scraps from the cookies she had laid out. "I wish I had an answer for you, Barbara."

We sat in silence for a moment or two and she reached into her shirt pocket and handed me a check.

"You know, I don't feel right about this," I said. "Especially considering what happened."

"No, you brought me some closure, Mr. Collins. I'm grateful for that."

We finished our tea and chatted for a few more minutes, then I gave her a hug, told her I would keep in touch, and walked down the driveway. Dottie gave me a wave as I approached my car. I was sure that Barbara McAndrews would withstand the loss of her daughter. As to whether or not the mothers of the other girls would, I couldn't be certain. For decades, mothers and fathers have kissed their daughters and bid them farewell as they set out for Hollywood and the hope of fame and fortune in this crazy, mixed-up town. Meredith Paulson wouldn't be the last. They would keep coming. Hopefully, they wouldn't run into the likes of Ken Thompson, Vic Benedetti, David Forbes, and Roger Iverson.

I turned right on Foothill Boulevard and headed for the I-5. The check Barbara McAndrews had given me burned a hole in my shirt pocket. Before I got back to my office, I went through my bank's drive-up teller and deposited it. Once behind my desk, I went online, found a women's shelter and made a donation. It wasn't a substantial contribution, but my hope was that it would somehow provide help to others like Meredith Paulson.

THE END

ABOUT THE AUTHOR

Clive Rosengren is a "recovering" actor, whose career spanned more than forty years, eighteen of them pounding many of the same streets as his fictional private eye Eddie Collins. Movie credits include Ed Wood, Soapdish, Cobb, and Bugsy. Among numerous television credits are Seinfeld, Home Improvement, and Cheers, where he played the only person to throw Sam Malone out of his own bar. Rosengren has written four books in the Eddie Collins Mystery series: *Murder Unscripted*, *Red Desert*, *Velvet on a Tuesday Afternoon*, and *Martini Shot*. Books one and two were finalists for the Shamus Award from the Private Eye Writers of America.

CPSIA information can be obtained
at www.ICGtesting.com
Printed in the USA
LVHW030059260821
696068LV00013B/738

9 781603 812627